SWEETEST IN THE GALE

A MARYSBURG STORY COLLECTION

OLIVIA DADE

PRAISE FOR OLIVIA DADE

Achingly romantic, and beautifully written.

"Cover Me" is an absolute gem—a marriage-of-convenience story with a giant heart! It's a story to treasure!

Beautifully written with intensely felt characters whose dedication is restorative and heartwarming. This is just the romance we need right now.

ISBN: 978-1-945836-16-9

❀ Created with Vellum

SWEETEST IN THE GALE

ABOUT "SWEETEST IN THE GALE"

Much ado about love...

Candy Albright has always stomped confidently through the halls of Marysburg High, passionate and loud and entirely devoted to her students and her various English department initiatives. From his first day as her colleague, Griff Conover couldn't look away, despite his best efforts.

After a summer apart, though, Candy returns to school a changed woman. Muted. Dimmed. Bowed by a grief Griff recognizes all too well, but doesn't yet understand. And when they're thrown together to coordinate a poetry project, he can't resist the urge to read between her lines once and for all—even if doing so means he'll have to confront his own loss...and his own lonely, longing heart.

For all those who grieve. May the other side of your and *bring you love and joy.*

ONE

THE FIRST TIME GRIFF TRULY NOTICED CANDY Albright, she was yelling about Frankenstein.

Well, maybe not yelling, per se. More issuing various pronouncements about Mary Shelley's magnum opus at such a volume that witnesses at that faculty meeting would never, ever again confuse the story's eponymous scientist with his vengeful, humanoid creation.

Over the course of five very loud, very entertaining minutes, she announced the various actions she'd taken to clarify the matter to the student body. Including—but by no means limited to—a planned puppet show. A goddamn *puppet show*, the apogee of her Frankenstein Is *Not* the Monster Initiative.

She was vibrating with passion, unabashedly herself, more alive than he'd felt in—

Well, that didn't matter.

What did matter: It was the first time since his move to Marysburg that he'd smiled.

In various start-of-the-school-year English department meetings, he'd only vaguely registered her presence and her name. Which was both a mystery and a travesty, given the way she seemed to gather all the light in the room, only to expel it in a sort of didactic supernova.

Overlooking Candy was a mistake he didn't intend to repeat.

For the rest of the school year, then, he made a point of observing her. Listening to her too, which wasn't difficult, given her admirable lung capacity.

She never disappointed. She always snapped his attention into sharp focus.

Stalwart. Stubborn. Shrewish, some might say, but they'd be wrong.

Since that first Marysburg High School faculty meeting, almost a year ago, the sight of her marching down the hall, all martial intensity and unshakeable confidence, had heartened him, even on his worst days. She cared about so much. Students and colleagues and stories and language. She was a constant reminder that determination and belief still existed in his world.

Which was why, when he saw her shuffle into the faculty lounge the following August, he immediately straightened in alarm.

"Good morning," Candy said, the words barely audible.

She'd spoken into Griff's right ear, but that wasn't the issue. His colleague's voice, so gloriously booming and decisive, normally made her angle of approach irrelevant.

Not today. She'd murmured the standard greeting, rather than making it seem like an order—you *will* have a good morning, *or else*—and she did so without her usual direct eye contact. Instead, she'd kept her head down, her gaze on the memos she'd just removed from her staff mailbox, still facing that honeycombed wall of wooden slots.

It didn't sound like a good morning. It didn't look like one either.

Nevertheless, he echoed her words, studying his colleague as discreetly as possible as she flipped through her mail.

8

With her shoulders slumped, her head bowed, and her hair shorn, the pale nape of her neck seemed...vulnerable. Not a word he'd have ever imagined using to describe her. Even more alarmingly, her usual schoolmarm cosplay, as he liked to think of it, had vanished.

Instead, she was wearing stretchy black pants, an oversized, faded tee, and sneakers. Which made total sense for a returning teacher prepared to set up her classroom for the upcoming school year. He'd donned worn jeans and his own faded t-shirt for this day's efforts, which would likely involve moving chairs, desks, and books between and within classrooms.

But Candy Albright didn't let good sense get in the way of her convictions, and at some point she'd evidently become convinced she should clothe her solid frame in a blouse, cardigan, pearls, and a long skirt each and every day she appeared at work. That she should pull her ashy brown hair back into a bun with the assistance of a wide headband, her eyebrow-length fringe of bangs brushed to the side. That she should secure her horn-rimmed glasses with a chain around her neck, even though she always, always had them perched on the bridge of her aquiline nose.

Rain, shine, school day, teacher work day, faculty retreat... it didn't matter. She altered not, as Shakespeare might have said.

Before this moment, then, he'd literally never seen her with her hair down. But sometime during the summer, she'd cut it too short for a bun. Instead, it framed her round face in smooth, jaw-length arcs. With her chin down, that swoop of hair swung forward, obscuring her expression from his sight.

The barrier bothered him more than it should.

It wasn't his business. He shouldn't inquire. The two of them were—and would remain—friendly colleagues, rather than friends. For so many reasons, his instincts had consistently guided him away from bridging that gap.

Still, he cleared his throat. Opened his mouth.

But before he said anything, she offered him a curt nod and trudged out the door of the faculty lounge. Belatedly recovering his own good sense, he waited sufficient time to ensure she'd reached her classroom before following her path to his.

Her room might adjoin his, and he might watch her from afar, but that was as much intimacy as he could handle.

Alas, I have grieved so I am hard to love.

Not that love had anything to do with it. Not at all.

THEY BOTH WORKED THE ENTIRE DAY AT THE school, sometimes encountering one another in the English department office or the copy room or—once again—in the faculty lounge, where he reheated the turkey sausage chili he'd made over the weekend while she retrieved a Diet Coke from the old, rattling refrigerator.

At each encounter, she greeted him with another dip of her chin and nothing more.

No talk of new department initiatives. No blustering insistence that he get more sleep, because she'd spotted the bags under his eyes. No demands that he tell her if he needed help moving or organizing anything.

She responded to his own offer of help with a mumbled assurance that she was fine, thank you anyway. He had to lip-read during that particular exchange, she was so muted.

He didn't want to worry. He wouldn't.

Most of their time, they spent inside their classrooms. And even through a wall, the screech of moving furniture told him what she was doing. Setting up her classroom, angling her desks and chairs just so. Exactly what he was doing.

Later in the afternoon, though, those bursts of sound

ceased. Like him, maybe she was fastening laminated posters to the wall or covering her bulletin board. Labeling folders and reviewing opening-day lesson plans.

At some point, as the sun sank toward the horizon outside his classroom windows, he took a break. Leaned his desk chair back. Snacked on a handful of pretzels.

Thought, unwillingly, about Candy. Again.

After their encounters today, he'd found himself loath to turn on music as he worked. He'd kept close to the wall adjoining their two rooms, his own newly-assigned classroom silent. Just in case.

He'd seen that particular greyness before. In the mirror, three years ago.

He reached for his reusable water bottle, which was sitting at the edge of his battered, paper-covered desk, and tipped it back. Swallowed hard.

If she needed him—

Rather, if she needed *anyone*, he wanted to hear. Especially since no other teacher had started their classroom setup quite so early, and the school echoed with emptiness after the administrators and maintenance staff went home for the evening.

Because of the encompassing silence that night, he heard the short, shocked cry, the crash, the thud. The awful moment of silence, followed by something that might have been a whimper.

He didn't have time to contemplate the matter further, because he was already racing out his door and wrenching hers open—why was it closed, when she never closed her door except when teaching?—and scanning her classroom for signs of trouble.

They weren't hard to locate or interpret. A chair rested on its side before her half-finished bulletin board, and Candy lay crumpled on the floor near its metal legs, eyes clenched shut.

She'd stood on the chair. Overbalanced. Fallen on the unforgiving tile.

Half a dozen strides, and he was there.

"Candy?" When he knelt beside her, that same tile bit into his aging knees. "Talk to me."

To his relief, her answer came immediately, its irony sharp enough to relieve his worst concerns about a concussion. "Certainly, Mr. Conover. Name your subject."

Normally, she called him Griff. Caught in such a helpless, vulnerable position, however, little wonder she'd grasped for the dignity and distance of his surname.

No blood. No unnatural angles in her limbs. Thank the heavens.

That said, some serious injuries weren't obvious to the untrained, naked eye. "Tell me where you're hurting."

She let out a single, heartrendingly raw sob, then pressed her wide mouth into a tight line and breathed hard through her nose. "I'm p-perfectly well, thank you."

If he hadn't been so worried, he would have yielded to the familiar, charming mulishness of her declaration. Given the circumstances, though, he couldn't let the clear falsehood stand.

"That seems more aspirational than truthful, I'm afraid." His hands hovered over her, his eagerness to help her from the hard floor at war with his common sense. He could cause further damage by lifting her head into his lap, and he knew it, but leaving her like this—if only for a moment longer—galled him. "Can you move?"

"Of course I can move." She sniffed, her pretense of unconcern only somewhat undercut by her trembling chin. "I'm a bit bruised, that's all."

Her legs shifted first, straightening in a seemingly easy motion. Then she raised her head. Rotated it cautiously but without signs of distress. Wiggled her torso.

"If your back and neck feel okay, do you want to try

sitting up?" He offered his hands, ignoring how they trembled fully as much as that stubborn chin. Jesus, she'd scared the hell out of him. "Here. Let me help."

She mustered a small smile. "Although I appreciate your offer of assistance, I'm more than capable of—*fuck!*"

With a gasping cry, her attempt to lever herself up ceased, and she curled in on herself once more, cradling her left arm against her body, panting through obvious pain.

He'd never heard her use an obscenity before. If only these sorts of situations prompted them, he hoped he never would again.

"Okay. Okay." Frantic, he peered out through the doorway, hoping to see their security guard, but he wasn't sure Carlotta even worked so late during the summer. "I'll call an ambulance. Or drive you to the emergency room."

"*No.*" It was an instant refusal. Firm and loud and definite.

He ignored it. Why weren't his keys in his jeans pocket? If he'd deposited them on top of his desk, he'd have to leave her long enough to get them. Shit.

"I'm going to my classroom for my keys, but I'll be right —" Already on his feet, he gaped down at her. "What the hell are you doing?"

Somehow, while he'd been patting his pockets, she'd raised herself to a sitting position using her right arm, her left still pressed against her chest. "Getting up, clearly."

She was trying to maneuver herself to her knees, her face deathly pale where it wasn't blotched with livid pink. Once more, he found himself reaching for her but unable to touch. This time, because she hadn't given him permission.

"Candy..." He met her red-rimmed gaze. Held it. "Please don't hurt yourself trying to do it alone. I can help. I *want* to help."

Her eyes turned glassy once more, and his gut churned at the sight.

Then she blinked hard, lifted a hand, and accepted his. "Okay. On the count of three. One...two...three."

Together, they got her kneeling. Her palm was damp against his, her grip firm, the skin-to-skin contact electric in a way he didn't have the time or inclination to parse.

He put her good arm around his shoulders. In halting movements, she rose to her feet with his assistance, still breathing hard through the pain.

For a few seconds, she remained huddled against him, allowing him to support some of her weight. He bore it gladly.

"Thank you," she eventually said.

The words were unadorned but decisive. Loud enough to hear easily.

He looked down at the graying crown of her head, wondering when that booming voice had become such a comfort to him. "You're welcome. Let's get you to the hospital."

She moved away from him then, her chin turning pugnacious in an entirely familiar way, and he braced himself for a fight.

After glancing down at her left arm, though, still bent protectively close to her chest, she sighed. "Your keys are in your classroom, you said?"

He let out a slow breath, almost giddy in his relief. "Yes."

"I'll gather everything I need and meet you in the hall." Her throat worked. "Thank you again. I don't—"

She cut herself off. Gazed up at him, brow creased in seeming confusion.

"Thank you," she repeated.

He forced himself to turn away from her.

"No problem," he said over his shoulder as he headed for the door.

Only he wasn't sure that was entirely true. Not for either of them.

"IF YOU DRIVE ME BACK TO THE SCHOOL, I CAN make it home just fine." Perched on the hospital bed, Candy pointed meaningfully at her left arm. "See? My arm might be broken, but the splint will keep everything stable until the swelling goes down and I can get a cast. And I didn't take anything but Tylenol, so my head is perfectly clear."

The doctor had wanted to write a prescription for stronger painkillers, but she'd refused with so much loud adamance, the man had taken an actual step backward, his white coat flapping.

A bit of missing context, Griff presumed. "Yes, but it's still going to be awkward. I'm happy to help you get settled, if you want."

"Thank you, but you've done enough," she said, looking down that straight nose at him.

The pronouncement did not invite argument, so he didn't offer one. Not about that, anyway.

He shoved his hair out of his eyes, recalling the doctor's instructions. Following his instincts. "Fine. But you'll need to elevate your arm above your heart whenever you can."

"Yes." Her gaze narrowed dangerously. "I also heard what the doctor said. There's nothing amiss with my hearing."

Well, that made one of them.

He deliberately ignored her growing ire. "You can put some ice in a towel or plastic bag to help with the swelling, but only over the splint. Fifteen to twenty minutes every few hours."

"I understand that." Each syllable sounded like ground glass. "I do not require you to reiterate all my instructions."

Apparently, his instincts when it came to Candy were surprisingly sound. As she grew more and more irritated, that awful grayness receded. Her cheeks turned rosy, her brown eyes sharp. Her shoulders squared, and her voice got louder.

Broken arm or no broken arm, she looked more herself right now than she had since June.

He wanted that confident, truculent Candy back. For her. For himself.

So he continued talking, injecting a bit of extra pompousness into his tone. "You should wiggle your fingers as much as possible."

"You—" Her brows snapped together, and she flung her uninjured arm in the air. "Are you aware that I was *in the room* while Dr. Marconi told me what I should and shouldn't do? Did you somehow *overlook* my *very presence?*"

Honestly, this was the most fun he'd had all day. "I thought I saw you, but I wasn't entirely certain. It's harder to recognize you without that whole bouffant thing"—he swirled his hand over the top of his head—"you used to have going on up here."

Her mouth dropped open in outrage. "A tiny bit of volume does not equal a *bouffant*. I'm not a refugee from the mid-1960s, Mr. Conover!"

"More late eighteenth-century France, then?" He sat back in his chair, crossing one ankle over his knee. "You *are* fond of proclamations. Very Marie Antoinette of you."

She sputtered, her nostrils flaring.

He smiled at her in a particularly obnoxious way. "Anyway, I won't go inside, but I'll follow you home, just in case. And I'll wait in your driveway until I see the lights come on."

"*Fine.*" It was more a growl than an actual word. "As long as you stop talking, right this second, you can follow me home."

That seemed like a fair tradeoff to him.

Besides, Shakespeare had the right of it. *Nothing can seem foul to those that win.*

So he obediently kept his mouth shut while she received

16

her discharge papers and swiped her credit card for her emergency room copay. Still silent, he drove her to the school parking lot, and then followed her small SUV across town.

It was after midnight, and she was returning to a dark, empty house. Just as he would, as soon as he ensured she was safely home.

After she let herself into the front door and flicked on the interior and porch lights, she lingered in the doorway. After a moment, she raised her good arm in something that wasn't quite a wave. More a gesture of acknowledgment.

Within that halo of golden light, he could read her lips. *Thank you, Griff.*

Then the door closed, and he drove home. Showered. Got in bed. Blinked at the ceiling as his brain inevitably returned to its favorite preoccupation.

Candy Albright. Again. Still.

She fascinated him for so many reasons.

Twenty-plus years of teaching, full to bursting with students and colleagues and discussions about poetry and plays and novels, had in turn taught him well. He'd learned at least one thing for certain.

Not everyone could decipher subtext.

Not even if they noticed its presence, which many people —too enmeshed in their own thoughts, their own concerns— did not. Not even when it was pointed out to them by, say, a longtime teacher who wanted his ninth graders to pass their end-of-year English proficiency test, and also wanted them to take pleasure in the way simple words could contain multitudes. Universes secreted away, but open to explorers with sufficient curiosity and persistence.

Even those who *could* decipher subtext didn't always wish to perform the labor. He hadn't required a teaching degree for that revelation. A decade of joyous, sometimes-contentious married life had clarified the matter sufficiently.

Yes, subtext was difficult. Fraught. No question about it.

17

Still. Since that first faculty meeting, he'd been amazed. Nay, stupefied.

People seemed to think Candy Albright was as straightforward and direct as her pronouncements, as if she possessed no subtext at all. No river running swift and hidden beneath the craggy, immovable, desert-dry boulders of her words.

Worse: No one, as far as he could tell, seemed to wonder about context either, or consider the simplest and most obvious question. The question he trained his ninth graders to ask over the course of a school year together.

Those times when he couldn't successfully occupy himself with other matters—times like these—he did wonder. He did consider. He asked himself *why*.

Why her students claimed to fear her, yet seemed entirely certain she would spend hours after the last bell working with them on their college application essays. Which she did. He'd seen her night after night, bent over a desk, red pen in hand, attention sharp as the tacks studding her bulletin board on the students and papers before her.

Why, when she worried and grew exasperated, she borrowed the words of mobsters instead of poets and threatened—unconvincingly—to put hits on those causing her distress. She, an English teacher of considerable repute, who guided her seniors inexorably through poetry and prose and the vagaries of the AP English Literature and Composition exam.

Why a woman, so often humorless as a dirge, had a laugh as loud and honking and unabashed as hers. A cascade of sound, its joyful draw undeniable. Though he had done his best to deny it anyway.

Why a woman so brash and unafraid and amusingly *certain*—a tidal wave in human form, a *force*—had arrived weeks early to set up her classroom, face grey and wan. Hair shorn, also greyer than the previous year. So quiet. Too quiet. Even before her injury.

Why, in short, Candy Albright was Candy Albright. The cocksure Candy Albright of last year, and the bafflingly diffident Candy Albright of today.

He shouldn't wonder, of course. It didn't speak well of him that he did. Or rather, *how* he did, with fascination and anxiety and something like urgency.

He wondered anyway.

Finally, once the bedside clock ticked past two in the morning, he punched his pillow, turned on his side, and forced his eyes shut.

This preoccupation—this foolish, damnable fascination with Candy—was a mere academic exercise, the allure of a puzzle yet to be solved. At most, the automatic, perfunctory concern of a coworker. Nothing more than that.

Please God, nothing more than that.

TWO

"WHY GREEN?" GRIFF ASKED IN LIEU OF ALL THE more important, more dangerous questions.

When Candy didn't answer right away, he held a letter against the paper-covered cork, using a level to ensure its straightness and a ruler to keep the spacing between letters even. With an emphatic bang, she stapled the last piece of the Jean Rhys quotation into place. Then she placed the stapler on the counter and gazed at the newly completed bulletin board as he climbed down from the stepstool.

Reading makes immigrants of us all. It takes us away from home, but more important, it finds homes for us everywhere. An assertion he both appreciated and seconded, naturally, although its selection was somehow... softer than he'd expected from his colleague. More openly sentimental.

With a quiet sigh, she removed her glasses and let them hang around her neck. Rubbed her eyes as he watched, struck by the sight of her without that barrier in place.

"Candy? Why green?" he repeated.

When she turned her head toward him, he could spot the thready lines and shadows underneath those sharp eyes, the way her brown eyelashes stood almost straight out instead of curling coquettishly. Defensive spikes, not an open fan.

A stray eyelash now rested above her round cheek, but he kept his hands to himself.

"I have no idea what you're talking about." She donned those horn-rimmed glasses once again and retreated behind her desk. "My bulletin board is blue."

Now he was even more intrigued. Deliberate obtuseness was not Candy's usual modus operandi. "So it is. Which is why I was referring to your cast, rather than your display."

After their late-night emergency room visit, she hadn't returned to school for the rest of the week. He'd fought against sending her an e-mail or concerned text every day. Every hour. But she'd arrived only minutes after him today, the following Monday, and his heart had uncramped a bit in his chest at the sound of her clomping footsteps in the hall, the sight of her rosy cheeks and tilted chin, even though she was wearing a t-shirt and stretchy pants again.

Apparently her swelling had diminished over the past week. Her lower left arm was now encased to the wrist in a forest-green fiberglass cast.

It seemed a curious choice for a woman who generally eschewed darker colors.

"Why is my cast green?" Her mouth pinched, she met his eyes for an electric moment. Then she looked away, those spiky eyelashes fluttering. "The whim of a moment, quickly regretted."

He leaned his butt against the counter and crossed his arms over his chest. Studied her.

The roses on her cheeks had turned blotchy, and they spread downward to the neckline of her t-shirt as she shuffled papers on her desk. "That said, it's a nice color. Attractive, I suppose."

Before he could inquire further, she went on the attack.

"Speaking of regrets, don't think I've missed those

caverns under your eyes, Griff," she said loudly, pointing an accusing forefinger at his face. "Either get more sleep soon, or I'll make sure you regr—"

To his shock, she cut herself off mid-threat.

The pinkness drained from her cheeks, and she was suddenly gray again, both arms limp at her sides. Her chin sank to her chest, and she was silent. One breath. Two. Five.

This time, he couldn't stop himself.

"Candy..." He got to his feet and rounded her desk, laying a careful hand on her good arm. "Are you okay? What's wrong?"

She didn't move away from the contact, although her fingers twitched. "I'm fine. My arm is hurting a bit, that's all."

To hear her response, he'd had to angle his head. Not a good sign.

"Just..." She made eye contact again, brow creased. "You'll make yourself sick, Griff. You need rest. I..."

He waited dumbstruck, dizzy at her proximity and the direct statement of concern. The meeting of intent stares. The kiss of flesh to flesh.

Her skin was softer than he'd imagined, giving and resilient beneath his fingertips.

Even if threatened with imminent destruction, he couldn't have spoken then. Not to save his life, much less his weary heart.

She cleared her throat, the sound raw and painful.

Still gazing into his eyes, face fierce with a determination he didn't understand, she finished her thought. "I worry about you."

The open admission somehow disconnected him from his own worries. His shame.

His hand moved of its own volition, lifting from her arm to her cheek.

"You have..." He gathered the stray eyelash from the thin,

fragile skin beneath her eye, careful not to smudge her glasses. "There. I got it."

Her chest hitched.

Upon his upturned forefinger, he presented his offering. "Make a wish."

She blinked up at him. Then she blew lightly, cool air rushing over his fingertip, and the eyelash took flight.

When she licked her pale lips, the sheen of moisture there drew his gaze like a lodestone. *My mistress' eyes are nothing like the sun; Coral is far more red than her lips' red…*

"I wished that you would get more sleep soon," she told him.

Her chin had turned mulish. Challenging in the most familiar, welcome way.

"If you say your wish, it won't come true." It was a gentle scolding, spoken through a thick throat.

Those dark eyes unexpectedly flooded, and she jerked back from him. He didn't beckon her closer again, didn't reach out to gather her into his arms, but he wanted to. Heaven help him, he wanted to.

She took a deep, shuddering breath. "But if you don't say it outright, directly, how can anyone know what you want? How you feel?"

Turning away, she gathered the last remaining poster from her desk, awkwardly removed the rubber band, and unrolled the laminated cylinder.

A portrait of Shakespeare, appropriately enough.

"Fair point," he managed to say, aching for them both.

It was also a point he'd heard before. Across a dinner table, the words patient and loving. Whispered into his good ear in the hush of a dark bedroom. Shouted during one of their rare arguments, her graceful hands flung wide in emphasis.

No, not everyone enjoyed interpreting subtext. Not all the time.

He closed his eyes.

Metaphors and poetry are wonderful. But sometimes people need to hear the actual words, love. Marianne had cupped his face, stroking her thumbs over his cheeks, her hair tumbled on a shared pillow. *Sometimes I need to hear the actual words. 'I'm scared. I'm angry. I'm sad. I love you.'*

Sometimes I can't find direct words that encompass everything I want to say, everything I feel, he'd protested.

Consider them handholds. Her fingers were warm and tender on his skin. *Easily grasped in hard moments. Easily understood. Easily supplemented with a few good metaphors or lines of poetry. I know your family didn't talk about feelings, but you're direct about everything else in your life, Griffin. You can do it. It'll just take some practice.*

She was almost always gentle, and she was always kind. To him, her family, the students she counseled, everyone.

I'll try harder, he'd told her. *I promise. I love you.*

Her smile was as sincere, as open, as she herself was. *Thank you, love.*

He'd nuzzled into her cupped hand. *And now, please stand by for metaphorical supplementation. Or, rather, lay by.*

Is that what you're calling it? Metaphorical supplementation? Really?

As she'd laughed, he'd surged forward to capture her mouth. Tumbled her beneath him. Marianne. His wife. His...everything.

He blinked his eyes open, bewildered and squinting in the harsh classroom lights.

The memory...

For the first time, it prompted a fierce ache, but didn't rend his heart anew. And somehow, that felt like yet another loss.

When had the sting of remembering his wife—his *wife*—become almost bearable? And what did that say about him, his constancy, his vows?

24

"Griff?" The word was loud. Sharp with concern.

He resurfaced and focused.

Candy. That was Candy, not Marianne.

Even lost in his past, there was no mistaking one for the other. The two women could hardly be more different, which burned like bile in his throat some nights.

Candy had set aside the poster. She was eyeing him carefully, somberly, her glasses glinting under the fluorescent lights.

"Sorry. I was thinking. About..." He fumbled. Shoved back his hair and grasped for words easier than the truth. "I was thinking about whether you'd have your Frankenstein initiative again this year."

Still watchful, she shook her head. "I've decided to implement four-year cycles."

"So most students experience each initiative during their time in Marysburg High, but you don't get bored doing the same thing year after year." He scratched his bearded chin, still fidgety. "Clever."

The slight curve of her lips was charmingly smug. "No need for more frequent repetition. Students don't tend to forget my initiatives."

"No." His unexpected bark of laughter hurt his tight chest. "I imagine they don't."

"Will you help me with this last poster?" She tilted her head to the left of the door. "I want it over there."

In response, he grabbed the level and tape dispenser and crossed the room, grateful for the opportunity to occupy his hands and distract himself from his troubling thoughts.

As they worked, he glanced over at her. Her eyes were a bit red-rimmed now, her face paler than when she'd arrived that morning. And just a minute or two ago, she'd been fighting tears again, slumped and mournful for reasons he hadn't yet discovered.

They could both use distraction, then. He would provide it.

"About your Frankenstein Is *Not* the Monster Initiative..." The top two corners secured, he began to make loops of tape for the bottom of the poster. "I've been meaning to discuss it with you. I think it could use some retooling."

Immediate, livid color filled her cheeks. Her eyes snapped to his, narrowed and sharp. "Is that so?"

It was more a warning than a question, and one he deliberately failed to heed. Their evening in the emergency room had taught him well.

"I think a convincing argument could be made that Victor Frankenstein *is* a monster. More so than his creation, in many ways." He quirked a brow at her before applying tape to the bottom of the poster and smoothing it against the wall. "There you go. All done."

"Thank you." The words were clearly begrudging, but she said them. She thought for a few moments before continuing to speak. "As far as my Frankenstein initiative... you may have a valid point." Then she pointed an accusing finger at him, her continued annoyance clear. "That said, you've deliberately misinterpreted the mission of the initiative, which is to stop students and certain intransigent faculty members from calling the misbegotten creature Frankenstein."

"By *certain intransigent faculty members*, you mean Mildred," he guessed.

Her nostrils flared. "I mean Mildred. The scourge of the art department."

Last Halloween, even after Candy's initiative, Mildred had assigned her students to make collage portraits of Frankenstein. And by *Frankenstein*, she meant the creature, not the scientist.

He had no idea whether Mildred was deliberately rattling her colleague's chain or was merely oblivious. Either way, the day Candy found out about the collage assignment, alien life forms in distant galaxies surely heard her infuriated howl and ran for cover.

All that week, she kept declaring, "There was a puppet show. A *puppet show*."

All that week, he had to duck into his classroom to stifle his hilarity, even as he sympathized with her frustration.

"If accurate identification of Victor Frankenstein is your primary goal, then maybe you should rename the initiative." He scratched his jaw again, dimly aware that he should either shave off his facial hair or care for it a little better. "I suggest something along the lines of: Victor Frankenstein May Be a Monster, But He's Not *the* Monster."

"I'll take that under advisement." Her baleful glare eased. "I've been considering whether I should clarify a few more matters about the creature next time. The misconceptions about him are maddening."

To her, he imagined they were. Candy did not suffer wrongness gladly. Or at all.

It was a wonder she could manage to spend any time on the internet, considering. If she ever came across the comments section beneath a YouTube video, she might literally explode on the spot. *Another victim of Acute Factual Outrage Syndrome*, the doctor would announce, shaking their head. *Such a shame*.

"You want everyone to know he's yellow in the book, rather than green?" An obvious guess, but the best one he had.

"Yes!" She gave a near-violent wave of her good arm. "*Thank you*. And he didn't have bolts in his neck either!"

Her awful sadness had disappeared, washed away by the intensity of her passion. Good.

"Well, you have plenty of time to rethink your initiative before it comes around again. By then, maybe Mildred will have retired."

Candy's lip curled. "Only the good retire young."

"I'm not sure anyone could describe Mildred as *young* anymore," he noted.

"Methuselah would." The corners of her eyes crinkled. "But only if he were lying."

He leaned into the wall, ready for further entertainment. "As long as we're discussing important literary and linguistic matters, I hear you tell your students not to split infinitives or leave dangling prepositions."

She sucked in a breath through her teeth, immediately on the defensive. "As it happens, I do tell them that. Your point, Mr. Conover?"

"People have been breaking those rules since English came into existence as a language."

She tilted her head so she could look down her nose at him. "People have done a lot of incorrect things since that time. I repeat: Your point, Mr. Conover?"

"Those rules made sense for the Romans, since sentences in Latin don't end with prepositions, and infinitives are one word. You literally can't split them." When her mouth opened, he raised his hand. "As I'm certain you're already aware. However, you may not realize how those strictures transferred to English."

Another glimpse of that faint, smug smile. "Because snobbish neoclassicists thought English should follow the same grammatical rules as Latin."

Triumph and aggravation suited her equally, he'd found. Both allowed her to draw straight and comfortably inhabit every inch of her tall, round body, rather than curling in on herself as she'd been doing since the summer.

In her own way, she was lovely. Striking and utterly unique.

Her brown hair shone as it swung to her jaw, and those glasses emphasized the intelligence in her gaze. Her rosy cheeks curved sweetly, and so did her br—

No. He wouldn't venture there, despite his recent, unwelcome discovery that physical need, the simple desire to touch and be touched intimately, hadn't died with his wife.

Walt Whitman's words unspooled in his mind. *The love of the body of man or woman balks account, the body itself balks account.*

When Candy stepped closer, his breath stalled in his lungs.

"You thought I didn't know about the origins of those grammatical rules? I do, of course. I also realize their inherent foolishness. That said"—leaning in until her bodily warmth became an inadvertent taunt, Candy tapped his chest with one short fingernail—"let me ask *you* a question, Griff. Do you think each and every AP grader in Salt Lake City considers those rules foolish? What about the people reading and rating college admission essays? What about old-school university professors grading student papers?"

Ah. Even in his muddled mind, that made a surprising amount of sense.

"So you may not personally care about split infinitives and dangling prepositions, but you're preparing your students for people who might." That single spot on his chest was aflame, but he tried to act normally. Like a colleague, not a man at war with himself. "I apologize for underestimating your knowledge and thoughtful consideration of these matters."

To his surprise, she laughed.

The room rang with it, the noise exuberant and irresistible. He found himself laughing too, and he had no idea why. Maybe because this was the first time he'd elicited that particular sound. Maybe because he was so tired of being sad all the damn time. Maybe because her body literally shook with the force of her mirth, and the sight was more charming than it should be.

It was fitting, too. Candy Albright didn't traffic in half-measures. Not in outrage, not in joy, not in anything.

Her laughter faded to a smile that pierced him with its

clear affection. "I'm just delighted to find someone who wants to talk about these issues with me. And as you've clearly realized, I relish a good argument. There's absolutely no need to apologize."

Before her, he would have said he avoided arguments whenever possible. That he found them stressful. But maybe…that wasn't entirely true.

Marianne, the gentlest of souls, a product of her parents' bitter divorce, had trembled when they argued. Cringed. Although she could handle moody teenagers in her guidance counselor's office, she didn't enjoy that kind of strife in her personal life.

Because he loved her, he'd done his best to shield her from any and all conflict—even verbal skirmishes conducted on an intellectual battlefield with no real rancor involved. She and Griff weren't one of those couples who bickered, either in fun or bitter enmity.

For the first time, though, he could picture how a relationship could work differently. How *he* could work differently in a relationship. How those differences might not constitute a hardship.

Which was rampant disloyalty, ugly and heartless. Wasn't it?

"That said, I'm afraid our continuing friendship may depend on one crucial question," he dimly heard Candy say, even though he hadn't realized they *were* friends. Not until just now, anyway. "How do you feel about the Oxford comma?"

"Indispensable," he muttered through numb lips.

Somehow she performed that trick again, gathering all the light in the room to herself. This time, she released all that brightness, all the energy, in her beaming smile. "Good. That's the correct answer, and I accept no other."

When a knock came from the doorway, only a foot or two away, he turned his head dazedly. Only to find their principal,

Tess Dunn, standing there, lounging comfortably against the doorframe. She looked as though she'd been lingering for quite some time, and they simply hadn't noticed her. A ridiculous thought, because of course they'd have seen her. With her standing that close, they couldn't possibly have missed her.

But her first words dispelled that notion. "I'm heartened you two came to an agreement on the important matters. Frankenstein, split infinitives, even comma usage. If only all conflicts were so easily resolved."

Her sharp gaze traveled to Candy. Lingered on that faded t-shirt, the jaw-length bob, the still-puffy eyes. Then she turned her attention to him, studying his shaggy hair and beard, the undeniable bags beneath his own eyes. Self-consciously, he scratched at his jaw again.

"You know…" The principal paused for several moments, brow crinkled, before encompassing both of them in a determined smile. "I'm so glad I caught the two of you together. I wanted to speak to you both about an upcoming project."

Candy's shoulders squared, and she straightened to her full height, a soldier standing at attention before her respected commander. "I enjoy projects, and I'm delighted to assist with whatever you need."

"I know you enjoy projects, Candy." The gentle, teasing affection in Tess's voice endeared her further to Griff—and he'd already formed a very high opinion of his head administrator. "Thank you for agreeing to one more, sight unseen. I appreciate your willingness to help."

At that point, he didn't really have much of a choice, did he?

"I'd be happy to help too." He raised his brows in inquiry. "What does the project entail?"

"Good question, Griff. Good…question." Tess bit her lip and glanced around Candy's room. "It's a very important task, involving—"

31

She frowned, seemingly distracted and bothered by her surroundings, and he had no idea why. Working together, he and Candy had finished her bulletin board, hung posters, and given each wall of her room a different focus: short fiction, poetry, novels, and drama. Everything was neat, colorful, and intelligently organized. No principal could ask for more, in his opinion.

Tess's face suddenly brightened. "I want you two to be in charge of the school's new, uh... Falling for Poetry Initiative." She gave a pleased little nod. "Since you're both here early, and your rooms are already in order, I'm hoping you'll have sufficient time to start planning together before the school year even begins. The initiative would take place in October, if that's acceptable to you both?"

"Falling for Poetry is a pun, I take it? Because of autumn?" Candy tapped her chin. "It's relatively short notice, but I think I could pull something together."

"With Griff's help, don't forget. I don't want you working too hard or putting any stress on that arm, so his assistance will prove invaluable." Tess pinned him with her stare. "That is, if he's willing to participate. Are you, Griff?"

Again, there was only one right answer. It was also the answer he wanted to give, even though it scared him.

"Yes," he said. "I'll do it."

Tess's grin was triumphant in a way he didn't fully understand, but he supposed that was why he was a lifelong teacher, rather than an administrator. How did he know what made principals gleeful and smug?

"What would be our budgetary—" he began.

Tess interrupted hastily. "Let's save all the details for an official meeting next week. Check your calendars and get back to me with times you're both available. In the meantime, I want you to consider—"

Still talking, she turned her back, walked over to Candy's desk, and scrawled something on a pad of sticky notes. Even

32

pointing his good ear in her direction couldn't save him, not when her normal speaking voice was so much softer than Candy's.

When Tess swiveled to face them once more, sticky note in hand, he could hear her again. "—share your notes. Any questions?"

He shook his head and watched as she left.

Well, he supposed this moment was inevitable, if he and Candy were truly becoming friends and not simply friendly colleagues.

His hearing loss in his right ear wasn't exactly a secret, and it didn't shame him in any way. That said, he didn't share the information freely either. As long as it didn't impact his ability to teach effectively, it was no one's business but his.

Unless he chose otherwise.

He supposed he was doing that now. Choosing.

When he closed the classroom door behind Tess, the action drew Candy's immediate attention.

She looked up from where she'd been scribbling on a notepad, her brows raised above the rims of her glasses. "We need privacy for this discussion? How ominous." The bright determination in her face dimmed. "Listen, Griff. If you'd rather not do the project, I can handle it on my own. It's fine."

Ironic, that wording.

"I'm happy to do the project with you." He offered her a wry smile. "It's the whole *listen, Griff* part that's the problem."

Her brow beetled as she waited for him to clarify.

"I've had hearing loss in my right ear since I was a child," he told her. "Normally, if people speak loudly enough or I can do a bit of lip reading, I'm fine. When Tess turned her back, though, I missed some of what she was saying."

After a moment, Candy nodded. "She was mumbling."

He leaned against the whiteboard, struck by Candy's reaction to his revelation. Or rather, her lack thereof.

She readjusted her wide headband, mouth pursed in thought. "You didn't miss much. She was rambling, as well as mumbling." Leaning closer, as if sharing a confidence, she added, "Honestly, she seemed a bit distracted and disorganized today. I'm not certain she's fully thought through this project of hers."

He'd thought the same. "I'm sure the start of the school year pulls her in a lot of different directions."

"I suppose so." Candy lifted a round shoulder. "Anyway, she said to confer with one another about possible initiative activities, price out those ideas, and then share our notes at our meeting with her."

A quick glance at his watch told him they didn't have time for a real discussion now. His afternoon meeting with the other ninth-grade English teachers started soon. Too soon, dammit. "Fair enough. I have a meeting for the rest of today, but I should be available whenever you're free later this week. Including tomorrow."

She smiled at him, her cheeks pink as the peonies in his backyard. "Tomorrow works for me."

When he started to open her door, she lifted a hand to stop him.

"Wait, Griff." There was a fierceness in her stare he recognized. The protectiveness of a powerful creature defending its own. "Tell me how to make our conversations easier for you."

He didn't want to contemplate the warmth suffusing his chest at that look.

You already make things easier, just by being yourself, he wanted to say.

Instead, he listed the basics. "It's only a problem if I can't see your mouth, or if you speak softly in my right ear. If that happens, I don't want you to think I'm ignoring you."

"I'll make certain you can hear me." Her eyes locked to

34

his, she slowly bobbed her head, and it wasn't a mere nod. It was an avowal. An oath contained in a simple gesture. "Always."

He had no doubt. "Thank you."

He couldn't look away. Not until his phone chirped from her desk, a reminder of both his upcoming meeting and where he'd distractedly laid the device earlier.

Tearing his gaze from hers, he strode across the room. With a tap, the chirp fell silent. "I need to get going. I'm sorry."

As he reclaimed his cell and slid it into his pocket, a framed photo by her laptop caught his attention. It must have been a new addition from that morning, because he hadn't seen it before. He'd have noticed, the same way he noticed almost everything about her.

Suddenly, his concerns about lateness, about the turmoil in his head and heart, all vanished. His insatiable curiosity about Candy had reared its rampant head, and he couldn't deny it. Couldn't deny himself.

"Is this your sister?"

In the photo, the resemblance between the two was unmistakable. Both built like Valkyries, they stood bumping shoulders with one another, grinning as the sun reflected off their glasses. The other woman in the picture was blonder than Candy, a bit shorter, her glasses rounder, but otherwise could have been his colleague's twin.

After a pause, Candy cleared her throat once, then a second time. "Yes. Dee. Denise."

"You two look happy." He finally glanced up from the photo, only to find that Candy had turned her back. She was fiddling with the Shakespeare poster, tugging its already-straight edges. "I don't think I've heard you mention her before. Does she live close?"

Slowly, Candy swiveled toward him, and he knew.

He knew she was making eye contact only because she'd

promised to face him during conversation, and she was a woman who kept her promises, weeping be damned.

He knew why she'd returned to school a woman diminished and gray with pain, even if he didn't understand all the intricacies of her grief yet.

He knew her sister was gone. Recently.

"She lived in Oregon." Candy pronounced the verb carefully, even as her voice shook, and he knew something else. She still stumbled over the tense, just as he'd done for the first few months. "She died this summer."

No euphemisms. Candy was direct about everything but her emotions.

Like him, come to think of it.

"I'm so sorry," he said, trying to infuse all the sincerity he felt into the simple phrase, and she made a small sound in response. A noise, more than a word. A whimper, wrenched from her resisting throat as she tried so damn hard not to sob out loud.

Shit, he couldn't just stand there and watch her crumple. Fuck his doubts and fears. Fuck his own grief. Fuck everything but what she needed from him—from someone—right this second.

"Oh, Candy." He reached for her with both hands, the desire to give comfort instinctive and urgent. "I—"

When she backed away from his touch, it hurt. More than it should have. He, of all people, understood how kindness could wreck someone in mourning, more thoroughly than the most vicious insult.

"It's fine," she told him, dashing away tears with her knuckles. "I'm fine."

He tore his hand through his hair, helpless and frustrated. Unwilling to leave her in this state, but aware that he had no choice, not if she didn't want him to stay.

"Don't you have a meeting?" Her brown eyes, lashes now

spiked with moisture, were pleading with him to go, to allow her some dignity. "You'll be late."

After one last, long look, he surrendered to the inevitable. "I'll see you tomorrow."

She dipped her trembling chin in acknowledgment, and then he left.

The door closed behind him, and he was entirely certain she was about to retreat to her desk, out of sight to passersby who might peer through the window in her door. She would cry alone, where no one could see, no one could hear. No one could offer her support or affection or anything else she needed, other than her pride and her privacy.

Dammit. He understood that too.

He needed a minute before entering the meeting, despite his increasing tardiness. So he went to the men's faculty bathroom. Splashed water on his face. Dried himself with a paper towel. Pushed an overlong hank of hair behind his ear and studied his own damp reflection.

How long since he'd last cut his hair or groomed his growing beard?

How long since he'd seen himself without those dark pits beneath his eyes?

Gripping the sink with both hands, his knuckles nearly as white as the chipped porcelain, he acknowledged another unwelcome truth, asked himself another agonizing question.

How long since his own grayness had disappeared? Because he might be unkempt, but Candy's particular stage of numb, half-dead sadness had passed at some point.

Part of his brain kept insisting he should be ashamed of that.

Marianne wouldn't have wanted him to mire himself in his grief forever, though. It was a cliché, but also the hard, hard, truth.

Now he had to decide what he wanted for himself.

And as he met his own gaze clearly for the first time in—

Well, he didn't know how long.

But he noted, as if viewing a stranger, that he had green eyes. Weary, complete with bursts of lines at their corners, but green nevertheless.

Forest green, one might say.

At some point, he was going to have to look at that bit of subtext. Decipher it. Then decide whether he wanted to make it text instead. Clear. Undeniable.

Loud as life.

THREE

"I THINK WE HAVE THE POETRY SLAM MOSTLY planned out. So that brings us to our next task: the morning announcements." Candy hooked a finger in her pearl neck-lace, rotating one of the milky spheres idly as she frowned at her notebook. "Which poems do you propose to include? Either they have to be short, or we have to choose brief selections from longer poems."

To Griff's relief, Candy had resumed her schoolmarm cosplay when the official report day for teachers arrived. Other than the bun and her cast, everything remained the same from last year. Her eyebrow-length bangs swept diagonally across her high forehead, the rest of her hair tamed by a wide headband. Her pearl necklace nestled just above the collar of her blouse, while her cardigan and long skirt covered almost every inch of her sturdy frame.

He considered that bit of reclaimed normality a good sign, even though she didn't quite seem herself yet. That, of course, would take time. Months. Maybe years.

To his surprise, he kind of missed some aspects of her more casual clothing. The way those stretchy pants clung to her long, dimpled thighs. The squeak of her sneakers, and

necklines. How her t-shirts cupped her
tried not to notice.

small triangle of bare flesh at the base of
er collar gaped open, drew his eye again
ne pale stretch of her neck, and the peek of
r nape.

es distracted him during conversations with
Candy, and sometimes missed questions and cues to
speak. Luckily, she didn't get impatient, most likely because
she blamed his slow reactions on his hearing loss. A convenient excuse, he had to admit.

"Griff?"

Especially at times like these. "I'm sorry. I was just trying
to remember my list of poems."

"Why are you trying to remember it?" Behind her bangs,
he could just barely spot the wrinkle of her brow. "Didn't you
write it down?"

"Oh. Yes." Hurriedly, he flipped open his notebook. "Yes,
of course I did."

Now she was definitely side-eyeing him, and he couldn't
blame her.

"Okay," she said, drawing out the word. "So tell me one
of the poems you chose."

Dammit, he needed to be a professional, not a man
absurdly fixated on a patch of creamy skin he couldn't—
wouldn't—touch. "A few of my favorites weren't appropriate
for the morning announcements. Notably, Philip Larkin's—"

"'This Be the Verse.'" She tilted her head, expectant. "Did
I guess right?"

He laughed, absurdly happy that she somehow knew the
exact poem he'd been poised to name. "Students would love
it. *Love* it. But we'd also get fired, and I enjoy eating."

"As do I." She grinned at him. "It's a shame, though."

He thought for a moment. "'Those Winter Sundays' by

Robert Hayden is a worthy alternative. Or 'Good Bones' by Maggie Smith."

"Agreed." Letting go of her necklace, she put a check next to something on her paper. "I had those poems in mind as possibilities too."

He nodded toward her notebook. "Why don't you tell me about your choices? I'll fill in any gaps, as necessary."

Given his dubious attention span, better for her to spearhead the discussion as much as possible. Besides, he was curious about her selections and what they said about her, and about the way her mind worked, free of possible cross-contamination from his own choices.

Clicking her pen open and shut a few times, she frowned down at her list. "I had trouble narrowing the field of contenders, frankly. There are the usual suspects. Shakespeare, Emily Dickinson, Robert Frost, Elizabeth Barrett Browning, Christopher Marlowe, Phillis Wheatley, etc. Poems and poets who are part of any standard English curriculum."

He'd been afraid of this. Worried her sometimes-rigid notions about literature would leave her stranded in the classics from now-distant centuries. They were classics for a reason, of course, but sometimes not the most immediately engaging choices for students, especially at seven-thirty in the morning.

"Honestly, though, I think modern poetry more often connects with high schoolers, and standardized testing ensures they'll encounter the older classics at some point anyway." With a little shrug, she dismissed her obligation to those poems. "So the majority of my suggestions are from the past century. Maya Angelou's 'Still I Rise.' 'I Am Offering this Poem' by Jimmy Santiago Baca. 'Who Said It Was Simple' by Audre Lorde, and '[i carry your heart with me(i carry it in]' by Cummings. 'I, Too' by Langston Hughes. 'Love

41

is Not All' by Edna St. Vincent Millay. 'The friend' by Marge Piercy."

She went on for another minute or two, listing authors and poems he hadn't realized she'd know, or hadn't realized she'd appreciate. Lyrical poems, rage-filled poems, lovestruck poems, poems about marginalization and identity and humanity.

His favorites. So many of his favorites.

Oh, this was undiluted pleasure. To share a common language, to exult together in a searing turn of phrase, to find a kindred soul in poetry.

Still, he tried to hide his foolish giddiness and remain somber. Collegial.

"You've, uh, covered most of my suggestions already." He checked his own list again. "I'd add 'The Changeling's Lament' by Shira Lipkin and 'Instructions on Not Giving Up' by Ada Limón."

"Those are new to me." With a few taps of her screen, she brought the poems up on her cell and read them, eyes intent on the words. "They're important additions. Thank you, Griff. I'm bookmarking them."

Which left only the last batch of poems he'd earmarked for possible use.

"There are a few…" He licked his dry lips and looked down at the scrawled titles on his paper, formulating what he would say. Hoping he didn't injure her further. "I don't know how comfortable you'd be with Mary Oliver's 'In Blackwater Woods,' Sharon Olds's 'Cambridge Elegy,' or possibly 'One Art' by Elizabeth Bishop. Maybe 'The Watch' by Danusha Laméris."

All poems about loss and grief and death. Gorgeous poems. Heartrending poems.

She was silent.

"It's just…" He tapped his pen against his notebook. "Students respond well to those particular poems, because mortality, the reality of death, is becoming so much clearer to them by high school. And for kids who've experienced loss, poetry can help them work through their emotions and maybe find comfort."

Maybe you'd find comfort in those poems too, however fleeting, he carefully didn't say. *Just as I have.*

At the time he'd jotted them on the paper, he hadn't been sure Candy would know them. Now he was certain she did, but whether she'd turned to them or not, he couldn't say.

"I reread—" She hesitated. "I reread Mary Oliver all the time. 'Wild Geese' and 'In Blackwater Woods' especially. They're...important to me." Her mouth trembled, but she pressed her lips tight and took a deep breath. "Those are great choices. Let's add 'To a Sad Daughter' by Michael Ondaatje too."

"I don't think I've read that." He stole her phone to look it up, then wrote himself a reminder to savor it more thoroughly later. "It'll end up in this year's curriculum, I think."

Once he returned her cell, she claimed it. She stared down at the screen, where the Ondaatje poem remained on display, but he didn't think she was reading it.

She was fidgeting in her chair, free hand clenched. Then she nodded, seemingly to herself, and made direct eye contact with him. "Yesterday, a parent came to school for a meeting with Principal Dunn."

She paused for a moment, mouth white around the edges.

"From behind, I thought she looked like Dee. My sister. When I saw her, my heart..." She placed a palm over her chest. "It felt like being electrocuted. I called out to her, but she turned, and it wasn't—It wasn't her. The woman was a total stranger. Face to face, she didn't look anything like my sister. I barely got to the bathroom before I started crying. And it was—"

Her jaw worked, and she stared up at the ceiling for a moment.

"It was horrible," she finally said. "Humiliating and…"

This time, he filled in the word, so she didn't have to. "Heartbreaking."

Another nod.

He sank into his own chair, stunned by her unprompted admission. By the way she'd just tilted up her chin, bared that pale neck to him, and waited to find out whether he'd cut it.

This wasn't an iteration of Candy he'd met before.

This was the river beneath her boulders. Swift and deep. Full of beauty. Teeming with terrors.

Deliberately, he leaned forward from across Candy's desk and laid his hands flat between them. "Did it make you wonder whether you were losing your grip on reality?"

She cringed away from him, and it was unbearable. He hated it. *Hated* it.

He would never mock her. Never use such an intimate, painful confession against her. She didn't know that yet, but she would. He would make certain of it, starting now.

"My wife, Marianne, died three years ago," he said.

Candy swayed in his direction once more, her stricken wince gone. Instead, her expression had become as open and unguarded as he'd ever seen it. Sad again, this time for his sake.

"Oh, Griff." She spoke so softly, he had to read her lips.

"Brain aneurysm. Totally unexpected." The words were abrupt and hoarse, but he couldn't help that. He didn't talk about his grief to anyone who didn't already share it. Marianne's family, mostly. Maybe if he did, he could discuss it more easily.

Instead, the story clawed at his throat, unwilling to emerge. He forced it out anyway.

"She had a terrible headache all day, but we thought it was just the stress of the holidays." One final opportunity for intervention—for life—lost, though neither of them had

44

known it. "She died sometime during the night. When I woke up the next morning, she was already gone."

The horror of that awakening, Candy didn't need to hear about. Not now, anyway. Sharing that particular experience wasn't the point of his revelation.

"For months afterward, I saw her everywhere." *This* was the point. The reassurance that Candy wasn't experiencing anything unusual, anything that should embarrass her, anything that indicated acute mental instability, at least not by itself. "At gas stations. In the cars ahead of me at drive-throughs. At school. In malls and doctors' offices and sometimes even in our house. In our bed."

Candy's utter stillness, her sympathetic silence, allowed him to keep going, keep baring himself in the hopes she might recognize herself in his nakedness.

"It felt like being haunted. I thought I might be, uh, losing my faculties." When he forced out a dry, strangled sort of laugh, Candy's good hand covered his. Broad, strong, sheltering. "But the grief counselor said it was common. That for most people, those moments would eventually diminish, and then disappear entirely."

Her deep green cast seemed to absorb the sunlight beaming through her classroom windows, the color as warm and comforting as her hand on his. And beneath that fiberglass, her broken ulna was healing. Quickly, he hoped.

The clean fracture they'd both seen on the emergency room x-ray would cease to exist at some point. Maybe evidence of the damage would appear on future x-rays, or in a marrow-deep ache on rainy days, but maybe not. Her acute pain would become a mere memory, and they'd both welcome its retreat into the past. He certainly didn't want her to hurt any longer than necessary.

He didn't want her to hurt at all, but that wasn't an option.

Why couldn't he seem to feel the same about his own

fracture, his own pain? Why couldn't he greet his own healing with uncomplicated relief?

Her voice was loud enough for him to hear, but gentle. So gentle. "Did you stop seeing your wife at some point?"

"After a few months."

At first, he went a few days in between sightings. Then weeks.

Then, without him noticing, she'd slipped away entirely. Again.

"Was that a good thing? Or—" Candy bit her lip and thought for a moment. "Or did you miss that moment of possibility? The sense that she might be close, despite everything?"

So incisive. Like a surgeon, she'd sliced directly to his heart, bound in scars but frantically beating despite the damage.

"Those moments wrecked me." The bright burst of hope was never, ever worth the darkness afterward. "But when they were gone, when I didn't see her anywhere outside memories and photos anymore, I—"

When he didn't finish, she tilted her head, a line scored deep between her brows. "It felt like another loss?"

"Yes, but not just that. The guilt…" He forced himself to slide his hand out from beneath hers, and his arms immediately prickled with cold. The damn school kept its air conditioning way too chilly. "It gutted me."

At that, she sat back and sighed. "Ah, guilt. My newfound, constant companion."

The contours of his own guilt, he understood—the way his love of and loyalty to Marianne, his sense of who he was as a husband and a man, became fraught and disorienting as her death steadily receded into the past. But what possible reason could Candy have for feeling guilty about her sister's death?

"Why do you—" he began to say.

The speaker over the whiteboard abruptly crackled to life, the voice of their principal coming through loud and clear. "To all faculty and staff, this is a reminder that our meeting begins in ten minutes in the cafeteria. As promised, we're providing sandwiches, fresh veggies, and brownies. I'm not saying you should hurry, but I *am* saying swarms of locusts are slower and less comprehensive in their consumption of available foodstuffs than you are. Again, you have ten minutes. Then the floodgates open, and no sandwich is safe. Also, someone better save me a brownie, or you're going to have a very cranky principal for the rest of the week. You've been warned."

The speaker went silent, and Candy snorted.

"She's funny," he said, "and a vast improvement over my previous principal."

"Before she was a great principal, she was a great teacher." Candy's brow compressed. "I need to run a couple of errands before the faculty meeting starts. I don't mean to cut off our conversation, but—"

He heaved himself to his feet, suddenly tired enough to sleep right there, sprawled over her desk. "No worries. I have a few things I should do before then too. And as Tess noted, lateness is not a good strategy for this particular meeting, not if we want free lunch."

"Which we do." Her pale lips curved. "Even though we'll only bitch about its inferior quality and quantity afterward."

Somehow, despite his exhaustion, despite having dredged up and shared memories of Marianne, he discovered he was grinning too. "As mandated by teacherly tradition, hallowed and ancient."

"I'm sure Mildred was there when they carved the appropriate runes." She gathered her purse and notebook. "As one of the village elders, naturally."

Somehow, he'd never suspected Candy might contain this

brand of humor. He should have, though, given that ringing, wholehearted laugh of hers.

Shoving his hair back from his face—dammit, he really did need a cut—he huffed out an amused breath and followed her out the door. "It's a wonder she didn't clarify the Frankenstein issue with Mary Shelley herself."

"They didn't frequent the same social circles." She produced her room key and locked the door behind them. "Shelley was too young and vibrant, and"—getting up on tiptoe, she whispered into his left ear—"Mildred didn't approve of that whippersnapper Byron."

She'd remembered. Remembered and spoken so he could hear her, her rush of breath against his skin minty and damp and rippling through his body in a shockwave.

When he bent and leaned close to whisper in her own ear, her fine, soft hair caught on his beard. "I hate to tell you this, but I think you just made Mildred the hero of this particular tale."

Apple. Her hair smelled like an apple, surprisingly sweet and clean.

He could have stood there and inhaled that scent all day.

"Dammit." With that murmur, her lips must have been a hairsbreadth away from his skin, and he squeezed his eyes shut at the bolt of sensation down his spine. "Byron *was* a complete dick. I guess Mildred got it right. For once."

He indulged himself with one last comment, one last lungful of fragrant air near her pink, plump earlobe. "Maybe you should make that a new project: the Byron and Most of the Romantic Poets *Were* Total Dicks Initiative."

Then he moved one painful step back. Another. Even though she was cackling now, her frame shaking as her laughter echoed in the halls, and he wanted so badly to know how that felt up close, one body to another.

"Oh, God," she wheezed, "they're *the worst*, Griff. Such incredible, unrepentant *assholes*."

"They really are," he managed to say.

Then he was laughing too, hard enough that the guilt couldn't dig in its claws and gain purchase in his flesh.

It would find him again, he knew. Sooner or later. Probably sooner.

So he'd bask in this respite, the sunshine of their shared mirth, while he could.

FOUR

In his peripheral vision, Griff spotted Candy the moment she appeared in his open doorway. But he couldn't interrupt the student in front of him, not given the young woman's current state of distress.

Out of the student's sight, he held up a forefinger, requesting a minute.

Then he listened with his full attention once more, not only because his hearing loss necessitated that kind of concentration, but also because Shantae Kingsley—like every other student—deserved it.

"I did the assignment, I *swear*, Mr. Conover." When he passed her the tissue box, she snatched several and dabbed her eyes. "I don't know where it went, though. I checked my locker, I checked my backpack, I went back to my homeroom to see if I'd left it there—"

From almost the beginning of his career, he'd instinctively gravitated toward teaching ninth graders. Maybe because his calmness counterbalanced their sometimes-frenetic energy. Maybe because some of them were still grappling with the hormonal surges of puberty, and while he demanded a certain level of kindness and respect in his classroom, he didn't tend

to take moodiness personally. Maybe because he loved literature, but he also loved watching students take vast leaps in
their communication abilities—both written and oral—
during their first year of high school.

Sometimes, students struggled with the transition from
middle school. The sheer size of the school and the student
body, the number of classes, the way they had to keep track
of and take responsibility for their own assignments without
much outside help, could be intimidating for some kids.

But they would learn, and he could help. He loved
that too.

When Shantae finally wound down and took a breath, he
smiled at her.

"I believe you," he said, handing her another tissue.

Even after only a week of classes, he'd already noticed
how diligently she took notes and how fully she concentrated
on each assignment. He considered each of his students
special in their own way, of course, but Shantae—hand high
in the air to ask a question, eyes bright behind her glasses—
had stood out from the beginning.

She released a shuddering breath. "I'm sorry."

"You're human, and the first week of school is over-
whelming. No need to apologize." Waving her to a seat, he
turned another student chair to face her. "If you can't find it
in the meantime, just redo the assignment and turn it in on
Monday."

Her shoulders visibly lowered. "I can still get full credit?"

"Yes." With his chin, he indicated her overflowing backpack, bristling with half-crumpled papers. "But while you're
here, let's talk about how you're organizing all your notes
and assignments. Do you have a separate notebook for each
class?"

She nodded, her breath no longer hitching.

"Good." If she'd said no, though, he had a few extras in a
cupboard for situations just like this. "Then let's figure out a

way to organize them that makes sense for you and makes finding your assignments easier."

Fifteen minutes later, Shantae offered him a grin bristling with braces and bounced toward the classroom door, her stray papers sorted into their respective notebooks and a system in place to help her remember where she'd put everything.

"Thanks again, Mr. Conover," she called over her shoulder.

"My pleasure. Have a great weekend, Shantae," he said as she disappeared into the hall.

They'd found the assignment, of course, balled up beneath her biology textbook. He'd skimmed the first paragraph discreetly, and was entirely unsurprised to find it both well-written and full of obvious effort.

His pen began fading as he scribbled himself a note. *Talk to Shantae about lit mag and/or school newspaper. E-mail/call her parents to praise good work.*

If she continued to struggle with organization, he could suggest a parent-teacher meeting to coordinate their efforts to support her. But he'd give her a few weeks to work out the kinks on her own first, as long as she didn't seem completely overwhelmed.

Which reminded him: He needed to contact the guidance counselor about Cameron in third period, who'd been tardy every day but refused to discuss the matter with him, and whose parents didn't respond to messages.

When he tried to write another note, though, his pen only made inkless scratches. After tossing it in the garbage can, he reached for another, only to find one already in front of his nose.

Candy was standing beside his desk, good arm stretched out to offer him one of her trademark red pens.

At the sight of her, steady and strong and waiting, something inside him bloomed. Wildflowers in what he'd considered an endless expanse of sere, cracked earth.

The growth prickled. Stung, despite the unexpected beauty.

"Thank you." He took the pen, scrawled a reminder to himself about Cameron, and handed it back. "I'm sorry I kept you waiting."

Her shoulder lifted in a small shrug. "Impromptu student help sessions are an occupational hazard. I wasn't going home anytime soon, anyway."

She took off her cat-eye glasses, letting them dangle from the chain around her neck. It was something she'd been doing more and more often when they were alone.

"I can't do that," she said abruptly.

Since she didn't appear to be sitting anytime soon, he stood too. "Do what?"

"Communicate that way with students." With a sigh, she scrubbed her face with her hands and leaned heavily against his desk. "Accept and handle their emotions so skillfully. Become soft when they need softness and offer structure when they don't."

Her arms dropped limply to her sides. "I'm all structure, no softness. Always the stick, never the carrot. With students, with colleagues. With everyone."

Last fall, he'd glanced through her doorway. Seen her dappled by the setting sun through her classroom windows, head bent close with a senior as they painstakingly crafted a college application essay. Heard the happy shouts in the hallway months later, as that same student announced her early-admission acceptance into UVA.

Last May, he'd stood unseen outside the school's bus entrance and watched Candy usher her students to the AP test. Her expression fierce, she'd informed them they should hold their heads high, because they were the best-prepared and hardest-working English Literature and Composition students in the country. She'd demanded their best efforts on the test, *or else*, because she wanted to see them rewarded for all their work.

"That said," she'd added, her voice ringing with authority, "my pride in your efforts and accomplishments does not depend on the score you may receive. You've labored and persevered for an entire school year. Less than four hours in a school cafeteria can't alter that."

The kids had stared at her, all nervous fiddling stilled.

Then, as the bus driver honked impatiently, Candy raised an imperative forefinger. "You should not be intimidated by this test." She looked them in the eye, every one of them. "You are *my* students. This test should be intimidated by *you*."

Their shoulders had straightened, feet braced wide as if for battle.

"Cry 'Havoc!' and let slip the dogs of war!" she'd roared, and her students had laughed and whooped and climbed onto the bus, looking as confident and steady as any group of test-bound kids he'd ever witnessed.

He'd pictured Candy in a toga then, laurels crowning her dark head, one shoulder exposed, her long arms bare and pale and strong. A distaff Julius Caesar, bursting with power and command. He'd immediately tried to dismiss the image, yet it had burned behind his eyelids for days.

Before she could turn back toward the school, he'd slunk away and hidden from her. Hidden from himself.

For over a year, he'd been repressing thoughts of one woman to keep the memory of another sacrosanct. But thoughts of Candy were the heads of a Hydra. Cut off one, and two more sprang forth. Sometimes in unexpected places and without warning.

At the faculty meeting last week, for instance, he'd arrived early. And to his shock, Rose Owens—accompanied by her devoted fiancé and fellow history teacher, Martin Krause—had settled herself in the seat beside his.

"You know," she'd said, adjusting the pristine cuffs of her satiny black blouse, "you should ask Candy about her AP pass rates. They're astounding."

Despite his confusion, he'd nodded. "Okay."

He didn't teach AP, and he didn't consider Candy's test results his business. But he also wasn't going to argue with Rose, who—quite frankly—scared him a little.

Her amber-brown eyes had locked onto his. "Too many people confuse surface and substance. They see only what's evident at first glance. Good historians, though, are trained to look harder. Dig deeper. Search for context and contradictions and alternative points of view. Some important tales can be told in a single look, a single sentence. Most can't."

Martin had been gaping at his fiancé, brows raised high, but he hadn't intervened.

Sitting back in his chair, Griff considered her. Evaluated her motivations. Fought his own desperate curiosity, his insatiable, maddening hunger for anything that would make Candy's subtext more easily decipherable.

Finally, he'd set his elbows on the table and turned his left ear toward Rose. "Tell me the rest of the tale, then."

So she had, at least until others joined their table.

That tale wasn't yet complete, he knew. But it was burgeoning, swelling with footnotes and the sort of context he couldn't have supplied on his own.

And he wasn't letting Candy's distorted view of herself stand unchallenged.

Before saying anything else, he closed his classroom door. For a variety of reasons, this conversation required privacy.

As he returned to his desk, he slanted her a stern look. "Your students adore you."

"No." Her fingers twisted together, but that obstinate chin jutted forward. "They fear me."

"Is that so?" He cocked his head. "Did you sleep through the speeches at graduation, Albright? Because I distinctly remember the valedictorian, salutatorian, *and* class president mentioning you by name."

She rolled her eyes, a gesture she rarely indulged. "To say I terrified them."

"Yes, that." Moving until he was directly in front of her, he waited until she made eye contact again. "But they said it while they were laughing. And two of them also thanked you for all your help and dedication and said they learned more in your class than anywhere else."

Her lips pursed, because she had no good rebuttal to that.

"Your carrot may not look like my carrot, but it's there, Candy." He paused. "Please allow me to clarify that I do not refer to any of my more intimate extremities as *my carrot*."

She snorted.

"My point is that your students know you care. Your means of expressing it is simply different from mine." He raised his brows. "Since you mentioned your relationship with our colleagues, Ms. All-Stick-No-Carrot, let's discuss that too. I know you mentor first-year teachers each and every fall. I know you sponsor the literary magazine because Khalid was depressed and needed to shoulder fewer responsibilities. I know you coordinated weekly meal drop-offs for Yelena all last year, as soon as her husband became ill and for months after his death."

Candy's mouth dropped open. "Who told you—"

"Furthermore, I saw you help with Rose's ridiculous promposal at that faculty meeting, and you were magnificent." He stabbed a forefinger into the desk. "If our colleagues don't realize you have a heart as big as the skies, that's on them. Not you."

He allowed his hand to rest on the desk, surrounding her on that one side, leaning in close. Her apple scent filled his lungs, and her heat wracked through him in a shudder.

"But—" Her eyes had turned glassy, her voice so quiet he could barely hear her. "Mildred called me a bully."

He knew. Rose had already told him. More importantly, Rose had told him *why*.

He put his other hand on the desk, surrounding her without a single inch of their skin touching. Providing the mute comfort of animal heat. Blocking out the world outside the two of them. Making certain he could hear her or read her lips, no matter how quietly she spoke.

Within the circle of his arms, she looked up at him and blinked, lips parted.

He lifted his shoulder a fraction. "Mildred called you a bully. Why? What's the context, Candy?"

She was an intelligent woman. She knew what he wanted her to articulate.

"She decided to skip her meal-delivery week for Yelena, but didn't alert me or find her own replacement. When I told her that was unacceptable, she got embarrassed, so she wanted to turn the blame on me. I get that, Griff." Her chin trembled, and the urge to duck his head and plant a comforting kiss there almost overwhelmed him. "But that doesn't mean she was wrong."

Dammit. More tears. "Candy…"

He couldn't stand it. He had to touch her somehow.

Lifting one hand, he gently thumbed away the tear creeping down her cheek. "What's going on? Why are you suddenly so determined to think ill of yourself?"

When she leaned into the contact, he maintained it. Cupped her cheek and watched her struggle to find words for a long, long time.

Finally, she sighed, still resting against his hand.

"Dee and I…" She swallowed back a rough, raw sound. "She's—she was—my baby sister. My only sibling. Just a year younger. Our mom died when I was three and she was two. A drunk driver. So Dad raised us, and he worked a lot, and he was—"

Her laugh broke in the middle. "He loved us, but he didn't know how to talk to us or what to say when we were sad or angry or lonely, and we didn't know how to talk about it either. We were just kids. So we mostly just sat and watched movies together, and at some point it became kind of a family game. Our own language, really."

He tipped his head, confused. "What became a family game?"

"To use stuff we'd seen from the movies to talk to each other. Especially when we got a little older, and he let us watch his favorite mobster films." Her lips stretched, but it didn't look much like a smile. "Instead of saying *I'm sorry you're sad*, we'd threaten to deliver a horse's head to whoever was teasing Dee at school. Instead of saying *I'm worried about you*, we'd tell Dad we were going to put a hit out on him if he didn't start sleeping more. He responded better to that than…"

When she bit her lip, he took a guess. "Emotions?"

She nodded. "He loved us, but the way he showed that was through service. Working hard. Helping us fix our bikes. Going to Dee's flute recitals. We didn't—we didn't talk about it." Her eyes searched his. "It was like reading a poem. A novel in a foreign language. Everything required interpretation and translation. Our words, what we did. And when we said we were fine, we were unreliable narrators."

Through the new lens she'd just offered him, he suspected he could see her more clearly. But he couldn't use it to study his memories of her, his observations. Not yet.

He needed to keep paying attention. Because she was still crying, and he still didn't know why. And somehow, while he'd been sorting through his thoughts, she'd entirely misinterpreted his expression and taken his silence for judgment.

"I-I'm not trying to excuse myself, Griff." She shrank back

against the desk, away from his touch, her face crumpling. "I swear on my mother's grave I'm not. I'm forty-seven years old. I've had plenty of time to learn better and find the right words. I'm just trying to explain why—"

For some reason, she was pleading with him, tears pooling beneath both eyes and dripping from her chin, and his scarred heart ripped open along a new axis.

"Sweetheart." He ducked his head to catch her gaze, hands hovering yet again. "I don't understand, but I also can't imagine why you would ever need an excuse for anything. You try your best, Candy. Always. You *care*. Always. Please stop crying. Please."

Leaning past her to snatch a tissue, he dried her tears, but they kept coming.

"Dee and I talk—talked—" The sob bucked her body against his, and he tentatively touched her shoulder. When she moved closer, he drew her into his arms. "We talked every week, and last winter, a few months after our father died, I knew something was wrong. Sometimes she was…off. Slurred and giggly one week, dull the next. Not herself."

The subtext was becoming text, at long last.

Once too spindly and faded to discern, the words were now stark and bold and black on a bone-white page, and he didn't want to read them. But he knew Candy was poring over them every day, flagellating herself as she read the same story, the same inevitable, tragic ending, again and again.

She deserved some company. Some respite. A new interpretation of the text.

She deserved—

That didn't bear contemplating, not right now.

Candy's fingers curled in the cotton of his button-down, and her eyes were huge and agonized. "I got worried, but she always had some reason for it. She had shoulder surgery the week after our father's funeral, and things went wrong, and they had to go back in. While she was recovering, the pain

59

meds they prescribed made her loopy. Then she said she was tired and punchy from long weeks at work, once she went back. Then she'd tell me she'd just come home from getting drinks with her friends, even though my sister didn't drink. Not ever, Griff, not after what happened to our mom."

Candy hadn't touched the wine at the faculty holiday party. He remembered that now.

Her laugh was sharp. Bitter. "Then she said I was imagining things. Eventually, she blew up at me for mentioning yet again how odd she sounded. She told me to stop h-harping on her and treat her like an adult."

The pain of that conversation lingered in the waver of her voice, but there was no soothing her now. Uglier revelations were appearing on the horizon, looming in the distance as they rocketed closer, word by word.

"You know what I did, Griff?" She didn't wait for a response. "I threatened her. Told her I'd fly to Oregon and kick her ass if she didn't sound more like herself soon. I said I'd put a hit out on her if she didn't stop worrying me. Because *that* was clearly going to fix the fucking problem. *That* was going to get her to talk to me."

Her hands were fisted now, her knuckles digging into his chest. "I hired a cleaning service to help her around the house while she recovered. I had food delivered. I researched the best post-operative physical therapists in her area."

Service. Love's austere and lonely offices.

But she couldn't see that. Not yet.

"You know what I *didn't* do?" She was sneering at herself now, face twisted in grief and self-loathing. "I didn't realize she'd become addicted to her pain meds, and I didn't tell her I loved her. M-my—"

Her words were garbled now by her sobbing, but he was paying attention as hard as he could. Holding her. Offering whatever mute comfort she'd accept.

She spat out each syllable like dirt in her mouth. "My *baby sister* died of an accidental opioid overdose alone in her apartment on July fucking fourteenth, and in our last conversation, I didn't once say *I love you*. I didn't tell her, Griff. I *didn't tell her*."

When she bowed her head for a moment, he kissed her crown. Rested his lips there. "Candy. Sweetheart—"

Her ragged, tear-soaked words were audible. Even now, she was keeping her promise, raising her head slightly from his chest and angling it toward his left ear so he could hear.

"She said not to come. She always said not to come, but that doesn't matter." Candy was trembling against him, and he ran his hands up and down her arms. Again. Again. "I should have showed up when I knew for sure something was wrong. And even if I couldn't get off my ass long enough to be a decent sister in person, I should have *asked*. I should have said, in plain, unmistakable words, *I love you. I'm worried about you. What's wrong? Please tell me.*"

He hitched her closer as she shook, silently supporting her in the only way he currently could.

Her lip curled in disgust at herself. "But I didn't. Dee died without getting what she needed from me, the one person she counted on in the entire world. Her big sister. And the least I can do now is take a hard fucking look at myself and try to be *b-better*."

When she stopped talking and began crying in earnest, he held her. As long as she needed him, he wasn't budging. Not one inch.

It all made a horrible sort of sense now.

Knowing how she thought, how she tended to make sense of her world, he could see how she'd interpreted the loss of her sister that way. He could even see a few glimmerings of real insight in the story.

Sometimes people need to hear the actual words, love, Marianne's voice whispered sweetly to him. *'I'm scared. I'm angry. I'm sad. I love you.'*

The rest of Candy's conclusions, though? Complete bullshit.

Once she'd calmed, he tenderly laid his left cheek against hers. "You're trying to be better...how? In the ways you communicate?"

Her small nod rubbed her smooth skin against his beard. "I've always known the way I express myself is different. But I thought that was okay. I thought the people who mattered understood me, but..." She sniffled, hard. "That's not true, Griff. I need to change. Completely."

For all her many, many strengths, nuance often escaped her.

He gathered his words carefully, examining each one for secondary meanings and unintended connotations and anything that could be misinterpreted.

"Candy, I'm so sorry. For your sister. For you. I think I understand what you're telling me, and I wish to heaven you weren't hurting like you are." He nuzzled his cheek against hers again, this time deliberately. "But sweetheart, I'm not certain I agree with you."

With a jerk, she pulled her face away from his and scowled at him blearily, her pale face blotchy and damp. "My life and my grief are *not* a matter for disagreement, Griff. I'm allowed to have my own feelings, regardless of your opinion."

"Of course you are."

The lure in sight, she waited a few seconds. Then she bit, as he'd anticipated. "But?"

How to say it without making it sound like judgment?

"You're drawn to dichotomies," he finally told her. "All or nothing. Right or wrong. Oxford comma enthusiasts or monsters."

She choked on a breath, coughing a little. "Don't make me laugh, Conover."

"Now you've sorted yourself, your communication style, into what you consider the just category. All wrong, nothing right." With his thumbs, he stroked the giving flesh of her upper arms, warm even through her blouse and cardigan. "But Candy, we both know nothing's that clean or obvious. Even you know it. It's why you acknowledge the stupidity of the split infinitive rule but teach it anyway. It's why you have your students read 'Ozymandias,' even though Shelley was a total dick. It's why you agree that Frankenstein may be one of two monsters in that story. Possibly more, if some of the other characters don't use the Oxford comma."

At that, her lips actually twitched upward at the corners. "Dammit, Griff. I told you not to do that."

He allowed himself to brush his lips against her temple, his victor's spoils.

"When it comes to your sister, I suspect you're being much too hard on yourself. But even if you could have done better, Candy, you tried. You did. As best you could, knowing what you knew then." His brows drew together, and he met her gaze directly. "Is there any conceivable way your sister didn't know you loved her? That she didn't carry that knowledge in the marrow of her bones?"

If Candy cared about anyone, anything, she informed the world at top volume. In her own way. Which didn't mean she couldn't or shouldn't use the direct words, but there was no mistaking her fierce brand of affection and protection.

Her loved ones would carry that devotion in each beat of their hearts, every breath they took. A benediction from a woman who somehow thought she offered too little, too faintly.

Candy's eyes flicked away from his, and he knew that gesture of avoidance, that mulish set of her chin, by now.

She knew he was right. She didn't want to admit it.

"I suppose…" With a sigh, she gave in. "I don't see any way she could have missed it."

He hated to remind her, but Candy sometimes needed

important points spelled out to her. "That last conversation, did your sister say she loved you?"

Her eyes filled again. "No."

That obviously hurt too, and he ached for it. "But she did love you."

"Yes." It wasn't a question, but she answered without hesitation. "Always."

And there it was. "Just like you knew, she knew. She *had* to know. That a threat to kick her ass meant *I love you*. That arranging a cleaning service meant *I love you*. That your phone call every week meant *I love you*. That your so-called harping meant *I love you*."

That particular subtext wouldn't be hard to decipher, especially not for a beloved sister.

"I want to believe that." Her lips quivered, puffy from crying. "I do."

"Get up off your knees, Candy." Just as she and her sister had shared a common language, she and Griff did too. Poetry. "Wild Geese," one of her favorites. "You don't have to be good. Besides, you already *are* good. You may not be perfect, but you're battling on the side of the angels more often than not."

She sputtered out a laugh. "No rational person would ever call me an angel."

Oh, he liked being able to contradict her.

"Yelena does. She smiles every time she says it." When Rose had told him that, he'd smiled too. "When her world was falling apart, you kept a few pieces of it safe for her, even though you two aren't close."

Leaning back, she pinned him with a narrow-eyed stare. "How do you even *know* all this? I've never seen you say more than hello to Yelena."

"Don't change the subject." He stroked a strand of hair back from her damp, sticky cheek, and let his fingertips linger there. "If you want to evolve, evolve. But please don't do so

64

from misplaced guilt and shame, because you don't deserve it. More than that, it's not—"

"—what Dee would have wanted," she finished, quietly.

"Not at all. Not if she's anything like you."

As he'd said before: both a cliché and the hard, hard truth.

"She is. Was." Biting that swollen lower lip, she looked up at him. Hesitated before speaking. "I still don't understand how you can do this."

Now she'd lost him. "Do what?"

Her voice was hoarse from her tears, but gloriously loud again. Strong in the way he loved. "Talk about emotions so directly. Handle mine with such ease."

Irony, that.

"Want to hear my secret?"

When she nodded, he traded vulnerability for vulnerability. A confidence to counterbalance all of hers, and yet another way in which they shared commonality.

"I'm comfortable discussing other people's emotions, but not my own. Not directly. Not with clarity. Instead, I reach for metaphors or"—shit, this made him sound insufferable —"poetry. It frustrated Marianne sometimes. And I didn't tell her I loved her as often as I should have. Not in those words. Instead, I'd turn to favorite poems or pertinent lines from novels."

The tips of his ears turned hot, and he fought the urge to squirm, to reassure Candy that he wasn't actually twee as fuck.

Her expression remained soft. Affectionate. Sure of him in a way he was equally sure he hadn't earned.

"But she knew she was loved," she said.

"Whatever my faults, she knew she was loved." For all his shame, he was suddenly certain of that. "In part because I kept quoting *Hamlet* to her."

Candy's head tilted, and she blinked at him for a minute.

"*Hamlet*? Of all Shakespeare's plays and sonnets, why would you—"

Then she paused. Nodded.

> "*Doubt thou the stars are fire,*
> *Doubt that the sun doth move,*
> *Doubt truth to be a liar,*
> *But never doubt I love.*"

Her clear, smooth recitation of those familiar lines washed over him. He could still hear himself saying them to Marianne on their honeymoon in Provence, lying together on a picnic blanket amidst sunlit fields of lavender, her head tucked beneath his chin, her breath sweet and precious on his neck. One of so many intimate, loving moments in their marriage.

It hurt.

But it didn't hurt nearly as much as it had months ago. Hours ago, even.

This hard, painful conversation with Candy had soothed something within him too. Through reassuring her, he'd inadvertently reassured himself.

Marianne had died by his side, in their warm, soft marriage bed, knowing he loved her in the marrow of her bones.

There was no way she couldn't have known.

"It's a lovely passage." A smile flirted with the corners of Candy's mouth. "However, I don't primarily associate *Hamlet* with romance. *Get thee to a nunnery* somewhat undercuts the swooniness of it all. And that's setting aside the whole drowning issue."

He had to laugh. "Marianne said exactly the same thing. *For God's sake, at least choose a damn* sonnet*, Griffin.* I'd tell her I already gave at the office."

Again, the familiar agony didn't appear. Not at the

mention of his wife's name. Not at the invocation of another precious memory.

He'd have to come to terms with that shift soon, one way or another. He'd have to make a decision about what he intended, and whether he could live with those intentions.

Especially since the feel of Candy in his arms, her softness and solidity and heat, the way her generous breasts molded to his chest and his legs tangled in her skirt, prickled at his nape and zapped down his spine to his—

Well.

The body electric, indeed.

Slowly, gently, Candy stepped out of his embrace. An arm's length away, she studied him with her hands on her hips. He had no idea what she was searching for.

Worse, he had no idea what she saw.

"Thank you," she finally said. "I feel…better. Not great, but better."

He nodded, his fingers curling in on emptiness, rather than warm flesh. "Like I told you, I talked to a grief counselor after Marianne was gone. If you start feeling worse again, you might want to consider—"

She held up a hand. "I know, I know. If I'm not more myself soon, I'll see a grief counselor or find a support group. I promise."

That was a vast leap for someone like her. Vaster than he even understood, probably.

"Good." He inclined his head, suddenly awkward. "You deserve to feel better."

Still watching him, she opened her mouth. Shut it.

"What?" he finally asked.

"Nothing." She shook her head. "You'll figure it out eventually."

Her words were unwontedly gentle. Tender in a way that stung more than a shout. Too frustratingly opaque for him to formulate a decent response.

"Let's talk about the initiative tomorrow, if that's doable for you." Gathering her notebook from his desk, she tapped it against her thigh. "I think we both need some time."

"All right," he said.

As she walked away, he didn't stop her, didn't ask her to explain herself, didn't—

"Griff?"

She paused in the doorframe, eyes swollen and reddened, blouse tearstained, chin resolute, her smile as small and warm and soft as a catkin on a pussy willow.

Beautiful.

Terrifying.

"Yes?" He raised his brows in inquiry.

That bloodshot gaze didn't waver. "It might be time to get up off your knees too."

Then she turned and left.

He stared after her.

Outside his windows, clouds scuttered across the sun, and his classroom abruptly dimmed. He hadn't noticed a chill even moments before, but now, between the shadows and the relentless air conditioning, his tear-soaked shirt prompted a shiver. Still, he didn't reach for his jacket. Didn't move.

Eventually, the echoing thuds of her steps faded to nothing, leaving him only the analog tick of his classroom clock as company.

As a metaphor enthusiast, he had to admit: That seemed fair.

FIVE

WHEN CANDY WALKED INTO GRIFF'S CLASSROOM and saw him sitting behind his desk the next day, her smile was a bit crooked. Wry in a way he couldn't interpret.

He tipped his head to the side. "What? Do I have something in my beard?"

After eating, he always checked carefully for residue. Especially now, with his facial hair bushier and less tamed. Still, he could have missed something.

In all honesty, he didn't even like the way it looked anymore. He didn't like how it felt, either.

Last night, he'd reached for his clippers. Then shied away, as the task began to seem much too metaphorical. Much too fraught.

Marianne had always liked him clean-shaven.

As he'd eyed the clippers, though, he'd been considering another woman entirely.

"Your beard remains pristine." After closing the door, she lowered herself into the student chair nearest his desk with a thump. "I was just...thinking about something. Nothing important."

Despite her emotional upheaval yesterday, she didn't

69

appear especially tired or sad today. Her fawn-brown eyes were alert, no shadows beneath them. Even better, that horrible grayness had vanished entirely in the last several weeks, the unceasing demands of a new school year perhaps distracting her from her grief. Or maybe the simple passage of time was eroding her pain, like a tide over stone.

If their late-afternoon conversation in his room had helped too, he was glad.

Under his scrutiny, she shifted in her seat a bit, and he frowned.

Marysburg High didn't use chairs with built-in writing surfaces, and thank heaven for that. Those damn desks had tormented bigger students at his previous school. Some kids couldn't fit in them at all, while others had squeezed themselves into the openings with such difficulty, they must have left his class bruised and aching each time.

Over the years, he'd quietly gathered alternative seating. Beanbags. A few freestanding chairs. But even that, he knew, was humiliating in its own way, the need for special accommodation. And teenagers could be so damn cruel sometimes. Not in front of him, of course, because under no circumstances did he allow cruelty in his classroom. But in the halls, by the lockers, he knew at least some of those kids must suffer.

Even apart from the emotional toll exacted by the desks, how exactly did the school expect larger students to pay attention and learn under those circumstances? How could they become their best selves in the midst of perpetual discomfort and pain?

He'd left his old school to escape the sight of someone else's name on Marianne's office door. To flee from the way she glided down every hallway and perched at every table and lingered in every doorway, populating every corner of the workplace they'd shared for over a decade. He'd left his old home, even his old time zone, for much the same reason.

The move had drained his scant remaining resources, emotional and physical.

That said, his former administration's casual unconcern for vulnerable students, the incidental cruelties he and his late wife had tried to combat for years, had made the professional aspect of his transition easier than he'd feared. He was glad to be teaching at Marysburg High, under a principal like Tess Dunn. Proud, actually.

His students didn't always leave his classroom delighted, but they never left it bruised and humiliated. Or hungry, for that matter, due to Tess's relentless advocacy on that topic.

He wondered what Candy had looked like as a teenager. Whether she'd spent school days in pain. Whether she'd demanded better options, or simply tried to shove herself into a spot that would always be too small for her.

Whatever her experiences in high school, the woman she'd become took up space unapologetically and did not suffer quietly. He loved that about her.

So she probably wasn't actively hurting right now. Still, her frame was large enough that the student seat didn't look entirely comfortable for her.

Easily remedied, that, as long as she didn't get stubborn on him.

Getting to his feet, he rolled his desk chair in her direction. "Here. Take this."

She didn't argue, and it felt like victory. Especially when her smile widened, plumping her cheeks and crinkling the corners of her eyes. "Thanks. I've been eyeing this chair for a year now, wondering how it felt."

They switched places, and he watched, pleased, as she sank into the extra-wide, cushioned seat.

His old desk chair had collapsed right before the move from Wisconsin, and his former mother-in-law had insisted on ordering him a new one as a sort of going-away present.

She'd had it delivered directly to Virginia, and he'd known why as soon as he saw it.

It was more appropriate for a CEO than a public school teacher, all tufted, plush, gleaming leather and generous lines. Incredibly comfortable. Undeniably expensive. Huge.

It didn't fit under his desk, of course. After a year of hard use, that leather was already scuffed and damaged. One of the casters had never quite recovered from an encounter with gum over the winter. By springtime, his students had felt comfortable enough to tease him about his *fancy-man chair* and inquire about the whereabouts of his butler.

But Marianne's mother had wanted to do something nice for him, and she had. Even though, if she'd asked his opinion, he'd have requested a mesh chair like Candy's. Which was, of course, why she hadn't asked.

"This…" Candy smoothed her palm down the padded-leather length of the chair arm, her touch lingering. Caressing. "This is the most gorgeous, comfortable piece of furniture that's ever deigned to inhabit Marysburg High. Aren't you worried it might be stripped and sold for parts on our faculty gray market?"

He followed the movement of her hand, swallowing over a throat as dry as chalk dust. "We had one of those at my old school, but I hadn't seen any evidence of it here."

"Most exchanges are kept pretty quiet. A file cabinet for a work table. A new desk in return for sponsoring the Latin Club." She shook her head. "That was an ill-advised agreement, by the way. Poor Magistra Anderson. Between the two of us, it wasn't grape juice in her clay cup at the Saturnalia feast last year. Otherwise, she wouldn't have been shouting that particular Catullus poem from her dining couch."

He tried to imagine Magistra Anderson, nearing retirement age and seemingly frail, drunk and shouting semi-obscene poetry in a retrofitted sheet.

Yeah, that sounded about right. Especially given the

Faculty Holiday Party Incident, as his colleagues chose to refer to the event. Like any good Roman, the woman enjoyed her wine.

But that wasn't the point.

"Are you saying my chair may not be safe here over the summer?" He pursed his lips. "I took it home last year, but I was hoping to leave it from now on, because that thing is a behemoth."

She tilted her head back against the lavishly cushioned seat, her eyes closing. A small, blissful smile teased the corners of her mouth. "Outright theft is rare, and your chair is too distinctive to offer plausible deniability. Normally, I'd say you're fine. But now, having sat in it..."

With her lips parted, her face soft with pleasure, Candy wasn't simply striking.

A reckless surge of heat incinerated his thoughts and left him tangle-tongued.

"Now I think you'd better research how to install LoJack on a desk chair, Griff. Otherwise, it may go missing." Her eyes opened, and her smile turned into a wide, deliciously wicked grin. "If it does, don't check next door."

Despite his ever-increasing agitation, he had to respond. "Should I prepare for the My New Desk Chair Is Definitely *Not* Griff's Purloined Possession Initiative?"

"Perhaps." Leaning the chair back, she heaved a lusty sigh. "Oh, yes. Flights of angels would definitely sing me to my rest in this seat."

Distracted from his own lust, he frowned at her.

She snickered. "Rest in the most literal sense, Griff. I'm not actually going to die of excessive comfort in your desk chair." Then she sobered and levered herself back to vertical. "Which is a terrible, awkward, tone-deaf segue, but by now, you should know not to expect better from me."

Whatever this conversation would contain, he'd likely prefer to avoid. But avoiding something Candy wished to discuss was much like attempting to avoid an incoming, foot-ball-field-size asteroid by dodging a few feet to the left. Ultimately pointless. Guaranteed to be loud and fiery and painful.

So he crossed his arms over his chest and waited.

"Thank you. For yesterday." Resting both forearms on his desk, she tapped her cast with the fingertips of her right hand. "I'm still…"

Her gulp shifted the shadows contouring her throat. "I'm still, um…sad." She bit her lip, then forced herself to continue. "Guilty. Angry at myself and her. But I didn't have nightmares last night. I didn't wake up crying. Talking helped. So thank you."

She was trying so hard. Using the direct words they both avoided at all costs.

That determination of hers could heave mountains from the flat earth.

He inclined his head, honoring her efforts. "You're welcome."

Tap, tap, tap.

Desperate to forestall further gratitude, he jerked his chin toward her cast.

"What are you doing?" When her dark eyebrow cocked in mute answer, he amended, "What are you attempting to accomplish with what you're doing?"

She glared down at her cast. "My skin itches beneath this albatross."

"Because you're healing." And thank heavens for it. "Good."

Now the scowl transferred to him. "I'm itching because I can't wash under there, and I'm dirty." More tapping, now a bit more forceful. "It's a travesty that modern medicine hasn't made this process less onerous."

Tap, tap, *tap*.

She was going to damage something if she didn't stop.

"Candy—" he began.

"It's unbearable." Her mouth sulky, she returned her attention to her forearm. "The doctor said not to use a pencil or ruler to reach the right spot, but by God, I will make this infernal itching stop *somehow*."

Tap, tap, TAP.

He couldn't stand it. Lunging forward, he claimed her busy fingers and lifted them away from her cast. "Stop that."

Her brow beetled, she promised retribution with a fulminating glower.

But she didn't remove her hand from his. And he didn't let her go.

"As you say, you can't stick anything inside the cast, because it might break the skin and cause an infection." He'd done his research after their night in the emergency room, to understand better what she'd be experiencing in the coming weeks. "What are your other options for dealing with the itch?"

"Tapping." Each syllable was crystalline and distinct, etched with ire.

Nevertheless, her hand didn't so much as twitch in his, while he was suddenly floundering. For words, for purchase, as her spike-lashed stare and long-fingered grip dragged him to sea.

Eyes locked to his, she swayed closer. Closer still.

Her lips were parted again, full and soft, pink as the tide of color washing onto her round cheeks. Within his grip, her hand turned. Clasped his.

The slide of flesh against flesh, his fingers spearing through hers, opening them wide, all shadowed clefts and damp warmth...

The metaphor might be earthy and unbefitting, but it turned him hard.

"What else?" he whispered.

He'd tried for assurance, but instead produced the

desperate gasp of a man sinking beneath the waves. It would be humiliating, if his mind could acknowledge anything but her.

"I can…" Her glare had metamorphosed into a different sort of heat, and her nostrils narrowed in a deep, deep inhalation. "I can blow cool air from a hair dryer around the cast's edges."

His eyelids had turned heavy. So heavy.

"No hair dryer here."

Slowly, she shook her head. "No."

Her lips puckered as she formed the word.

When he placed her hand back on his desk, her chin dropped to her chest. Only to snap upward again when he claimed her other hand instead.

He carefully, slowly sank his fingers between hers a second time. The cast covered most of her palm and crossed between her thumb and forefinger, but everything else was bare. Vulnerable. His.

He lifted their clasped hands. Rested them against his bristly cheek.

Then he blew into the edge of her cast. Cool air, where she couldn't reach. Relief for her itch as his became agony. Again. Again.

Her hand trembled against his, and he rubbed his beard against that tangle of interlaced fingers. Abraded her skin to see the bob of her long, pale throat as she swallowed in silence.

"Better?" A murmured word against her thumb.

He could take the pad of that thumb between his teeth so easily.

Silently, she shook her head and rolled his chair closer, until her skirt brushed against his pants. Closer, until his knee was between hers, pinning that skirt tight to her long thighs.

He blew again, cool air against hot skin, and they both

shook.

"It still itches."

She'd whispered that, but he read it in the movements of her lips.

"Make it better, Griff," she said.

Her cheek was fiery beneath his stroking knuckles, her hair soft in his fist, her mouth plush and wide and entirely hers. Quintessentially Candy's. Not quiescent or accepting under his own mouth, not even from the first moment, but full of demand and passion and obvious, heartbreaking *caring*.

He sucked on her tongue, swallowed her moan, and it was just like her. Exactly like her.

Unexpectedly sweet. Irresistible.

There was no mistaking her for another. No doubt in his mind whose lips he'd claimed, whose breath filled his straining lungs, whose whimper of need drew his open mouth over her stubborn jaw and down that fragrant throat in hungry, wet kisses.

And in the end, that was what made him stop.

His hand splayed and gliding over the silky cotton of her blouse, an inch away from the swell of her breast, he froze, arrested by sudden realization.

He'd done it again. Touched her without thought, without conscious intent.

Candy. Clearly, unmistakably Candy. Not Marianne.

For these past minutes, Marianne might never have existed at all, except as a sweet memory stored in the dimmest recesses of his lust-clouded mind.

His wife.

He'd forgotten his wife.

And only a careless, selfish man touched without thought, without understanding his own intentions. Without making sure those intentions wouldn't hurt the woman beneath his hands.

Unsteady and flushed and embarrassingly erect, he

heaved himself away from Candy. As she stared up at him in silence from his desk chair, hugging herself awkwardly, he stumbled over a brief apology, and then—

His own damn classroom. The kiss he'd initiated. The woman he desired.

He fled them all.

SIX

It was the choice of a coward, Griff knew.

Instead of discussing his ignominious flight from his own classroom face-to-face with Candy, or even calling her to discuss it over the phone, he e-mailed her that night instead.

In writing, sometimes the directness that eluded him in conversation became possible. And in such an important matter, with such an important person, he needed plain words and clarity more than ever.

His hand on the mouse shook as he clicked *send*.

FROM: griffin.conover@qc.k12.va.us
TO: candice.albright@qc.k12.va.us
SUBJECT: An explanation and apology

Candy, I owe you an avalanche of apologies, but please let me start with this one, inadequate though it may be. I will try to be as direct as I can, because I owe that to both of us, and because I need to learn. Finally, I need to learn.

I like you. I admire you. I care about you. I want you.

That's why I kissed you. No other reason.

I'm sorry if I caused you to doubt that. I'm sorry I left so abruptly. I'm sorry if I hurt you. I'm sorry I started us down a path I couldn't explore to its end, wholeheartedly and with clear purpose. I didn't mean to mislead you, although we both know that's the facile excuse of a scoundrel. It's also—at least in this case—true.

I ran because—

Fuck, this is hard.

I ran because my feelings for you still sometimes seem like a betrayal of Marianne, our marriage, my love for her, and her love for me.

My desire and affection for you are mixed with shame, and that's not right. For either of us. I don't intend to become emotionally or physically intimate with you again until that shame is gone, and I can stand before you a man free and eager to offer what you need and what I want to give.

In the meantime, we're still colleagues. If you're willing, we will continue to work together on the poetry initiative, although I'd prefer to do as much of the planning as possible via e-mail. Unless you wish it, I don't intend to avoid you, because you're my friend. If you need help with anything —*anything*—please call on me. Extended interludes alone together can't happen, however, since I find you—

Well, I find you irresistible. Even when I should resist.

I need time, Candy. I don't know how long. It may be a week. It may be a year. It may be the rest of my life.

Since I know we speak the same language, I'll allow myself this: Of the three things I need to do to live in this world, I've accomplished two. Not the third. Not quite yet, even though I know the time has come.

Whatever happens next, please believe I regret any harm I've caused you, and I wish you only good things. You deserve

time and attention and understanding and effort a͟
affection.

You deserve love, Candy. Full-throated, devoted love.

I hope I can offer that someday.

If you're not still waiting if and when I'm ready, I'll understand. I want your happiness, and you are not a toy for me to stow away until I'm free to play.

(Not that I consider anything we've said or done together a game. Let me be clear about that.)

I'm so sorry.
Griff

No NOVEL, NO TELEVISION SHOW, NO AMOUNT OF internet noodling could hold his attention.

It flowed like a river to sea, inexorably, back to Candy. Always. Back to his mouth on her flesh in his classroom, and back to an e-mailed response that might come at any moment or never, depending on how she'd reacted to his flight that afternoon and his subsequent message.

Leaning back on his couch, he propped an ankle on his knee and jiggled his leg. Tunneled his fingers through his hair, which was beginning to resemble straw at the ends. Stared in the general direction of the television, where—because of the popularity of the *Gods of the Gates* series—historians were discussing the *Aeneid*.

Specifically, Dido. How, left behind by the man she loved, she stabbed herself atop a funeral pyre and burned to ash as Aeneas's fleet sailed from her harbor.

Candy was no Dido. With or without a lover, heartbroken or not, she'd forge ahead, stalwart and determined. She was the rightful hero of an epic poem, rather than a secondary character or simple love interest.

Griff, though...hmmm.

He'd never considered harming himself. Not directly. But whether he resembled the queen of Carthage in other discomfiting ways—

Well, that was less clear to him.

Or maybe it *was* clear, and he simply didn't want to acknowledge the clarity.

Candy's e-mail arrived before the end of the documentary, and relief mingled with renewed terror as he clicked on the message.

But he should have known, really. Terror had no place and held no purpose in his relationship with her.

A heart as big as the skies, he'd said, and here lay further proof.

———

FROM: candice.albright@qc.k12.va.us
TO: griffin.conover@qc.k12.va.us
SUBJECT: Re: An explanation and apology

GRIFF, YOU MADE ME NO PROMISES, AND YOU OWE me no apologies. Any hurt I may feel, I'm experiencing because of my own choices. Thank you for caring about my feelings, though, and thank you for caring about me. Thank you for making your position clear.

Now let me do the same.

I understand that you may not be ready for a relationship in the immediate future, or conceivably ever, and I don't want to force myself upon you or make your life more difficult than it already is. I also don't want to interfere with your grieving and/or recovery processes.

Any boundaries you specify, I promise to honor. As you know, I am a woman of my word.

If you'd prefer to cease non-professional contact entirely, I will accept that too. In case that's your preference, let me say this now:

I like you. I admire you. I care about you. I want you.

That's why I kissed you. No other reason.

(It's unrepentant plagiarism, I know. Write me up for an honor code violation at the front office, as desired.)

In my own words, I also want you to know something else: I don't expect you to forget about Marianne. I don't want you to somehow pretend that she, your marriage, and your love for one another never existed, or that they no longer possess importance, meaning, and emotional weight for you.

To misquote Whitman, our hearts are large. They contain multitudes.

I don't expect yours to be empty of anyone but me.

My feelings toward you don't erase my love and grief for Dee. I carry both with me. I always will. I don't expect you to be any different.

Until you indicate a desire for further intimacy, that's all I'll say concerning non-professional matters. As to the poetry initiative: I am more than willing to continue working together, and we can do so via e-mail.

At the moment, I am contemplating whether we should add an Impromptu Haiku activity to our plans. With Tess's permission, we could designate one specific day and time for all students to write a haiku about whatever class they happen to be attending. Kids in my class might write a haiku about Shakespeare, then, while kids in biology might write about the Krebs cycle. Kids in Mildred's class might write, quite justifiably, about her ignorance when it comes to seminal literature in the science-fiction genre.

I am eager to hear your thoughts on the matter.

Take care, Griff. I would threaten you with mobster-style retaliation should you fail to do so, but that is no longer the language I wish to use when speaking to those I care about.

Instead, I'll simply say: I worry about you. If you wish to alleviate that worry, you'll get more sleep and eat regular meals.

See? All carrot, no stick. I'm learning.

Yours,
Candy

HE DROPPED HIS CHIN TO HIS CHEST AND TOOK A few shuddering breaths. Then he sent a quick message back.

FROM: griffin.conover@qc.k12.va.us
TO: candice.albright@qc.k12.va.us
SUBJECT: Thank you

I ABSOLUTELY WANT TO REMAIN YOUR FRIEND AS well as your colleague, Candy. I know you'll honor your word and my boundaries, and I appreciate that. I appreciate you.

The Impromptu Haiku idea (and title) is brilliant. I'll speak to Principal Dunn about it tomorrow.

Griff

A MINUTE LATER, HER RESPONSE ARRIVED. *THEN WE have a plan. See you at school.*

That was all she wrote, each word friendly enough but distant. Businesslike. Already, she was making good on her vows.

No physical intimacies. No emotional intimacies. Exactly as he'd requested.

He showered and changed his bed linens, always willing to indulge a metaphor. When he slid under the covers, they were gratifyingly unwrinkled. Pristine.

Also cold. Very cold.

Our hearts are large. They contain multitudes.

I don't expect yours to be empty of anyone but me.

The words wouldn't leave him be. All night, they chased him through the darkness, scrolling across his ceiling. Echoing in Candy's stentorian boom, then whispering with Marianne's gentle murmur. Haunting him, even though he'd never believed in spirits.

Or, rather, he'd always believed humans conjured their own ghosts, haunting themselves with creations born out of need and grief and anger and shame.

His restlessness rumpled those spotless sheets. They twisted around his legs in a bind that bit into his flesh. With a hissed curse, he kicked free and went to sleep on his couch instead.

He'd expected to find serenity in the decision he'd made. A certain restfulness in having set limits and protected himself, despite how fervently he'd come to want Candy.

Instead, he found a disquieting emptiness, cold as those damn sheets.

It wasn't the same emptiness he'd experienced upon Marianne's death.

But it wasn't as far removed as he'd have imagined.

THE NEXT MORNING, GRIFF ENCOUNTERED CANDY outside their classrooms.

Other than a quick stutter in her step upon seeing him, she betrayed no nervousness, no hurt, no particular reaction to his appearance.

"Good morning, Griff." Her briefcase swinging from her

shoulder, she unlocked her door before he could offer assistance. "You're here early."

He fiddled with his own keys. "I, uh"—*couldn't sleep, because I kept thinking of you*—"had some items to knock off my to-do list before kids started arriving for the day. You're here early too."

"Yes." A polite confirmation as she flicked on her lights. "I have a few errands to run."

When he didn't move or say more, she directed a look of bland inquiry his way. "Did you want to discuss the poetry initiative? I have about ten minutes, if you'd like to talk in the department office or the library."

He might have been any colleague working with her on a project.

It was what he wanted. What he needed.

It felt precisely the same as those sheets last night.

And for some reason, he was scrambling to keep her talking. Keep her with him. At least for one more minute.

"We can talk here in the hall, if you want." When she didn't object, her gaze as inscrutable as before, he attempted to remember anything relevant to say. "Um…I'll finalize the logistics of the poetry slam in the next day or two. The venue, required tech, refreshments, et cetera. Any changes to our plans or new information, I'll send along. I'll also let you know what Principal Dunn says about the Impromptu Haiku activity."

She smiled, and it was friendly. Nothing more. "That would be appreciated. Thank you. I'll work on creating advertisements for the poetry slam and the Verses vs. Verses poetry bracket contest, which I'll send for your approval before running them by the front office. As far as the poems for the morning announcements, I have the preliminary list somewhere on my desk—"

When she shifted to peer inside her classroom, the overloaded briefcase slid off her shoulder, the strap falling to her forearm. The one with a cast.

She gasped at the impact.

"Dammit." Instinctively, he reached for her, but she jerked back from him. "Candy—"

She cut him off. "I'm fine."

Withdrawing his hand, he tore it through his hair and welcomed the sting of his scalp.

Even through the barrier of her glasses, he could easily spy arcs of shadows beneath those pained fawn-brown eyes. Her bangs, neatly side-swept as always, were more effective at obscuring the lines etched across her forehead as she grimaced.

After squeezing her eyes shut for a moment, she carefully placed the bag back on her shoulder and met his gaze again.

"As I was saying, I have the initial list we made, but I think you have one that's updated. If you could send it to me, I'd be appreciative." She stepped into her room. "When you do, feel free to mention any other questions or updates. Have a great day, Griff."

She didn't give him an opportunity to delay her further. In a blink, her classroom door was clicking shut behind her, the sound quiet but unmistakable.

LATER THAT DAY, HE E-MAILED SOME UPDATED information and raised one last question. *At our next department meeting, do you want to speak to everyone about emphasizing poetry in their classes during the appropriate week, or shall I?*

Her response was pure Candy, crystallized into a single sentence. *Would you rather charm them or employ blunt force trauma in verbal form?*

He laughed out loud, even as that emptiness inside him ballooned further.

Your brand of blunt force trauma is a pleasure to observe, always. Bring on the carnage, Candy.

He waited for a response. When it came, it was brief.

Very well. Take care, Griff.

Five words. He stared at them for a very, very long time.

OVER THE NEXT FEW DAYS, HE AND CANDY ORBITED each other from a safe distance. They sat at opposite ends of tables during faculty gatherings, greeted each other in passing as they walked down the halls of the school, and e-mailed documents and updates on the initiative rather than discussing them in person.

Sometimes brief, bright glimpses of their old rapport shone through the veil he'd placed between them—

It appears I bludgeoned our department members into submission, she'd written after the meeting, and he'd snickered at both the memory and her choice of wording. *I hope you enjoyed the show.*

—but for the most part, their new relationship was everything he'd told her he wanted, and nothing he hadn't.

To quote Shakespeare: *When you depart from me sorrow abides, and happiness takes his leave.*

To quote his students: It sucked.

One more week of emptiness. Two.

By the time their Falling for Poetry Initiative actually began, he was coming out of his skin, agitated and exhausted and confused. Still, all their plans and activities ran smoothly the first two days of the week. He and Candy hadn't needed to confer in person once.

In all honesty, by Tuesday afternoon, he was kind of hoping something would go wrong.

When he saw Candy after school that day, though, he regretted his wish.

Something clearly *had* gone wrong. That horrible grayness had leached the rosy color from her skin once more, and her face was closed as a fist. And if that wasn't enough to alarm him, she was wearing *pants*. Her fine, ash-brown hair, sans headband, flopped around the sides of her stiff, still features, and she didn't push it out of the way.

She was passing by him in the hall outside their rooms.

They made eye contact. Hers were red-rimmed.

She offered no polite smile, as she usually did. No simple, friendly greeting. Nothing but a bare nod as they crossed paths and continued in their separate directions, farther and farther apart.

He couldn't take it.

"Candy." Catching her good arm, he gently urged her to a stop. "Hold on a minute."

Obediently, she turned to face him, but said nothing.

Her total lack of expression kicked his heart into a panicked gallop. Dammit, what the hell had happened to her?

He stepped closer. "Are you okay? Because I haven't seen you look like this in—"

"It's the three-month anniversary," she told him in a monotone. "Now if you'll excuse me, I need to make a phone call."

Shit. *Shit.* He should have remembered.

July fucking fourteenth, she'd spat. *My baby sister.*

When she turned away, he moved in front of her.

"Candy, please." Ducking his head, he caught her eye again. "Is there something I can do to help? Do you want to talk, or—"

Once more, she didn't let him finish.

"I appreciate your offer. I mean that." Her face had softened a fraction. "However, you wanted time without physical or emotional intimacy. I'm respecting your wishes. Please don't make that process harder than it already is."

Without further ado, she removed her arm from his loose grasp and reclaimed a step's worth of distance.

She might as well have belted him in the gut. The formality of her words, the rejection of his offered comfort, his touch, drove the breath from his lungs.

"You're right." He forced out the words. "Of course you're right. I'm sorry."

He wanted to vomit.

He'd done this. No one but him.

He'd erected this barricade between them, scared of what might happen without it, and now he couldn't reach her. Not even when she needed affection and understanding and everything else he had to offer her. Everything else he *wanted* to offer her.

And if he ever decided to tear down that barricade, he had no idea whether she'd still be waiting on the other side. If she wasn't, he wouldn't blame her.

"Griff..." She sighed, her bloodshot eyes sharp on his face. "It's fine. I'm not angry. Just...trying to do what's right."

Fuck, why was *she* reassuring *him*?

Her attempted smile didn't last more than a breath. "Don't worry about me. I suppose I simply need some time too."

Stupidly, he'd never considered how it would feel to let her hurt alone.

That was his sole option, however. At least for the moment.

"I'll get out of your way, then." His legs leaden weights, he moved to the side of the hall. "Please take care of yourself. And if you want me to handle more of our activities this week, just let me know. I'd be happy to help."

Looking at the state of her, he could hardly believe she'd survived two full days of teaching and various Falling for Poetry projects. If he could ease any of her burdens for the

90

rest of the week, the ones he could still access, he would. Gratefully.

Already turning away, she suddenly snapped her fingers and swiveled back to him. "God, I almost forgot. Yes. Yes, I could use your help."

"What can I do?" Whatever she needed, he'd take care of it. Anything. Everything.

"My doctor's office called this afternoon and left a message on my cell. They moved my cast-removal appointment to late tomorrow, when I'd planned to help set up for the poetry slam." With her thumb and forefinger, she pinched her temples, looking even more tired than before. "I can reschedule the appointment, obviously. If at all possible, however, I'd prefer to keep it, because the itch beneath this damn contraption"—she glared down at her cast—"may well drive me to madness soon."

He didn't hesitate. "By all means, get your cast removed as soon as possible. I'll make certain the poetry slam preparations happen without a hitch." Removing his phone from his pocket, he tapped out a note to himself. "Do you want to skip the event entirely and just go home after your appointment?"

"No. I want to see all our hard work pay off." Her tone discouraged further discussion. "My appointment's at five. I have no idea how long it takes to remove a cast, but I hope to be back at school by six-thirty at the latest."

He lifted a shoulder. "However long it takes is fine."

Despite his reassurances, she frowned up at him. "Are you positive you can coordinate all the prep without my assistance?"

He'd have thought she didn't trust him, but he knew her too well by now.

The woman hated shirking responsibilities. That wasn't what she was currently doing, of course, but she would perceive it that way anyway.

"Don't worry, Candy," he said. "I'll take care of everything."

Her long, slow exhalation left her slumped. "Thank you, Griff. Okay, now I really do need to go."

He smiled. "You're more than welcome."

With a nod, she turned a second time and began to walk away, her stride more a shuffle than her usual stomp. Moment by moment, her figure got smaller in his sight, her footsteps fainter in his hearing.

She was disappearing from him, bit by bit.

When she was halfway down the hall, he couldn't stop himself.

"I swear to you, Candy, the anniversaries hurt less over time," he called out.

She halted for a moment, her back stiff. Then she lifted a hand in acknowledgment and kept walking.

LATE THAT NIGHT, HE LAY ON HIS COUCH AND ached for Candy and her loss.

He also ached for his own losses. Old and new. Unavoidable and self-inflicted. Marianne and Candy. The woman he'd loved and married, and the woman he—

Well, he hadn't let it get that far, had he?

The space he'd imposed between them, the time he'd requested to think and recover, he'd considered rational. But maybe it wasn't. Maybe it had nothing whatsoever to do with reason.

Maybe it was a total dodge, born of fear. The instinct of a wounded creature swiping wildly at anything and anyone that came near, forestalling any further chance of pain.

He could love Candy.

He could. If he let himself.

Did he intend to wait until he no longer grieved Marianne's death?

Did he intend to wait until he no longer thought of Marianne at all?

Did he intend to wait until he no longer feared another loss?

If so, he'd never move on. Never fall in love again.

Our hearts are large. They contain multitudes.

I don't expect yours to be empty of anyone but me.

Did he really think Marianne would consider his attachment to another woman a betrayal? The same Marianne who'd always, always wanted only good things, only joy, for him? The gentle, generous woman he'd sworn fidelity to until death did them part?

Death had parted them in a brutal, sudden rupture. Three years ago.

Did he really think Marianne wanted him to throw himself on a figurative funeral pyre to prove his grief and loyalty to her?

In his dreams these past weeks, she raged at him in a way she'd never done in life. He'd woken with a pounding skull and wet cheeks, entirely ignorant of what she was trying to tell him in his sleep. What his brain was trying to tell him.

Now he understood.

For all her gentleness, Marianne would be fucking *furious* at him. At the *waste* of it all. At the very *idea* she wouldn't know he loved her still, even if he grew to love someone else.

The second part of his life was beginning, like it or not, and the two halves were going to be conjoined somehow. And all this time, when he'd fearfully considered the juncture, he'd thought in terms of *or*.

He grieved Marianne, or he desired Candy. Marianne was his beloved wife, or he could find joy in his life after her death. He loved the wonderful, empathetic woman he'd married, or he could fall in love with the wonderful, indomitable woman in the classroom next door.

But his heart contained multitudes. It did.

Or was a false dichotomy, as he'd once tried to tell Candy.

He'd chosen the wrong conjunction.

His heart, his life, his future—they were *and*. Not *or*.

He grieved Marianne, and he desired Candy. Marianne was his beloved wife, and he could find joy in his life after her death. He loved Marianne, always would—and he was falling in love with Candy.

Candy. Loud, opinionated, sexy, whip-smart, devoted, hilarious Candy. Sweet as her name, although not everyone saw that.

Then again, not everyone could recognize or decipher subtext.

He could. Thank heavens, he could.

But he wasn't going to make her do the same. Not any longer.

BEFORE DAWN, GRIFF HAD FORMULATED HIS PLAN.

No more dithering or delays. He was ready to act, before Candy slipped away from him in the darkness.

As soon as he arrived at school, he tracked down Rose and Martin, who were waiting for their turn in the second-floor copy room. As he'd hoped, they were happy to help with the setup for the poetry slam that evening. Or so Martin claimed, although Rose did not second the statement.

"If Candy needs me, I'll be there," she said instead. "Just send instructions."

He wondered if Candy knew she'd earned that brand of fierce loyalty from her history department colleague. Somehow, he doubted it.

During lunch, he called to make an appointment of his

own. The receptionist squawked at the short notice, but he promised to bring decorated cookies from his favorite local bakery, Sweet Elizabeth, and his blatant bribery worked.

Immediately after school, he drove home. Dropped his briefcase just inside the door. Stripped off his jacket and button-down and tossed them onto his bed. Strode into the master bathroom.

He had just enough time to do this before his appointment.

Bracing his fists on the edge of the vanity, he leaned forward and stared at himself in the mirror, all itchy, shaggy beard and overlong hair.

If Marianne walked through the door right now, she'd barely recognize him. Hell, he barely recognized himself some days.

That hadn't mattered to him, though. Not really, not for the longest time. Even if the man in the mirror hadn't matched his past self, the reflection had matched how he felt inside. Who he was, down to his soul.

An abandoned husk, empty and useless.

It'd seemed like symmetry, somehow. Like justice. Like an act of love, even though seeing him this way would have gutted Marianne.

One final, hard look. He had to know for sure.

Then he did. At long last, he did.

That man was a stranger, and not just on the outside. Not anymore.

He reached into his under-sink cabinet, hand steady as a surgeon's.

And without another second of hesitation or doubt, he unearthed his clippers and got to work.

SEVEN

DESPITE HIS BEST EFFORTS, GRIFF RAN LATE.

Because they were fitting his appointment in between those already scheduled, it took longer than he'd hoped. The department store's checkout line was slow too. And although he'd well remembered the name of Candy's doctor—*Dr. Payne?* he'd said wonderingly in the emergency room after the nurse asked where Candy's records should be sent, and despite her injury, Candy had laughed and agreed on the name's insalubrity—actually locating the correct office also required some time.

When he finally entered the practice's waiting room, she'd already been called back. Unable to do anything else, he tunneled his fingers through his hair and took a seat against the wall. Crossed his ankle over his knee and jiggled his leg, a nervous habit that had occasionally irritated Marianne. Plucked at the side seams of his new jeans, the placket of his new shirt.

They were the first items of clothing he'd bought since moving to Marysburg.

Previously, he'd always chosen muted shades for his attire. His new shirt was a rich blue. A jewel tone because

Candy loved vibrant colors. Blue because, in a fit of dressing-room vanity and optimism, he'd decided it flattered the green of his eyes.

Candy liked his eyes. He thought. He hoped.

Hopefully she'd like his haircut too. After some consideration and a consultation with the stylist, he'd left it longish, but neatly trimmed. The women working and waiting at the salon had extended their wolf-whistled approval at his transformation, but Candy was an entity unto herself. The opinion of others wouldn't drive her reaction.

Another reason to adore her. Another reason for nervousness.

Casting yet another glance at the door she'd eventually exit from, he crossed his arms and drummed his fingers against his biceps, discontented.

He'd wanted to be with her as the doctor removed her cast. Wanted to offer support at the end of her injury as he had at its beginning. The potential symmetry had pleased him.

Nothing in actual human life, rather than literature, was that neat, of course. Today wasn't truly the end of her recovery. She'd require time and effort to regain full movement and strength in her limb. But her healing was well on its way.

As was his.

He supposed that was enough of a metaphor for him.

Minutes ticked by. A quarter hour. A half hour. Forty-five minutes.

Then, finally, the nerve-racking wait ended. She burst into the waiting room in full flight, eyes on her phone as she tapped rapidly at the screen.

Immediately, he spied at least one reason for her lengthy time in the back. She'd rolled the left sleeve of her blouse above her elbow, but even so, the edges of the fabric were wet.

Her new skin appeared a bit pink and damp, but not flaky

or peeling. With her typical efficiency, she'd already scrubbed off whatever unfortunateness lurked beneath her cast. Probably for the best, because they both knew teenagers would like nothing more than to tell tales of fearsome Ms. Albright's crusty, possibly smelly arm.

That forearm was a bit withered, true. Straight as a soldier at attention, though, and still as capable as any limb he'd ever seen. Although perhaps that was indulging in a bit of synecdoche.

With one final, decisive tap, she looked up from her phone and spotted him.

In that same moment, his own cell dinged with a new message.

"What the—" She stumbled to a halt, her brow puckered. "Griff, what—"

He stood. Strove for archness. "Fancy meeting you here."

Shaking her head, she tried again. "I just texted to tell you I was on my way. What are you doing here? And what happened to your—" Sudden panic widened her eyes. "Oh, God. If you're here, who's setting up for the poetry slam? Dammit, Griff—"

He raised a soothing hand. "It's being taken care of. Rose and Martin are coordinating the preparations until we arrive."

Utterly unappeased, she glared at him. "You said *you* were doing the setup."

"I said I would take care of the setup," he corrected. "Which I did, through judicious use of delegation."

The unintentional ambiguity of that verb choice had suited his purposes nicely.

"But how do they even know what we intended?" Her mouth pinched tight, she started for the exit. "I'd planned to stop home and change, but now I guess I shouldn't."

Shoving open the glass door, she stomped onto the sidewalk outside.

He fell into step beside her. "Candy, please stop and listen for a moment. Please."

At that second *please*, she slowed and swung to face him.

"If this is about why you're here and why you look so..." Her voice trailed off, and she bit her lip, her gaze tracing him from crown to toe. "Anyway. That can wait. We have responsibilities."

He smiled at her. "Do you really think I'd let them handle setup without a detailed explanation of what we wanted? Do you really think Rose or Martin would skimp in their efforts to make the poetry slam successful?"

Her gaze flicked away even as the set of her chin turned truculent. Which meant, as always, she knew he was right but was loath to admit it.

"Fine," she eventually allowed. "I suppose you make a salient point."

It was a begrudging admission, but he didn't care. He'd already wasted too much time, and he was seizing this opportunity. Right here. Right now.

Gather ye mulish, delicious English teachers while ye may.

Her face had regained some of its color since yesterday, although she still appeared a bit pale, her hair a tad rumpled. Those wide headbands usually held everything precisely in place, but she'd skipped using one again today. Her students had probably marveled at the sight.

Tenderly, he smoothed a stray strand back behind her ear. "We can spare five minutes, Candy. Ten. As many as we need."

"Why..." Her swallow worked her throat, and he wanted to trace the shifting shadows with his tongue. "Why do we need ten minutes?"

Screw your courage to the sticking-place, he instructed himself, *and you'll not fail.*

"I have some updates to discuss with you." Ones not

related to the poetry initiative, but she'd realize that soon enough. "But first, I want to hear what your doctor said."

With a light touch to her arm, he ushered her toward a bench near the sidewalk, beneath a tree blazing with autumn color. At the contact, she cast him another befuddled glance, but she didn't move away from him, and she sat without protest.

"Umm..." She kept darting glances at him. His hair. His face. His clothing. "Dr. Payne said I should start physical therapy so I can regain my full range of motion and rebuild my strength. As everything heals, I can start lifting weights."

Exactly what his research had indicated. "But overall, everything looks good?"

"Yes." Plucking her glasses from her nose, she let them hang around her neck. Her spike-lashed eyes searched his. "Griff, we agreed to share updates via e-mail. We agreed not to exchange physical intimacies. So what in the world are you doing here? Why did you—"

She cut herself off, her eyes turning glassy.

Her hand fluttered to the spot on her cheek where he'd smoothed away her hair. The exact place on her arm he'd touched to guide her to the bench.

"This isn't fair." She was whispering, but he could lip-read the words, because she was facing him as they talked. Keeping her promises, yet again. "You're taunting me with what I can't have, and it hurts. It's cruel, Griff, and you're not a cruel person. So why—"

When he cupped her soft cheek in his palm, she bit her lip again and leaned into his hand. But she was crying silently, her eyes stricken, and he chose his words carefully.

This was the fulcrum of his life, his heart, his future. The moment he crossed over to the other side of his *and*. If only she'd still have him.

"I told you I have significant hearing loss in my right ear."

He stroked along her cheekbone with his thumb. "I have since I was a child."

Her brow knitted, but she hitched her head in a little nod.

"That hearing loss hasn't gone away over time. It never will. It's changed who I am, forever. And in some ways, it's made my life harder." He watched her carefully. Saw when her eyes sharpened in recognition of their common language. "But when someone is speaking to me, my hearing loss ensures I pay them total attention. It makes me extraordinarily, consistently protective and careful of the hearing I do have, because I don't want to damage it."

He repeated himself with deliberate slowness. "I never, *ever* want to damage it."

Tears spilled over her lashes again.

Leaning in close, he paused. When she didn't move, when she simply stared up at him, lips parted, he kissed away a stray tear gleaming at the top of her cheek and leaned his forehead against hers.

"Because of my hearing loss," he added, "I also tend to appreciate those who speak clearly and loudly. Very loudly."

At that, her lips tipped in a trembling smile.

"Someone who speaks clearly deserves clarity in return." He gulped. "I—"

And, he reminded himself. *And*.

"I'm falling in love with you." There. There it was. "It's not a betrayal of Marianne, and I've accepted that. Our hearts are large. My heart is large. I can keep her there and still love you, still devote myself to any life we might make together, still do my damnedest to make you happy each and every day on this earth."

She sniffed loudly, and her hand covered his.

"Are you certain?" Her eyes were the stars in his firmament, bright and true. "You have to be certain."

It was a plea and a demand both. Scared but determined. Essentially, gorgeously Candy.

"If you'll have me," he told her, "I would not wish any companion in the world but you. May I woo you?"

"Woo me?" She huffed out a laugh, and its warmth banished the chill of endless weeks without her. "Really?"

He inclined his head. "Woo. Court. Seduce, as necessary."

She ran her fingertips lightly over his beard, and he shivered at the carnal pleasure of it. "Consider me seduced. You were already devastating, but now..."

Studying himself in the mirror earlier that afternoon, he'd considered removing all his facial hair. Going clean-shaven, as Marianne had preferred. Then he'd remembered how Candy had reacted to the abrasion of his beard against their entwined fingers. Her parted lips. Her desperate swallow.

If that beard earned him open, unguarded *heat* from Candy, he'd keep it forever.

In the end, then, he'd merely tamed it. Made clear it was a choice, not the exhausted shrug of a broken man. He liked it now, more than he'd expected.

He suspected he'd like it even more soon, once he'd rubbed it against the most tender, sensitive reaches of Candy's body and felt her shudder and gasp and break.

She murmured into his good ear, her mouth brushing his lobe with every syllable, and he had to close his eyes. "Now you're irresistible."

He'd once said the same to her. He'd meant it.

When her fingers sifted through his hair, he let out a hard breath. "A haircut and beard trim are nothing. I'll do whatever it takes to make you mine and be yours."

The words were rough. Hoarse. Honest.

"Griff." She moved back far enough to see his face, to trace it lovingly with her gaze, her smile wide and piercing in its sweetness. "Don't be obtuse, dearest. I'm already yours."

Then she kissed him, and the world vanished.

LATE THAT NIGHT, AFTER SHE'D FALLEN ASLEEP IN his arms, in his bed, he e-mailed her the first of many poems. Tokens of his love, in a language they both spoke. Something to start her new morning once they'd arrived at work together and walked to their classrooms hand in hand.

All day, she could keep it cupped safe within her heart, a light to guide her through more hard hours to come. A reminder that no matter how the wind whipped and tore at her, she was beloved. His beloved.

There was love. There was hope. And the birdsong of that hope, as Emily Dickinson once wrote, was sweetest in the gale.

He knew that down to his marrow, because Candy had showed him.

UNRAVELED

ABOUT "UNRAVELED"

The more tightly wound a man is, the faster he unravels…

Math teacher Simon Burnham—cool, calm, controlled—can't abide problems with no good solution. Which makes his current work assignment, mentoring art teacher Poppy Wick, nothing short of torture. She's warm but sharp. Chaotic but meticulous. Simultaneously the most frustrating and most alluring woman he's ever known. And in her free time, she makes murder dioramas. *Murder dioramas*, for heaven's sake. But the more tightly wound a man is, the faster he unravels —and despite his best efforts, he soon finds himself attempting to solve three separate mysteries: a murder in miniature, the unexplained disappearance of a colleague…and the unexpected theft of his cold, cold heart.

This story is dedicated to my mom, the sort of elementary school teacher kids hugged around the knees in the grocery store, faces alight with joy at seeing her. I love you.

ONE

A MERE TEN MINUTES AFTER FIRST SETTING EYES on her, Simon had already drawn his initial conclusion: In terms of professional appearance and deportment, Ms. Poppy Wick was a disgrace.

In defiance of the faculty dress code, she was wearing jeans. Not even dark, trouser-style jeans, which at a casual glance might be mistaken for appropriate work pants. No, hers clung faithfully to her ample hips and bottom. More importantly, they were faded and splotched with…what *was* that? Some sort of floury glue concoction? And now that he was looking more closely, flecks of paint revealed themselves on the denim covering her round thighs. A rainbow of color, and a silent testament to her defiance of necessary rules.

On Fridays, to be fair, teachers could donate money to charity in exchange for wearing jeans. But today was Tuesday, and the entire faculty of Marysburg High was sitting around cafeteria tables listening to the superintendent's latest consultant drone on while wearing a suit more expensive than any teacher could ever afford, and Ms. Wick was *doodling*.

He glanced closer.

A skull, surrounded by ivy. Dear Lord.

At the very least, she might have had the dignity to sketch cubes or other three-dimensional geometric shapes, as he sometimes did. Although not during faculty meetings, and never with his hair in two wispy, drooping little reddish-blond buns, perched high on either side of the head. He kept his own dark hair neatly trimmed every two weeks and in strict order, despite its distressing tendency to wave.

She'd had a free seat beside her for the faculty meeting, and he'd taken it in hopes of observing her at least once before their respective positions became clear. Which was optimal, since knowledge of his scrutiny and its purpose would naturally change her behavior. Heisenberg's Uncertainty Principle: The Teacher Observation Corollary.

He sighed and began making a list of topics he and Ms. Wick would need to address in their initial consultation.

Why their principal, Tess Dunn, had assigned him as the mentor to an art teacher, he hadn't the faintest clue. Yes, Ms. Wick had recently joined the faculty, and all first-year teachers at MHS received a mentor, no matter how long they'd taught in other school districts. Yes, mentors were chosen at random. But he was the chair of the math department, unsuited for—

Something was nudging his arm.

When he looked up and to the right, his mentee winked at him, hazel eyes sparkling above rosy cheeks. She nudged him again, and he looked down at her spiral-bound notebook, currently poking against his forearm.

Her looping script wasn't difficult to read. *Want to play Hangman?*

Ms. Wick appeared to be in her mid-forties, perhaps a year or two older than him. Still, she'd passed him a note, invited him to play a juvenile game, as if she were one of their sophomores.

He stared at her, aghast.

Retrieving her notebook, she added more, then slid it back in his direction.

C'mon. You're obviously distracted too.

Well, yes. But that was her fault entirely. Especially since, now that they were face-to-face, he could spot yet more paint flecks dappling her high, broad forehead and rounded chin. There was even a little blue smear just above the bow of her curved lips.

Another quick note. *I'll let you choose the word or phrase.*

Sighing, he turned to a fresh page in his own legal pad, determined to quash her unacceptable behavior.

Ms. Wick, we are in a professional sett—

The legal pad was yanked out from beneath his hand, and she jotted something beneath his half-finished scold. On *his* paper.

How did you know my name? She paused, then huffed out an amused breath. *I'm that memorable, am I?*

Eyes narrowed at her audaciousness, he reclaimed his notebook with a decisive tug.

Not at all. Earlier today, I was assigned to be your first-year mentor.

There. That should put an end to her unprofessionalism.

She tilted her head for a moment, forehead crinkled, before her impish grin flickered back to full brightness. *Damn. I was hoping for Candy Albright.*

Well, she'd at least written it on her own notebook this time. Small victories.

He shouldn't ask. He wouldn't ask.

Yet the word somehow appeared on his paper, in his usual, careful print. *Why?*

She's equally terrifying, but in a FUN way.

Ms. Wick had underlined *FUN* three times.

He paused, unable to understand why that stung. Being fun had never constituted one of his goals, and if he terrified her, wouldn't that better assure her compliance with faculty rules and regulations?

He should be glad he both bored and terrified her, after a mere quarter-hour in her presence. He *was* glad.

Odd, though. She didn't *seem* terrified. In fact, she seemed to be writing him yet another note, despite his scowling disfavor.

Candy cornered me about Oxford commas last week. It was a memorable discussion.

Yes, he imagined so. Candy's opinions on grammar were both numerous and intense, and usually shared at top volume.

Ms. Wick still wasn't done writing. *She left me an informative pamphlet on my desk. Then she told me how glad she was that I'd replaced Mildred, cackled, and shouted DING-DONG, THE WITCH IS DEAD.*

She beamed at him, as if inviting him to share the humor, and for a moment he almost smiled back.

Clearing his throat, he turned away instead, as if preoccupied by the consultant's PowerPoint slides. No, he would not encourage his mentee's behavior. This conversation was done, at least until after the faculty meeting.

But minutes later, when he again glanced at his legal pad, he discovered that she'd managed to write a question there without him noticing, a question so simple he'd be churlish not to answer.

I should know my mentor's name. What is it?

Dammit. He had to respond. The rules of politeness required it, as did a smoothly functioning mentor-mentee relationship.

Simon Burnham, he wrote on his paper. *Chair of the Math Department.*

At some point, she'd returned to her doodling. Now the ivy swept across the page, sliding through openings in the skull, the vines encroaching and ominous, edged and shad-owed in black.

She wasn't paying him a bit of attention anymore, and he stared at her profile for a moment, unable to reconcile her blend of cheer and macabre sensibilities, unable to determine why he suddenly wanted her eyes back on him.

His dignity wouldn't allow him to poke her with his note-book, as she'd done to him. Instead, he lightly tapped her bare arm with his fingertips, just below where she'd pushed up the sleeves of her cardigan.

Her skin was warm and giving, even under such a tenta-tive touch. When he withdrew his hand, he clenched it around an unexpected burn.

As she turned those bright eyes back to him, he pointed to his paper. She read his note, then contemplated him for a moment, smile absent, her scrutiny uncomfortably sharp.

Shall I call you Simon or Mr. Burnham? she finally wrote in her notebook.

He knew trouble when it nudged him in the arm.

If first impressions proved accurate, Ms. Wick was a problem with no clear solution, a human version of the Riemann Hypothesis, and he wanted none of it. None of her.

Mr. Burnham, he wrote, and determinedly ignored her for the rest of the faculty meeting.

WHEN THE LENGTHY MEETING ENDED, MS. WICK tucked her notebook beneath her arm, slung her purse over her shoulder, and raised a pale eyebrow. "Have I passed initial inspection, Mr. Burnham?"

Her voice was slightly hoarse, low and warm with amuse-ment. It seemed expressly designed for sharing confidences and laughter. But Simon had never indulged in those sorts of dangerous intimacies, and he didn't intend to start now. Especially with someone like her.

"I'll meet you in your room shortly," he said.

At that, she snorted. "I'll take that as a no."

The prospect didn't seem to bother her. She left the table after a saucy salute in his direction, and within a dozen confident strides, she was linking arms with one of the other art teachers and whispering briefly before they both convulsed with mirth as they left the cafeteria.

Maybe she was laughing at him. His rigidity. His coldness.

Fortunately, he didn't care about her good opinion. He cared about professionalism and hard work and creating an orderly, calm environment for himself and his students alike. As long as the personal lives and judgments of his colleagues didn't affect job performance, they were irrelevant. Hell, he didn't even know why Mildred had left, or why Candy was so happy to see the older woman gone. He didn't need to know, and he didn't want to.

Although Mildred, as of last year, hadn't mentioned the prospect of leaving, and the customary ceremonies accompanying the retirement of such a longtime teacher hadn't occurred. No announcement in a faculty meeting or presentation of flowers and a gift. No potluck in the library, which he visited only to offer a handshake before promptly departing once more.

Odd. Very odd.

Considering the matter, he slowly walked to the cafeteria door, only to find himself beside Candy and one of the newer English teachers—Greg? Griff? It didn't matter.

"Ms. Albright." Simon was speaking to her. Why was he speaking to her? "Please pardon the interruption. I was wondering—"

No, he wasn't a gossip, and he didn't care.

Her brows rose behind her horn-rimmed glasses. "Yes, Mr. Burnham?"

He wrestled with himself for a moment.

"Mildred. Mrs. Krackel." There. That wasn't a question. Thus, he wasn't a gossip.

Greg-Griff-Whoever turned away to cough into his fist, shoulders shaking, while a tiny, evil smile curved Ms. Albright's mouth.

"Mildred got what she deserved," she declared. "Mary Shelley would be pleased."

Then she marched down the hall without another word, her English Department colleague at her shoulder.

Terrifying, Ms. Wick had called Ms. Albright.

Mary Shelley had written *Frankenstein*, a story of horror and violence and transgression. And the author would be pleased about what happened to Mrs. Krackel? What precisely had Ms. Albright thought Mildred *deserved*?

The halls of the school seemed to empty with astonishing quickness that evening, and by the time he'd stopped by his room to gather his briefcase and journeyed to the opposite end of the school, where Ms. Wick's classroom was located, shadows were amassing in the corners. His footsteps echoed in an unsettling way as he strode down halls he'd rarely visited.

His pace quickened as he neared her door. It was getting late, and he didn't intend to spend longer with his mentee than absolutely necessary.

She was sitting at her desk, her high forehead crinkled as she typed on her laptop. Another man, one less intent on the business at hand, one interested in such matters, might have called that evidence of her concentration *endearing*.

Her shades were closed against the gathering dusk outside, and the overhead fluorescent lights didn't entirely banish the gloom. To his surprise, however, the expansive room, stuffed with work tables and cabinets, was neater than Ms. Wick herself upon first glance.

He'd have time to inspect her classroom organization

later. His first priority: making the rules and expectations regarding their relationship—their mentor-mentee relationship, that is—clear.

When he knocked on her doorframe, she looked up from her laptop placidly, with no sign of startlement.

Even as he approached her desk, he began instructing her. "Per Principal Dunn's request, I will observe your seventh period class for five consecutive days, beginning this upcoming Monday. Since seventh period is one of my planning periods, I will stay the entire length of the class. As I observe, I will evaluate your performance based on criteria outlined in the memo you should have received via e-mail about the mentorship program last month. If you need another copy, I can forward one to you."

"I don't need one." Her lips quivering, she shook her head. "Shockingly, I managed to keep track of the memo."

Ignoring her impertinent choice of adverb, he continued. "After class, assuming you don't have to leave for any necessary meetings, I will share my observations with you, and at the end of the week, I will write my initial evaluation, which, once approved by Principal Dunn, will be sent to you. After next week, we will meet monthly to discuss your progress or lack thereof. Other observations may occur, based on necessity. Any questions?"

If he'd expected her to be cowed by his blunt speech, intimidated into silence by the prospect of his judgment, he would have been disappointed. If anything, those hazel eyes of hers had brightened further, alight with...challenge? Amusement?

"Of course I have questions." She propped her elbows on her desk and rested her chin on her entwined, paint-flecked fingers. "How long have you been teaching, Mr. Burnham?"

His frown pinched his brows. "Twenty years last fall. How is that relevant? Are you concerned I have insufficient expertise in pedagogy to serve as your mentor?"

"No," she said, one of her little buns now sagging half an inch above her left ear. "I was merely curious."

To return her question in kind would not in_____ curiosity of his own, but instead provide necessary context for his mentoring efforts. Professionalism demanded more information, and he was always, always a consummate professional.

"And yourself, Ms. Wick? How many years have you been a teacher?"

"Twenty-four." Her gaze remained solely on him, and he found himself shifting beneath its keen sharpness. "Before this, I taught near D.C., but I wanted to move closer to my parents. I'm an only child, and their health is getting more precarious by the year."

Fortunately, she'd answered the question he wouldn't have allowed himself to ask: *Why did you change schools?*

"Any other concerns or queries?" If not, he intended to perform a preliminary inspection of her room and evaluate her organizational system and abilities.

"Oh, countless. But we have plenty of time for those." She smiled at him, very slowly. One might almost have called the expression *smug*. "That said, I should probably warn you about the unit we're starting next week."

He merely looked at her, waiting for whatever had prompted that mischievous curve of her pink, pink mouth.

Her explanation didn't provide any clarity. "We're tackling three-dimensional representation of objects and scenes and discussing the intersection of art and public service."

That all sounded completely, laudably appropriate and professional to him. So why—

"Specifically," she continued, "we're studying Frances Glessner Lee's mid-century efforts to advance forensic science through her Nutshell Studies of Unexplained Death. Then the students will create their own educational dioramas, upon topics of their choosing."

Unexplained death? What the hell?

She waved a casual hand. "And, of course, I'll bring in an example of my own work as further inspiration."

He blinked at her, still stuck on the *unexplained death* bit. "Your...own work?"

"During summers and in my spare time, I create and sell my own dioramas." Her smile was no longer merely smug. It was now a wide, gleaming, toothy taunt. "If I didn't enjoy teaching so much, I might consider doing my dioramas full-time, since I've amassed an appreciative audience for my work."

This. This was why she was pleased, why her rosy cheeks glowed so cheerily. He could tell that much, but he still didn't understand *why*.

And she wasn't offering him the necessary context. Not this time. Oh, no, her soft lips were pressed shut as she waited for the question. Waited for him to break.

Ten minutes ago, he'd have sworn he never would. But that stupid, wispy bun was almost touching the flushed tip of her ear, and the blue streak above her mouth was mocking him, and her delighted grin plumped those round cheeks, and he had to ask. He *had* to.

"What—" He cleared his throat, studying her file cabinet as if it held vast importance in his eventual evaluation of her teaching. "What is your work, specifically?"

She didn't answer until he met her gaze again, and he didn't know whether to admire or despise her for it.

"Murder dioramas," she said.

As soon as he noticed he was gaping at her, open-mouthed, he snapped his jaw shut.

Deep breath. Raise an eyebrow. Seem only distantly engaged in the discussion.

"Murder dioramas?" he repeated coolly. "I'm afraid I'll require more detail, so as to determine the appropriateness of your work for a classroom setting."

Her grin only widened. "Oh, naturally."

She made him wait again, because of course she did.

"Yes, Ms. Wick?" he eventually prodded.

"Sorry. My mind must have wandered for a moment. It's getting late, isn't it?" She glanced at the clock on the wall, and then gave what seemed to be a genuine gasp. "Oh, damn, I'm going to be late for my oil change."

Jumping to her feet, she began shoving papers into a tote and searching for her keys.

From all appearances, she intended to leave him without further explanation, and that was unacceptable. Completely and utterly unacceptable.

He stepped close enough to interrupt her frantic efforts. "An explanation, Ms. Wick."

"Fine." Apparently lacking the time to taunt him further, she met his eyes and quickly summarized her ghoulish hobby. "My business is called Crafting the Perfect Murder. I imagine and recreate a violent crime in miniature form, complete with subtle clues as to what happened, why, and who was responsible. I also provide witness statements. People buy the dioramas and attempt to solve the mystery, and I can either send them the solution or not, as they desire."

His mouth temporarily refused to form words.

"My dioramas are art, but people with plenty of spending money also buy them as a party game, especially around Halloween. You know, competing as to who can solve the case first." Glancing down, she finally located her keys and brandished them in triumph. "There they are!"

Finally, his tongue came untethered.

"People *pay* for that?" he asked, incredulous.

Immediately, he wished he'd bitten that tongue instead, because she took a step backward and flinched, her smile vanishing in a microsecond. At the sudden movement, her failing bun unraveled entirely, the spiral of fine hair falling over her ear and against her reddening cheek.

Dammit.

The remark hadn't been intended as a referendum on the quality of her work, as he had no way of judging that. He hadn't even meant it as an insult, although he undoubtedly found such a hobby macabre in the extreme. More, he'd been confused as to why anyone would invite violence and confusion into their home if they had a choice not to, and wondering whether she could possibly get paid enough for her work to defray the costs of her creations.

But she'd clearly taken his thoughtless comment as a slight against her work, and perhaps rightly so. Politeness required that he make amends. Immediately. Before the memory of the hurt in her eyes, however quickly masked, twisted his gut further.

"Ms. Wick, please for—"

But it was too late for apologies. She was already speaking, already headed for the door.

"If you think what I do deserves so little respect, I dare you to solve the mystery in the diorama I'm bringing to class next week. Maybe then you'll have a better idea why people *pay for that*, as you so charmingly put it." When she reached the door, she swiveled to face him. "I have to leave. Are you coming or not?"

He dropped his chin to his chest for a moment. "I, uh— I'd planned to evaluate the layout and organization of your classroom, if that's acceptable."

The inspection could have occurred next week, of course, but he needed to sit and think a minute. Wait until solid ground formed beneath him once more.

She shrugged. "Knock yourself out. Just ask a custodian to lock up behind you, please."

"I will." He didn't offer another apology. Instead, he

simply watched her flee from his presence, her rapid footsteps retreating into silence.

Terrifying. Not in a fun way.

That was him.

He sat in her desk chair, and it was still warm from her body.

Math. That would clear his troubled thoughts. Seven squared was forty-nine. Seven cubed was 343. Seven to the fourth power was 2,401. Seven to the fifth power was—

The overhead lights went out. In the evening, the hallway lights were dim, and they barely penetrated the sudden, choking blackness of the classroom.

"Hello?" he called. "I'm still here."

There were footsteps in the distance, shuffling and steady. Coming closer.

"Hello!" he called again.

No one answered, but someone was approaching. Only steps away now.

Mildred got what she deserved.

Involuntarily, he shivered and leapt to his feet. He wasn't staying any longer in a dark room, with mysterious footsteps—

The lights flickered back on, and a moment later, Mrs. Denham, one of the custodians, poked her head in the doorway. "Did you say something?"

His heart was rabbiting, and he gripped the edge of Ms. Wick's desk with both hands. "The lights…" He pointed at them, as if the custodian couldn't locate them for herself. "There's a problem with them. They went out without warning."

Mrs. Denham's smile was kind, if a bit patronizing. "In this wing of the school, the overheads use motion sensors to reduce energy consumption. If you don't move for a while, they'll go out, but as soon as you wave an arm, they'll come right back on. Don't worry."

"Oh." Of course. Of course. "Thank you."

"Next summer, they'll install the sensors on your side of the school," the custodian added. "Why are you here, anyway, instead of your own classroom?"

It was yet another question that didn't have a single, clear answer.

He hated those sorts of questions. Always had, always would.

So before he could make a fool of himself yet again, before he spent another moment contemplating a problem with no solution, he said goodbye to Mrs. Denham and left.

TWO

By the following Monday, Simon's mind had settled itself, regaining its accustomed calm clarity.

Or at least it would have, had he not overheard part of a murmured conversation in the faculty lounge, as he was removing his usual healthy-but-filling lunch from the shared refrigerator. Two members of the science department were huddled up close at the round table, brows furrowed in…was that concern? Fear?

When he heard the word *Mildred*, he lingered in front of the refrigerator. Bending at the waist, he extended an arm, as if unable to locate the insulated bag positioned directly in front of him, in its normal spot.

"…such a shame, what happened," one of his colleagues whispered.

The other teacher nodded emphatically. "I feel so much less safe now."

At that moment, he happened to accidentally knock over a can of Diet Coke in the refrigerator, and the noise halted the conversation behind him. When it didn't resume after a moment, he admitted defeat, righted the can of soda, gathered his lunch, and left to eat in his classroom.

If the incident left him rattled, that was only to be expected. Anyone would be distressed by the possibility that a longtime coworker had mysteriously vanished, or possibly even met a violent end.

And if the memory of how Ms. Wick had cringed and stepped back from him, hurt dousing the sparkle in those hazel eyes, also came to mind uncomfortably often, surely that was natural under the circumstances. For the purposes of a productive mentor-mentee relationship, open lines of communication would prove crucial. Any logical professional would feel compelled to apologize and make necessary amends as soon as possible.

Accordingly, he'd hoped to arrive in her classroom several minutes before the start of seventh period, allowing him enough time to speak privately with her and offer his regrets for his unguarded, hurtful remark. But one of his sixth-period students had appeared distressed at the results of the test he'd handed back earlier in the period, and he needed to talk with her at the end of class to reiterate the various ways she could receive extra help and/or raise her grade. His regular after-school hours for struggling students, for example, or extra credit work—or even the option of retaking the test at a future date, when she felt more confident in the mathematical concepts covered.

"You can rectify the situation," he'd calmly promised, after outlining her various avenues for assistance. "I will help."

By the time the student departed his classroom, no longer near tears, he had no hopes of a private discussion with Ms. Wick. In fact, he arrived at her doorway just as the bell rang for the start of seventh period. Closing the door behind him, he leaned against it and observed.

Her students had already settled at their two-person tables and were beginning to write in notebooks they'd evidently retrieved from the open cabinet near the doorway. On the whiteboard, Ms. Wick had written their initial task for the class, a five-minute writing prompt to settle them down and channel their thoughts toward the day's lesson: *What one topic do you wish people understood more fully? Why? What do you wish they knew about that topic?*

He'd known, of course, what work awaited the students. Ms. Wick had e-mailed him her week's lesson plans on Saturday, attaching the agendas and objectives for each day and listing the state standards her lessons satisfied.

Her thoroughness had surprised him, although perhaps it shouldn't have. Not once he'd seen the orderliness of her classroom, despite all the potential for mess and chaos inherent in art classes.

He blamed those droopy buns for misleading him so badly.

Today, as she set up her laptop and prepared her presentation about Frances Glessner Lee, she looked much more professional in her clothing choices and overall appearance. Her black dress fell softly to her calves, swirling as she bustled around the room. Her chunky amber-colored necklace and dangling earrings framed her round, lively face.

Only one bun today, it seemed. It perched high atop her head, still messy, but in a way that looked somehow deliberate and neat nevertheless. Wavy, fine tendrils caressed her cheeks.

She was the prettiest witch in the forest.

Startled by his uncharacteristic flight of fancy, he jotted a note in his legal pad: *Discuss faculty dress code.*

Speaking of witchy, there was an unusual number of young women clad entirely in black in this class. If he wasn't mistaken, all members of the state-champion girls' softball team.

When Ms. Wick turned away for a minute, producing

something large and cloth-covered from behind her desk and setting it on an empty table nearby, he heard one girl whispering to another.

"Freakin' finally," the student with cornrows hissed excitedly. "The murder unit."

The other young woman, her skin powdered pale, extended her fist for bumping. "This is our moment, Tori."

Then Ms. Wick called the class to order, and he watched over twenty years of teaching experience at work. Using a well-organized PowerPoint presentation, she relayed Frances Glessner Lee's story with enthusiasm, covering various objectives while inviting student interaction and gearing it toward their interests whenever possible.

And their interests all appeared to tend toward one topic, and one topic alone: bloodshed.

"Dude," Tori muttered to her friend. "Look at those stab wounds."

In the current slide, projected onto the whiteboard, a male doll lay face-down on the floor of a meticulously crafted and detailed bedroom, red splotches marring his blue-striped pajamas. A female doll lay equally dead and bloody in the bed nearby.

"—included witness statements," Ms. Wick said. "Her attention to detail was remarkable, as you can see. Let's focus on another scene, which includes a calendar with flippable pages. Using a single-hair paintbrush, she would write tiny letters, one by one. And please note those amazing stockings on the victim here, knitted by hand with straight pins, as well as the working locks she created for windows and—"

Given the subject, Ms. Wick's enthusiasm was inappropriate at best.

Nevertheless, her students seemed enthralled. Whenever she paused, various hands waved in the air, while other kids took feverish notes.

"Wasn't it weird for a woman to do things like that, back in the '40s and '50s?" the pale-powdered girl asked.

Ms. Wick considered her answer for a moment. "Although forensic science was a relatively new field then, police work was dominated almost entirely by men. Some bristled at her intrusion into that domain, yes."

A greasy-haired kid, slouched in his chair, raised his hand. "I bet it helped that she was rich."

"You're exactly right, Travis." Ms. Wick smiled at him. "Because of her family's prominence, she had influential supporters. Her money also allowed her to woo students to her week-long courses, complete with a concluding banquet at the Ritz-Carlton."

Several students groaned at that, while one boy in a hoodie muttered, "The Ritz? Sweet."

"But whatever encouraged investigators to take her classes," she continued, "by the end of their week of instruction, after studying her dioramas, those students found themselves much better able to evaluate crime scenes in a systematic way, gather evidence, and draw logical conclusions from what they'd seen. And her work was so brilliant, her Nutshell Studies are used to train investigators to this day. That's why the solutions aren't publicly available."

A girl at the table next to him twitched suddenly. As her hand shot into the air, her face alight, she began to grin.

Revelation. Watching it dawn on a student's face was a privilege, one he didn't take for granted. He'd been chasing that particular expression for over twenty years, day by day.

"Go ahead, Amanda," Ms. Wick said to the young woman.

"If you think about it, what she did was really clever." Amanda waved an impatient, dismissive hand. "I mean, obviously her dioramas were smart, and awesome in an artistic sense and all, but that's not what I'm talking about."

Ms. Wick rested her elbows on her lectern. "Okay."

"If she was going to barge into a male-dominated field, what better way to do it than with dollhouses? Something that was considered girly or whatever." Amanda twisted her mouth, trying to find the right words. "She used the things girls were allowed to do, the things they were taught, to elbow her way into things she wasn't supposed to do."

If he'd been the recipient of such an approving beam from Ms. Wick, he imagined he'd feel exactly as pleased as her student currently looked.

"I think you've touched on a key point there, Amanda," she said. "Let's talk a bit more about that, and then discuss the specific techniques Lee used to recreate her scenes in three dimensions, as well as how art and public service are often intertwined. After that, you'll have some time to consider what you'd like your own educational dioramas to include. I've also brought one of my own dioramas for your inspection. If any of you manage to solve its mystery before the end of the week, I have a reward for you."

Over twenty heads swiveled toward the table near her desk, where her cloth-covered diorama was evidently waiting.

"I Googled her dioramas, and they're extra-gory," Tori whispered to her friend. "This is the best day ever."

"Bring on the carnage," the pale girl declared with unmistakable glee. "Do you think the reward is, like, an invitation to watch an autopsy?"

Pinching the bridge of his nose between thumb and forefinger, Simon sighed.

As the students spent the end of the class planning their own dioramas, Simon claimed one of the magnifying glasses provided by Ms. Wick and studied her work up close.

The diorama she'd created included three rooms of a small house: a bedroom, a bathroom, and a living room. The living room was charred almost beyond recognition, with a blackened corpse on the floor. The edges of the bedroom also showed evidence of fire, but the room hadn't been incinerated in the same way as the living room. The bathroom, in contrast, appeared entirely undamaged, pristine other than the hair clippings glistening with faux-moisture in the marble sink's drain.

According to the written information provided, two brothers had lived in the house. One, Kaden, lay dead in the living room. The other—Barron—had managed to escape through the bedroom window in a panic, the encroaching flames too intense to attempt to save his sibling.

Outside the dwelling, a police officer stood near her four primary witnesses and suspects. The surviving brother, of course, but also an ex-girlfriend of the victim, who was suspected of having violated the restraining order Kaden had filed against her. Lingering nearby were a neighbor with a grudge—the two brothers had a habit of throwing loud parties late at night, evidently—and a landlord who'd threatened consequences if Kaden didn't stop smoking inside the unit.

Simon had all week to solve the mystery, so he decided to study the witness statements another day and focus on the diorama itself today. Not so much the evidence of murder contained within and outside the miniature home, but rather the evidence of Ms. Wick's labors. The diorama as a piece of art, rather than a crime scene.

Simon could not claim to be an aesthete, by any means.

Still. Her artistry, however macabre its inspiration, was… astonishing. Rigorous precision coupled with unbounded creativity and skill. Some of the furnishings she'd bought as is, perhaps, but no miniature store provided half-burned recliners or stacks of papers on a desk, their written contents just visible with a magnifying glass and the use of tweezers, or the impression of a heeled shoe in the dirt outside the living room window, or a bandage on an elderly landlord's arm.

He would have bet his 401K that the suspects' clothes were hand-stitched. She hadn't missed a detail, not the miniscule lighter just poking out of the neighbor's back pocket, not the way all the men's shoelaces were double-knotted, not the spurned ex-girlfriend's choppy haircut.

To complete her gruesome creation, Ms. Wick had to have mastered an astounding array of mediums and techniques, and her hands must have been steady as a neurosurgeon's.

Everything was exactly in scale, which required mathematical skill too.

The realization pleased him more than it should have.

The final bell rang while he was still lost in contemplation, but he barely noted the buzz of students chatting, packing up their backpacks, and heading out the door, bound toward home or work or extracurricular activities.

"Are you ready to make an arrest?"

Her voice, though mischievous, didn't quite contain the warmth of their previous meeting, and he knew why. But her body next to his, their shoulders almost—almost—touching, radiated heat in a way that made him want to close his eyes and simply breathe in her faint scent of turpentine and soap.

He didn't, of course. Instead, ignoring her question, he turned stiffly and gestured toward the nearest table. "Let's discuss my initial observations."

With a mocking little bow of her head, she sat in a student chair. Tempted to choose the one beside her, he instead selected a seat safely across the table.

They were both professionals. No small talk was necessary.

"If today's lesson is any indication, you're obviously a teacher of great experience and skill, well able to keep the attention of a roomful of students while covering all necessary topics and meeting all required objectives. Your rapport with your students is remarkable, as is your ability to elicit participation from them. Your classroom is impeccably organized." He kept his voice cool, as befitted an objective mentor. "If the rest of this week's lessons prove similar to today's, I can only conclude that Marysburg High is fortunate to have you amongst its faculty."

He flicked a glance up from his notes, meeting her wide eyes.

An unkind observer might have described her mouth as agape, and a more whimsical man might have been tempted to throw a grape in there.

Those soft lips snapped shut quickly enough, however, when he continued.

"That said, the faculty's dress code appears to have escaped you. Today's outfit is appropriate and very, uh, becoming—"

Shit.

"—um, becoming *for a professional teacher*." There. Saved it. No room for misinterpretation. "But your clothing at the faculty meeting did not meet the standards set by school guidelines. No jeans, except on Denim Fridays, and all garments worn by teachers must be clean."

Since her eyes were currently narrowed slits of hazel affront, he was smart enough not to mention the faculty meeting's droopy buns. Those could wait for a debriefing session later in the week.

In the spirit of tearing off a bandage as quickly as possible, he continued hastily, before her glare lasered actual holes through his skull. "The contents of today's lecture, while fascinating and well-presented, also put you at risk for student and parental complaints. The topic was, in short, overly macabre and ghoulish. I would suggest you pick more school-appropriate topics in the future."

One of her pale eyebrows arched high. "Would you?"

She'd settled back in her chair, affront replaced by steely calm.

The expression bolted down his spine in a way he couldn't interpret. Was that electric jolt warning him he'd erred somehow? Was it a visceral response to the challenge betrayed by her pugnacious, upturned chin and haughty stare? Was it because, beneath that witchy, alluring dress, her plump thighs had shifted and rubbed—

No, it wasn't excitement. Professional evaluations did not prompt passion of any sort. Not for him, anyway.

If his tie suddenly constricted his breath, he'd merely fastened it a bit too tightly that morning. The prickling heat spreading lower and lower, making his button-down tease against every nerve ending his skin possessed, was simply the result of the school's inadequate HVAC system. Nothing more.

His throat might be dry, but he would remain entirely businesslike.

"I also believe you left the student diorama assignment too open-ended, given the limited time available for this unit. You might consider providing a handout of preapproved topics in the future." That was the last item on today's list, but he continued looking down at his legal pad. "Finally, I inadvertently insulted both you and your work last week. My remark was rude and uncollegial."

After sketching a tiny, perfect cube on the edge of his paper, he continued. "Furthermore, my study of your work today elucidated my comment's essential injustice. I might consider the subject matter disturbing, but it was quite evident why consumers would pay a great deal of money to possess such a wondrous, meticulous piece of artistry."

Two squared is four. Two cubed is eight. Two to the fourth power is sixteen.

He raised an expressionless face. "Please accept my sincere apologies."

Her face had also turned unreadable, but at least she wasn't openly scowling at him anymore. As always, small victories.

After a lengthy pause, she spoke slowly. "I'll address your feedback one topic at a time, if that's acceptable to you?"

He gave her a jerky nod, and somehow he already knew.

By the end of this conversation, he'd feel like a fool once more.

"Last Tuesday, the day of the faculty meeting, my students were making papier-mâché masks using paper plates, aluminum foil, hot glue guns, newspapers, flour, water, and paint. I defy anyone to oversee the making of those masks without finding their clothing soiled in some fashion, protective apron be damned." Her lips tilted up in a little, satisfied smile, a silent warning that this entire conversation was only going to get worse for him. "More importantly, if you'd consulted with Principal Dunn, you'd have discovered that we already discussed the issue of appropriate clothing and came to a mutual agreement on the matter."

Yes. This was definitely worse.

"On days like today, when I'm lecturing and likely to remain clean, I follow the standard dress code." She swept a hand downward, indicating her current outfit. "On days when my clothing is likely to get stained, I'm allowed to wear jeans and more casual tops. Because, as we both concluded, asking me to replenish my work wardrobe every time an item became slightly soiled was both unreasonable and cost-prohibitive."

No amount of exponential multiplication was going to save him now. "It appears I owe you another ap—"

"If I were you, I'd save further apologies until we're

finished," she interrupted, still smiling. "You might as well beg forgiveness for everything at once. For the sake of efficiency, which I know is of the utmost importance to you."

Shit. *Worse* appeared to be an understatement.

"Now onto your next critique, concerning the inappropriateness of today's lesson." She ticked off her multipart response on her fingers. "First, inappropriateness is very much a subjective matter. I'm surprised a man like you, who seems to prize objectivity, would use such a nebulous, essentially undefinable concept as part of your feedback. Second, I ran the unit and its contents by Principal Dunn before the school year even began. She gave her approval. She did so because, third, I sent a letter home to the parents and guardians of my students weeks ago, one that described this week's topic in detail and required their signatures for student participation."

How he'd fucked up so badly, he couldn't even say. All he could do was keep listening, silent, as she enumerated the flaws in his conclusions.

"As far as listing a set of preapproved diorama topics—I agree such a list would contribute to greater efficiency in my classroom." She leaned forward, elbows on the desk. "But it would detract from the actual experience of making art, which is as much about the creative process as it is about the final result. I want my students to find topics that speak to them on an individual level, and I certainly don't know them well enough to be able to predict the contents of their hearts or the subjects that consume their innermost thoughts. I'm happy to guide them if they have difficulty choosing a topic, but I don't want to prematurely limit the expanse of their imaginations."

It all sounded like chaos to him. Total and complete chaos.

She tapped a fingertip on the table. "This isn't a math problem with one right answer, Mr. Burnham. There aren't even ten right answers, or a million right answers. There are *infinite* right answers."

That lack of surety was discomfiting at best. Terrifying at worst.

But it didn't matter how much he feared problems without a clear solution. What mattered: the wrong he'd done his colleague by presuming her less a professional than she actually was.

"I apologize, Ms. Wick. Again." He maintained eye contact as a reassurance of his sincerity, despite his desire to turn away in shame. "I've underestimated you, and I promise to try my best not to do so in the future."

He wouldn't make excuses for himself. He wouldn't. But she needed to understand, if only to comprehend—

Well, not the contents of his heart. But maybe his innermost thoughts. Some of them, anyway.

"I just—" Under her scrutiny, he fumbled for the right words. "As you said, maybe I should have talked to Principal Dunn before offering my critique. But I didn't want to get..."

No, he should just keep his mouth shut. His innermost thoughts were his to keep.

But it was too late. That same glow of revelation he'd seen on her student transfused Ms. Wick's expression, and her mouth pursed in a silent *oh*.

She blinked at him, her throat shifting as she swallowed.

"You didn't want to get me into trouble," she finally finished for him, her voice hoarse and warm and so liquid he could have bathed in it.

Yes. Yes, that was exactly what he'd tried not to say.

After giving herself a little shake, she sat up straighter. "I appreciate your consideration, Mr. Burnham, but you still could have *asked* me if I'd somehow addressed your concerns ahead of time, instead of assuming I hadn't."

He could have. It would, in fact, have been the logical way to handle the situation.

Which was…a disturbing realization.

An outside observer would almost conclude that he was, for some reason, *trying* to think badly of Ms. Wick. *Determined* to see flaws where they didn't necessarily exist.

It was yet another problem whose answer wasn't quite clear to him. Yet another mystery to unravel, when he'd never, ever, been good at interpreting clues.

"You're right." He didn't equivocate. "That's what I should have done."

Her chin dipped in a firm little nod. "Graciously conceded, Mr. Burnham. I forgive you. For everything."

The chunky amber spheres of her necklace glowed against her pale skin, and her eyes were fathomless.

"Please call me Simon," he said.

"Gladly." The curve of her lips was small and sweet. "And I'm Poppy."

She offered her hand, as if they were meeting for the first time, and he shook it. Her fingers were long and blunt, her palm warm and slightly rough, her grip firm.

He couldn't breathe.

As quickly as was polite, he let go and met her gaze. "If you're leaving soon, why don't I walk you to your car? The sun's going down earlier and earlier these days."

Shuffling steps in the darkness.

I feel so much less safe now.

Mildred got what she deserved.

No, Poppy wasn't going to that deserted parking lot alone. Not if he could help it.

"All right," she said after a moment, her gaze tentative, the words halting. "I just need five minutes, if you don't mind waiting."

He shook his head. "I don't."

The rules of gentlemanly behavior were clear under the circumstances, and he followed them. After she'd packed her belongings in her tote, he offered to carry it for her. As she

140

locked her classroom door behind them, he scanned the dim hallway to ensure her safety. Once they reached her car, he made certain she left the lot before driving away himself.

The entire time, he tried to hide the disconcerting truth.

Her touch had incinerated him so thoroughly, he might as well be the house in her diorama. And the burn had left him feeling anything—anything—but gentlemanly and professional.

THREE

As the seventh period bell rang on Wednesday, Simon sat at his usual table and congratulated himself on having remained cool, calm, and controlled for almost a full forty-eight hours, despite having spent several of those hours in Poppy's unsettling presence.

Yesterday, the students had begun creating their dioramas. *Controlled chaos* was perhaps the best way to describe her classroom then. Or possibly *paint-bedecked* and *glue-soaked*.

No wonder she'd worn her faded jeans again. That pretty black dress would have been absolutely *ruined*.

At the end of class, he'd asked whether she knew of any reasonable way to limit the mess created by her students during their projects. Not so much because the mess was excessive—which it wasn't, under the circumstances—or because mess bothered him in general—which it did, of course—but rather because cleaning up that mess required a considerable chunk of student time at the end of the period and an even more considerable chunk of Poppy's time after the students left.

"Well, I can't leave everything to the custodial staff. Mildred, the teacher I replaced, apparently used to have poor

Mrs. Denham do all the cleanup, but that's just cruel. No wonder they hated her so much." Poppy had patted him on the arm then, the gesture not quite pitying, but not quite *not* pitying either. "Besides, Simon, mess is both inevitable and part of the artistic process for most people. Don't worry."

Yes, the contact burned, but her near-pity had helped temper the worst of it.

He'd helped her clean and made a quick stop back in his own classroom to gather the night's grading. Then once again, he'd walked her to her car, and once again, he'd been forced to recite prime numbers to himself that night before he could fall asleep.

Still, he'd neither insulted her nor pinned her against the classroom wall to claim that wide, impish mouth of hers. He hadn't even buried his fingers in her drooping bun and angled her head to reveal her soft neck, hadn't sucked at her rapid pulse there, hadn't left a mark with his teeth on her pale flesh.

Small victories. Small, small victories.

Today, he hoped, would prove equally satisfying.

Or, rather, *un*satisfying, but predictable. Understandable and under control.

The students were hard at work again this period, their educational dioramas beginning to take shape minute by minute. Occasionally, someone paused a moment to peruse the half-charred diorama perched at his table, but for the most part, no one went near him.

Which, now that he considered the matter, was rather odd.

Two students shared each work station, and space was tight. He'd deliberately placed himself at the very end of his long table, right next to the diorama, to leave Poppy's kids as much room as possible. But no one had moved to claim the open space or even bothered to deposit an overflow of supplies there.

Maybe she'd previously told them not to spread out on his table. It was the closest one to her desk, so maybe she reserved it for her sole use. Or maybe the students were simply too terrified of him, *not in a fun way*, to share the space.

Or maybe—

He could swear some of the Goth softball players kept looking at the table. Not him, not the diorama, the *table*. In fact, Tori was saying something to her pale-powdered friend right now, in between glances at the faux-wood surface. In response, the poor girl blanched even further, her black-lined eyes round with horror.

Casually, Simon got to his feet and wandered closer.

"I mean…" Tori said with a shudder. "Can you believe it?"

"I—" The other young woman clapped a hand to her belly. "I think I'm going to be sick."

Tori corralled a nearby trash can with her boot, nudging it toward their work station. "Here you go. If you have to hork, keep it as clean as possible."

Very practical. Simon was growing fonder of Tori by the minute.

"I'll never be able to use that table again." Nausea apparently conquered for the moment, the pale girl wrinkled her nose. "Not without picturing what happened…there."

He couldn't deny it any longer, even to himself. He really, really wanted a full explanation for Mildred's departure, because some of his imaginings were…

Well, he'd clearly seen one too many blood-soaked dioramas.

Just as Simon was mentally urging the Goth girls to elaborate, *elaborate*, they caught sight of him and hurriedly turned back to their dioramas-in-progress.

"So as I was telling you," Tori said a bit too loudly, "art often serves a crucial societal role when it comes to dissemination of important information."

"Why, yes," her friend affirmed. "I remember you saying that very thing only moments ago, as we discussed our class objectives for the day."

No point in lingering, except for the sheer entertainment value of their faux-conversation. He wasn't going to get any more information out of them.

Accordingly, he returned to the diorama and studied the booklet containing witness statements, looking for information he hadn't properly registered the first time. But no new clues stood out to him. Not a surprise, given his lack of—

Poppy gasped loudly, and his head jerked up.

He knew exactly where she was. Of course he did. If she was within sight, part of his attention never, ever left her.

"Ms. Wick, are you—" a tall young man with thick-framed glasses was asking, but she was already striding toward the classroom sink, her forehead pinched in seeming distress.

Simon intercepted her along the way. "What happened?"

"I'm fine, Demetrius. Don't worry," she called over her shoulder, and then answered Simon. "Hot-glue-gun burn on the back of my hand. I just need to—"

With a flick of his wrist, the water was running and set to a cool temperature. He guided her right hand beneath the spray, pulse hammering in his ears.

A reddening blotch marked the spot of her injury, visible even through the streaming water, and he scowled at it.

"Simon." Her voice was low and gentle. "To an art teacher, hot-glue-gun burns are basically badges of honor. They're inevitable and nothing to be concerned about."

His scowl only deepened. "You're in pain. Do you need to see the nurse?"

"No, Simon." Her hand moved, and suddenly he wasn't supporting it anymore. Instead, she was holding his, as if comforting *him*. "No. It's already feeling better. But I'll cover the spot with a bandage, if that would make you less worried."

If that would make you less worried.

The utter ridiculousness of his reaction—his *over*reaction —struck him in that moment, and he dropped her hand as if he'd been scorched himself.

Despite her minor injury, she was in complete control of herself and the situation, while he—he—

He wasn't. He wasn't in control of himself.

Spinning away from her, he hurried to the classroom door. "I'll get you a bandage from the nurse's office."

"But I—Simon!" She was calling out to him, trying to flag him down, but he pretended not to hear or see. "I already have ban—"

The door shut behind him, and he forced himself to walk, not run, away from her.

WHEN SIMON RETURNED TOWARD THE END OF THE period, a fresh box of bandages in hand, he found Poppy—no, Ms. Wick—bent over a student project, her burn already covered neatly.

At his arrival, she glanced up at him, but only for a moment before turning back to Amanda's diorama-in-progress. Which appeared, upon first glance, even more grisly than the murder scene on the table beside him. God help them all.

He settled in his usual spot, beside Ms. Wick's diorama. His heartbeat no longer echoed in his skull, and his hands were almost steady enough to create his own miniature crime scene. Not that he would ever employ his limited free time in such a disturbing manner.

Yes, fifteen minutes spent locked in his unlit room and mentally multiplying had accomplished wonders, as always. Outside his colleague's orbit, the impetus behind his urgent concern for her well-being had become clear, clear and comforting.

The rules of professional and gentlemanly conduct required him to assist a colleague in distress. Accordingly, he'd done so.

No need for either panic or anxiety.

In fact, he'd emerged from his classroom certain he could find rational solutions to all the mysteries cluttering his brain. With a little effort, he'd explain Mildred Krackel's disappearance, solve the miniature murder in Ms. Wick's diorama, and pinpoint precisely why the woman herself fascinated him so much. To accomplish the latter, he merely needed to determine the precise equation governing her behavior and the workings of her mind.

Then, solution in hand, he'd relegate her to the appropriate slot in his life.

Wick, Poppy. Talented but impertinent colleague. Best avoided for peace of mind.

Similarly, once he'd solved the other mysteries, he'd dismiss them from his thoughts. Simple as that.

And he could make progress this very moment, with the miniature crime scene. Given ample opportunity to observe the diorama and its clues more closely, surely he could discover the arsonist and murderer. Besides, P—*Ms. Wick* had dared him to solve the case. Doing so would prove his intelligence, and thus his ability to mentor her effectively.

Any professional would do the same.

With the help of a magnifying glass, he studied the blackened living room again. The shriveled corpse. The half-burned recliner. The bar cart, complete with tiny, tiny glass bottles full of amber liquid. The bookshelves. The overturned television. The ashtray. The neat row of shoes just inside the door. The charred jackets on a metal coat rack.

So much detail. She must have set those books on the

shelves and positioned those sneakers and shiny Oxford shoes on the floor one by one. A jacket's sleeve was inside out, as if stripped off in a hurry. The laces of the shoes were all untied. The books seemed shoved into place with a careless hand.

Because of her meticulous labor, Simon could picture it clearly. Two young brothers coming home from a jog or a day's work, hanging their coats, unlacing and removing their shoes before relaxing into their shared home. Going about their typical evening.

They'd settled onto the recliner and the couch, drinks in hand. Kaden had lit a cigarette, tapping its burning end into the ashtray. Together, they'd watched their favorite show and read timeworn paperbacks.

Finally, Barron had gone to bed. Kaden had stretched out in the recliner and inadvertently fallen asleep. Then: disaster. Arson.

Murder.

Simon tried not to shudder.

Inside the bedroom, he didn't spy anything remarkable other than Ms. Wick's artistry. Singed walls. Two narrow beds, their covers smoke-darkened. Two nightstands, with more paperbacks set atop them. Two dressers. A desk with scattered papers. The open window, where Barron had escaped in a panic. A closet filled with both professional and casual clothing, only a laundry hamper cluttering its floor.

The brothers had lived neatly, it seemed.

Which made the pile of glistening hair at the bottom of the bathroom sink—the cramped space otherwise spotless —rather odd.

Were they saving money by cutting their hair at home? Had Barron been doing some impromptu manscaping?

Flipping through the witness statements, Simon searched for an explanation.

There wasn't any. Huh.

As he scrutinized the outside of the home—the green

bushes, the faux-dirt under the windows, the suspects clustered around the police officer—the bell rang, and Poppy's students rushed out of the classroom.

Silently, he helped her sweep the floor and sponge down the work stations, doing his best to stay across the classroom from her whenever possible.

"You don't have to do this, Simon," she said after a minute, her voice cautious.

He didn't look up from an intransigent smear of brown paint. "I understand that, Ms. Wick."

"Ms. Wick," she repeated, so quietly he almost didn't hear her.

After that, she didn't speak either. Instead, brow puckered in apparent thought, she set her classroom in order.

When the room was relatively pristine, he approached her desk. She was shutting down her laptop and gathering papers in preparation to work at home. Because, as she'd told him yesterday, her wing of the school sometimes seemed a bit too empty and quiet for her in the late afternoon. After admitting that, she'd turned her face away and fallen uncharacteristically silent.

She hadn't used the word *lonely*, but he'd heard it anyway.

Her situation was easy enough to understand, even without further explanation. Most of her fellow teachers didn't know her well, not yet. She'd only moved to the area several months ago, leaving her former colleagues and friends behind. Her parents required her support, from what she'd indicated on Monday.

Did she have support of her own? Anyone to help her unpack or offer comfort or—

"I'm ready, Mr. Burnham." The words were a near-sigh, and she slumped in her office chair. "What are today's observations?"

Those dark smudges beneath her eyes weren't paint, and

her mouth was pale and pinched at the corners. Her hazel eyes had dulled.

Her wispy little buns were drooping. Not in a fun way.

Right now, as her mentor, he should be offering his thoughts about the lesson, giving guidance wherever necessary. Not that she really required any, from what he could tell.

Instead, he found himself asking, "Did it blister?"

She blinked up at him, confused.

"Your burn." He nodded down at her bandage. "Did it blister?"

"Oh." Her brow furrowed even more. "Uh, no. No blister. It barely even hurts anymore."

Which meant it *was* still hurting. He scowled at the cabinet containing her glue guns.

When he didn't say more, she added, "Thank you for bringing me a new package of bandages, by the way. It's good to have extras."

In the awkward silence that followed, the growl of her stomach was clearly audible.

No wonder she'd collapsed into her chair. She was hungry and hurting and tired and almost as alone as—

"Would you like to have dinner? With me?" He cleared his dry, dry throat. "We can go over my observations while we eat. Make it a working meal."

When she wrinkled her nose in an apologetic wince, he kept his expression blank.

A colleague refusing an invitation to a last-minute meeting did not and could not cause a pinch in his chest, and that twist in his gut indicated nothing but his own hunger.

"I'm sorry." Her round cheeks had pinkened, and she was smiling up at him now, eyes alight once more. "I'd love to, but I have dinner with my parents every Wednesday night. They like to eat early, so we wouldn't even have time to grab coffee before I'd need to go."

The painful tension in his shoulders eased. "I understand."

"How about tomorrow night?" Her brows arched in question.

His lungs filled with air, so much air he was suddenly buoyant, and the tips of his ears flushed with heat. The HVAC system in this wing of the building must be malfunctioning.

"Certainly." Working dinners needn't be confined to Wednesdays alone. "I'll make a note of the appointment in my calendar."

Her lips twitched. "Please do."

Another long pause as his entire body seemed to vibrate with every heartbeat.

"I should probably head out." She pushed up the sleeves of her cardigan. "Will you walk me to the parking lot?"

He inclined his head. "Of course."

Earlier, as he'd calmed himself in his classroom, he'd packed everything he needed in his briefcase. After locking her room, then, they said goodbye to Mrs. Denham and walked to Poppy's car without any detours.

In the half-empty lot, instead of immediately easing herself inside her bright red car—an electric vehicle, he noted —she turned to him. "Where would you have taken me?"

Where would he have *taken* her?

If he didn't know better? If he weren't a rational man and a professional?

Anywhere. God, anywhere. Anywhere and everywhere.

Last night, he'd dreamed about it. Woken in sweat-soaked sheets, so hard he'd ached and throbbed. Stroked himself in the shower until he'd shuddered and gasped out an obscenity, eyes closed beneath the stinging spray, breath stuttering.

He'd take her in a soft bed, her round thighs spread wide, wide enough for his shoulders, her agile hands clutching his headboard as she moaned and squirmed and came against his tongue. He'd take her over the desk in his home office, her eyes hot and heavy-lidded as she watched him over her pale shoulder, his fingertips firm on her hips while he—

"Simon?" She was squinting at him, head tilted.

He shook his head. Hard. "Excuse me?"

"If I'd been able to go to dinner tonight, where would you have taken me?" she clarified. "Where are you taking me tomorrow, for that matter?"

Oh. Oh, yes. Dinner.

"Um…" The afternoon sunlight was in her eyes, so he moved slightly to the side, until his shadow blocked the blinding rays. "Your choice."

Whatever she wanted, he could accommodate. Normally, he selected restaurants after careful study of both online reviews and sanitation grades, but a polite coworker bowed to the preferences of others.

Mischief sparked in her expression. "Uh-uh. I don't think so. You're not spoiling my fun, Mr. Burnham."

When she said his last name like that, it didn't sound distant or formal at all.

Instead, it was a tease. A dart of affection aimed right between his ribs, where it lodged and stung.

"Your—" He licked his lips. "Your fun?"

She rested that generous, gorgeous butt against the side of her car and tilted her chin in challenge. "I'm curious where you like to eat. More than that, I'm curious where you think *I'd* like to eat."

His mouth opened, then closed.

He didn't go out for dinner much, so his favorite restaurants offered both takeout and faultless inspection records. Which now seemed inadequate, not to mention boring as fuck.

No, he'd do better to focus on where *she* might like to eat. Places that would please *her*.

But how could he possibly predict something like that?

152

How could he solve a problem with so many unknown variables? They'd known each other less than two weeks, so how could he even try to guess what she'd want?

"Let's hear who you are and what you think of me, as expressed in restaurant form." She was grinning at him now, amused by his discomfiture. "C'mon. Out with it."

He couldn't help a tiny snort. "No pressure there."

What did he know about her, really? Other than how velvety her skin looked beneath the fluorescent lights, and how warmly she responded to student questions, and how focused and creative and patient she must be to create those bloody, bloody—

Wait. He had it.

At the sudden epiphany, a smug smile spread across his face.

For once, he'd put together clues and solved a mystery, and it tasted like victory. A small one, as always, but delicious nevertheless.

Delicious and morbid. So very morbid.

"Well..." His chest had puffed out a tad, and he didn't even care. "If you wouldn't mind driving into Richmond, there's a place you'd love."

He'd read about it months ago and cringed at the very thought of eating there. But, if his memory was correct, the review had praised the food and the restaurant's wholehearted commitment to its theme. Its terrible theme.

"Really?" Those reddish-gold brows arched again. "Tell me more."

Oh, this was going to feel *great*. "It's called That Good Night. It's only open for dinner."

"That Good Night." Her lips pressed together as she thought. "As in, *do not go gentle into?*"

He dipped his chin. "Exactly."

"So." She was gazing up at him, hair aglow in the sun,

with such rampant curiosity and *warmth*. "The restaurant's name refers to death?"

"It's a former mortuary," he told her. "If I'm remembering correctly, the knives are actually scalpels, the water comes in formaldehyde bottles, and they serve their food in little coffins. The whole restaurant is death-themed."

"That's…" Her whisper was barely audible, and her eyes were wide. "That's the most amazing thing I've ever heard. Yes. Yes, I'd love to go there tomorrow."

He resisted buffing his nails against his cotton button-down, but it was a close call. "Good. I'll make reservations."

"I really need to go, but—" Somehow, she was only inches away now, so close the heat from her body taunted him. "Where would you have picked? For yourself, I mean?"

Since she was still leaning against her car, he must have moved forward without conscious volition. As if he were a compass needle seeking true north, or a man irresistibly drawn to temptation and trouble.

Which he wasn't. He never had been, not once in over four decades.

"When I invite someone for dinner, it's about that person. Not me." It wasn't a real answer, but it wasn't a lie either. "Even in a professional context."

He didn't feel like a professional, though. In such close proximity to her, he felt like nothing more than a mammal in rut.

"Oh, I think your invitation says plenty about you." She wasn't smiling anymore. Instead, her gaze was solemn and fixed on him with such clarity, he had to fight a flinch. "More than you probably realize."

When she got into her car, he stepped safely away and watched her leave. She was long gone before he managed to think of the smartest response to her statement.

And by then, it was much too late to run.

FOUR

IF SIMON AND POPPY'S SHARED MEAL AT THAT GOOD
Night were a train, it remained safely on track for a full two
courses.

Over their Stopped Hearts of Palm bao bun appetizers and
Dismembered Duck Confit entrées—both her picks, both
unfamiliar to him, both served in coffins, both utterly delicious—they discussed the ways Marysburg High differed
from her previous school. How to operate most efficiently in
her new environment. When to visit the copy room, which
administrator to see for certain questions and concerns, the
most helpful front-desk secretary, and so forth.

As he'd learned through painful experience, she didn't
need assistance with teaching. Still, he could offer practical
tips about their specific school. And if he found himself
admiring how the flicker of candlelight highlighted the curve
of her neck, or noting the golden glow it imparted to her
strawberry blond hair, well, no one needed to know that but
him. It might constitute a weakness, but the chink in his
armor wasn't visible to the naked eye.

Then, with almost no warning, and entirely due to his

own negligence, their conversational train jumped the professional rails.

The server placed two thick slices of Murder by Chocolate cake in front of them, and Simon had no way to know they were speeding toward disaster with every bite.

"I'm sure you've noticed Amanda's diorama. Did you figure out the topic?" Poppy sipped at her mocktail, The Embalmer, between forkfuls of cake. "I'll give you a hint: Her mom's a nurse in the maternity ward of the local hospital."

With that information, everything he'd seen suddenly slotted into place. "Her diorama is about America's egregious maternal mortality rate."

That explained the stirrups, at least. He'd been concerned about those.

She pointed her fork at him. "Exactly. Nicely done, Mr. Burnham."

If he could, he would bathe in the warm approval of her smile.

Fuck, she was pretty. Her high buns exposed the sweet roundness of her rosy cheeks, the modest plunge of her neckline allowed a stunning, shadowy glimpse of cleavage every time she leaned forward, and her dangling jet earrings tickled the curves of her shoulders. Under the table, her leg brushed his, a moment of glancing, sliding contact that left him as dizzied as a blow to the head.

And somehow, before he thought through what he should say, he was asking her a personal question. "Why murder?"

She swallowed a bite before answering. "I'm not sure what you mean. In my lesson plans? In my dioramas? On a societal level?"

There it was. The smart way forward. He could steer the conversation back toward professionalism, back on track, with two words. *Lesson plans.*

In response, she'd say something about the inherent love of most teenagers for gore and drama, or about her years of gauging student response to different subjects, and he'd nod, and they'd get back to talking about which particular copier most often collated and stapled without overheating.

Instead, he said, "In your dioramas."

Because he was a fucking train wreck in human form, evidently. At least around her.

"Well..." With a muted *clink*, she set her fork down on the edge of her plate. "I'm not sure there's a simple, straightforward answer to that question."

"I don't need simple or straightforward," he told her, and that was news to him. He'd always wanted both. He'd wanted—needed—solvable problems he could comprehend and explain and set aside neatly at the end of the day.

Poppy Wick was many things, but she wasn't neat. Not in the ways that had long mattered to him. And so far, he'd been unable to comprehend her, explain her, or set her aside.

But he still wanted her.

To his horror, even *wanted* might not be a strong enough word for how he felt. Over the last few hours, he'd begun wondering whether—

"My best guess is that I've always been fascinated by things I don't quite understand. I think that's why I was drawn to art in the first place. Great artists..." Resting her elbows on the table, she set her chin on her clasped hands. "I don't understand how they find their inspiration, and I don't understand what allows them to translate that inspiration into art in such disparate, stunning ways."

He dipped his head in understanding. "And you don't understand murder either."

"No, I don't." Her forehead puckered in thought. "I understand motive and means and opportunity, at least enough to create my dioramas. I can even understand hatred and greed and lust. But how those emotions plunge over some invisible ledge and lead someone to shed blood, I don't get. I never will, I don't think. And I can't even *begin* to understand murderers with antisocial personality disorder, although I've read so many books about them."

"Of course you don't understand. You couldn't." Maybe he couldn't grasp Poppy in her complex entirety, but he knew that much. He'd seen her bent low, conferring with her students. He'd seen her in the grips of justified anger, directed his way, and then watched her forgive him minutes later after a single, inadequate apology. He'd seen her clean her classroom without complaint each afternoon, in lieu of unfairly burdening the custodial staff. "You care about other people too much. You'd never hurt someone without a damn good reason."

"Umm…" Her cheeks suddenly seemed pinker, but maybe that was a trick of the candlelight. "Thank you. I hope that's true."

"It is." His tone didn't allow for argument. "Are the dioramas your way of working through how people can do such terrible things to each other?"

The damage humans inflicted on one another didn't need to be physical, of course, much less murderous. But a diorama couldn't capture arguments conducted via shrieks and shouts and obscenities and slamming doors, or the terrible silence that descended on a home in the aftermath of rage.

"Maybe?" Her lips quirked. "But mostly I just think they're interesting, and they sell well. Plus, coming up with the crimes and clues is a good challenge, and so is putting it all together in miniature form. I'm damn good at what I do."

Why had he never realized how seductive confidence could be? "You are. Both in the classroom and as an artist. It's impressive."

No wonder she hadn't let his initial disapproval bow her. She knew her worth, and thank goodness for it.

She flicked a glance down at her plate, carefully

portioning another bite. "Thank you, Simon. Not everyone in my life has felt that way."

He frowned. Coworkers? Family? Lovers? Who'd disparaged her talent?

Other than him, of course, at their first meeting in her classroom. But he'd learned better quickly enough, even if the shame of the memory still prickled at the back of his neck.

"Would you..." Her swallow was visible, and she was still staring down at her plate. "Would you maybe like to, um, visit my workshop? Tonight? I could show you my diorama-in-progress."

It wasn't an invitation to bed her. He realized that.

Sadly, his erection didn't.

Before he could manage a coherent answer, she kept speaking, the words breathless and rapid. "Since we left right after work, it's still pretty early, and we could talk more about lesson plans or the school or..." Her pink tongue swiped a crumb from her bottom lip, and he almost choked on his own cake. "Or whatever."

Maybe she rented a studio of some sort? Or...was she inviting him home with her?

After clearing his throat once, then again, he managed to form actual, audible words. "You—you have a workshop in your house?"

She nodded and quickly took another huge bite of her cake, busily chewing while looking anywhere but at him.

Even when he ducked his head a bit, she didn't meet his eyes.

She was nervous?

No. That was unacceptable. She should never feel uncertain around him. Having just admired her pride and confidence, there was no goddamn way he'd let either be stripped from her.

159

His answer was abrupt, but he couldn't help that. "Yes. Of course. I'd like that."

"You would?" Her hazel eyes peeked at him through a darkened fan of lashes, but they were bright. Mesmerizing, really. "I mean, great. Okay. We can pick up my car in the school lot, and you can follow me home from there."

"That sounds, uh, good." His heart was skittering, and his hands weren't entirely steady. "Very logical."

In that moment, he could have been the same age as their students. A teenager fumbling for words, lost and confused and hopeful. So hopeful.

She tucked a tendril of hair behind the lovely curve of her ear. "Then it's a plan."

In his giddiness, he'd lost all his remaining appetite. He pushed away his plate, then set his napkin beside it.

"I'm almost done," she told him. "I know I'm a slow eater. Sorry."

He shook his head firmly. "Don't be sorry. Take your time."

The answering beam of her smile was so dazzling, so bursting with affection and happiness, he had to blink.

While Poppy finished her dessert, they sat in a silence that wasn't quite awkward. More...expectant. And then she was finally down to her last bite, and he couldn't seem to get enough oxygen to his straining lungs.

"If I'd known embalming fluid tasted like rosemary and ginger and lemon, I'd have been preserving myself decades ago." She tipped back her glass, draining the dregs of her mocktail. "I can only assume the carbonation keeps the skin of the deceased firm and supple."

He couldn't resist playing along. "That's just science."

Her laughter rang through the restaurant, and several nearby diners turned their way. He met their disapproving gazes with a hard stare, because he'd earned that laugh. No humorless assholes with scalpels were going to taint the moment.

"There may be a reason we don't teach biology," she said, still grinning.

With her fork, she scraped up the last crumbs of her cake. While she was distracted, he discreetly took care of the bill.

It's the least a mentor can do for his mentee, he told himself. But even he knew that was complete and utter bullshit.

None of this, not their walks to the parking lot or his panic over her hot-glue-gun burn or the way his gaze was drawn to the pale, plump curve of her earlobe, was entirely professional. Certainly not their dinner tonight, or their imminent trip to her home.

This time, he couldn't even fool himself.

And maybe—maybe—he was getting tired of trying.

FIVE

"I HAVEN'T FINISHED SETTING UP ALL THE ROOMS."
Poppy held the front door open for Simon, waving him ahead
of her. "There are still boxes stacked to the ceiling of the
guest bedroom. But the crucial spaces are done. The kitchen.
The den. The workroom. My, uh, bedroom."

At first glance, the home perfectly reflected the woman
who lived there: colorful, crammed full of interesting details,
and orderly despite the potential for absolute chaos.

Her entryway and den were the blue of a sunny day on the
beach, her kitchen the color of key lime pie. Further down
the shadowed hallway, he'd have bet his year's salary that the
open doorways to dark rooms promised yet more colors of
the rainbow.

Her hands twisting together at her waist, she led him
through the public spaces in her home. All the while, she
chattered about nothing in particular, her voice breathier
than normal. All the while, he observed. Her. Her home. His
reaction to both.

Built-in shelves lined almost the entire den. They
contained plenty of books, certainly, but also photo frames
and sculptures and geological specimens and what definitely

appeared to be a rodent of some sort, preserved through taxidermy.

He'd have to ask her about that...creature?...later, because she'd have a good reason for displaying it. He would bet good money on that too.

Other than its cleanliness, her home couldn't have provided a greater contrast to his own house, all of which he'd painted a pale gray. Upon moving in, he'd figured neutrals would prove soothing, so his furniture featured dark wood and forgettable colors, and he kept clutter to a minimum. No unnecessary decorative touches. Nothing breakable.

Years ago, one of the few women he'd ever brought home had deemed the space *monk-like* and *spartan*, and he hadn't disputed the assessment. Even though he'd realized it wasn't a compliment, it wasn't a comment about his home alone, and it also wasn't a good omen for the relationship as a whole.

There was no gray in sight here. Hundreds of objects and colors and textures competed for his attention, and he should have found it all disorienting. Chaotic. Objectionable.

"My workroom is down the hall," she said, shifting her weight from foot to foot. "If you—if you're still interested in seeing it."

His gaze caught on her, because how could it not? How could he *not* look at Poppy Wick, no matter the distractions surrounding them both?

Her hair was red-gold, her knit top the green of a wintry forest, her lips and cheeks pink, her wispy buns inevitably slipping, her jeans and sneakers splattered with paint. He was pretty sure that was chocolate cake smeared on the elbow of her cardigan.

A week ago, he'd have called her a mess.

A week ago, he'd have been a judgmental dick.

Tonight, he saw nothing but beauty, around him and

before him. She should know that, so she could stop wringing her hands and frowning at the sight of her own kitchen.

Her nose scrunched up. "I know my home is a lot."

"Your home is...homey," he told her.

She tilted her head, blinking owlishly, and then she was giggling, and he didn't blame her.

"Damned with faint praise!" The words were a gasp, barely intelligible.

"I meant—" He closed his eyes, impatient with himself. "It wasn't intended to—"

She was slightly bent at the waist, bracing herself against her refrigerator with one hand, eyes bright as a torch as she laughed at him.

He couldn't help it. He had to laugh with her, because, yes. *Homey.*

She wiped at her eyes, and he wanted to do it for her.

So he did.

Reaching out slowly, carefully, he cupped her sweet face in his hands. Her breath caught, and her eyes flew to his. He brushed away her tears of hilarity with a light, careful sweep of his thumbs.

Her skin was so fucking soft. So warm under his fingertips. As he stared down at her, those pink lips parted, and she wet them with her tongue.

He wasn't laughing anymore. Neither was she.

But he wasn't entirely certain yet, and he needed to be before this went any further.

When he lowered his hands and stepped back, she drew one shuddering breath. Another. He did the same.

When his control returned, so did his ability to speak. "May I visit your workroom?"

"Y—" Her swallow was audible in the stillness of her home. "Yes."

He followed her down the hall to the room at the very

164

end, forbidding his eyes to wander in search of her bed through the darkened doorways they passed.

When she flicked the light switch, he smiled at the vivid turquoise of her walls, then studied the space itself and how she'd transformed it.

This was her master bedroom. Or, at least, it had been. She'd made it her workspace instead, and no wonder. Given the multitude of windows and the French doors leading outside, the room no doubt received plenty of light. Perfect for an artist's studio. One of the walls was lined, floor to ceiling, with yet more white-painted shelves, each filled neatly with a labeled box.

She gestured to them. "I had a carpenter install the shelves before I moved in. I have so many supplies, it seemed like the best option."

Her work table was huge and solid, the wooden surface scarred, stained, and entirely free from dust. A mesh chair was positioned by its side. On top of the table sat her diorama-in-progress, complete with a male corpse sprawled on a rumpled bed, one who appeared to have been stabbed in his—

Involuntarily, Simon took a step backward.

She snickered. "Yeah, I imagine that will be most men's reaction."

"Did he deserve"—deep breath—"that?"

"Oh, definitely." Her cheeks plumped with her wicked grin. "Making this body anatomically correct was even more fun than usual."

He wanted to ask for more detail, but he also very much didn't.

Instead of contemplating the murder victim's mangled member, he studied the tools of her trade. She'd positioned a free-standing magnifier and a mug of paint brushes next to the miniature crime scene. A handful of other supplies—

tweezers, various glues, tubes of paint—also sat nearby her work in a tidy pile.

She nudged a single-hair brush with her blunt fingertip. "I try to put away anything I won't be using soon, because otherwise I don't have enough space to work. Or, worse, I'll inadvertently contaminate my scene with something that isn't supposed to be there."

Controlled, meticulous mess, just like her classroom.

There was no television in the room, no computer, no electronics of any sort—with one exception. On the shelf closest to her desk, she'd set up a little speaker for her cell phone.

Her eyes followed his. "I listen to music or podcasts while I work, usually." When he didn't respond, she let out a long breath. "Say something, Simon. Is this too creepy, or too—"

"You should put a comfortable chair in here." Frowning, he considered an unoccupied corner of the large room. "A chaise, perhaps. Near the windows."

With a charming tilt of her head, she studied the space too. "Huh. That's an idea."

He could see her laid full-length on that lounge already. It would be velvet, soft as her skin, and some color he'd never, ever choose. One that would complement both the turquoise and her beautiful, fine, reddish-gold hair. Mustard, maybe, or plum. She'd bask in the sun, eyes closed, a lazy smile indenting the corners of that tempting mouth. Or maybe she'd pluck one of those countless books from the shelves in her den and read while reclining, lips pursed in concentration.

Or maybe she could put a leather club chair in that spot instead. An ottoman too.

Suddenly, the image in his mind shifted.

Suddenly, he was the one in the leather chair. He was the one reading with his feet up, napping, smiling, laughing as Poppy worked on her crime scene at her sunny desk and probably sang along to her music badly and at top volume until, unable to resist any longer, he set aside his book and swiveled her work chair to face him and kissed her and kissed her—

He shook his head near-violently, dismissing the vision.

How he'd even imagined such an unlikely scenario, he had no idea. He'd never encountered that kind of affection, that kind of peaceful but passionate intimacy, anywhere outside of fiction. Certainly not in his own experience of home and family.

Which reminded him: He owed her an explanation, because he wouldn't let her continue to believe he'd insulted her in her own kitchen.

"When I said your house is homey, I meant it feels like a home." No, that didn't express what he wanted to say. He needed to abandon tautology in favor of specificity, no matter how uncomfortable he found it. "It feels—it feels like you. Warm and bright. Comfortable. Interesting. A place you can relax."

It feels like the home I would have wanted. The home some part of me still wants.

Her fingers curled slightly on her tabletop, but otherwise, she'd gone completely still. "So that *was* praise, after all. Not faint."

"No." He didn't smile, because he wasn't joking. "Not faint."

"Why math?"

It was an abrupt question, an echo of what he'd said at dinner: *Why murder?* It was also something no one had ever asked him before, probably because his interest in numbers had always seemed self-evident. Cold, logical man; cold, logical subject.

But it wasn't that simple. Nothing ever was, no matter what he'd prefer.

He held her gaze, unflinching. Flinty, his expression so

167

blank nothing could grab hold of its pristine surface. "My childhood was...chaotic."

His parents' arguments followed no logic. They happened after stressful days at work, and they happened on vacation weekends, at a peaceful beach. They circled recent offenses, and then addressed affronts from decades before, and then leaped to predictions of enraging future behavior.

The only things Simon himself could predict: He'd hide in his room. Something—a glass, a plate, a table—would end up in pieces on the floor. The shouted accusations would hurt his ears. The sobs would hurt his heart. And it would all happen again, the following day or week.

There was no end to their problems, no solution to their conflicts.

Poppy was still waiting, eyes solemn and expectant, so he elaborated. "Math was a comfort for me. It seemed clean. Orderly. Rational."

Safe.

"Okay." Although one droopy bun was unraveling above her ear, she paid it no heed. "But if you wanted rationality and order, why teach high school? Teenagers are chaos incarnate."

She was evaluating him like a crime scene, sharp as a sliver of broken glass on carpet. So sharp, she could make him bleed before he even knew she'd pierced his skin and burrowed beneath.

His shoulders had tightened to the point of pain. "Higher levels of math often involve problems with no clear solutions."

"You could have become an accountant instead."

No, she definitely wasn't accepting half-truths. Not after having let him see her most private space, displaying it for his judgment despite his disdain of less than a week ago.

Maybe he was wrong, but he suspected she'd consider

showing him her bedroom, her unclothed body, less intimate than guiding him inside her workroom.

Those hazel eyes flayed him, peeling away layer after layer until he stood shivering and exposed before her. He closed his eyes, because if he couldn't see her, she couldn't see him.

The illogic was galling and humiliating, but he clung to its scant protection.

"As a teacher—" His throat worked. "As a teacher, I can provide an orderly, quiet, safe space for children like me. Like the boy I was."

If he'd had his wish, he'd have slept at school. Camped out in Mrs. Delgado's classroom, which was always neat and clean. Her voice never rose. Her floor never cut his feet. Her hand was warm on his back as he worked on long division. Her questions always had answers, and he could provide them.

"I've seen you teach, you know," she said, her voice slightly muffled, and he blinked his eyes open.

She'd turned away from him, and was pretending to deposit something in one of her labeled boxes, but he knew better. She was giving him time to recover himself.

"When?" His voice was embarrassingly gravelly. "I would have noticed if—"

Wait. He knew.

"You were part of the group that observed me the second week of school." In his files, he still had their feedback forms. Now that he knew Poppy's was among them, he'd search for her comments and reread them. "For ten minutes, while we talked about derivatives."

He'd taken no notice of her, really, or any of the other observers. His students commanded his undivided attention between the bells, except in case of emergency.

It seemed impossible now—that he hadn't recognized her presence, hadn't acknowledged it, even without knowing her name or having exchanged a single word.

Somehow, he should have known. Should have seen.

"I stood in a corner and watched you discuss derivatives," she affirmed. "It was the quietest, most structured classroom and lesson I'd ever seen."

Terrifying. Not in a fun way.

But her eyes were soft, her lips curved. "You knew all their names already. You called them Ms. Blackwell and Mr. Jones and so on. Except for Sam, because those sorts of titles cause them gender dysphoria. Which I know, since Sam's in my second period class. Earlier this week, they told me you always used their preferred pronouns and name. From the moment you received their information form."

Her voice lowered almost to a whisper, as if they were sharing secrets, and maybe they were. "During the observation, when one kid didn't understand how you'd solved the problem on the board, you explained everything a second time, clearly and patiently."

Her praise was a warm tide in his chest, soaking into his limbs, spreading through his cold, aching bones. So welcome he had to fight against closing his eyes again.

"I was impressed. Beyond impressed. Those kids already adored you, Simon. After less than two weeks. If you wanted to provide them a peaceful, safe space..." In a graceful gesture, she spread her hands wide. "Mission accomplished."

The question was neither his business nor appropriate to ask. He shouldn't ask. Couldn't.

But *really*. She was standing there, fine wisps of disordered hair haloed around her head, round and kind and so very lovely, smart and funny and accomplished, and—

"How the hell are you single?" *Goddammit, Burnham.* "Not that it's any of my concern, and perhaps you have a partner you haven't mentioned, but—"

"Oh, I'm single." Her smile vanished. "No doubt about that."

Thank fuck.

"I am too," he told her without the slightest intention of doing so. "Never married."

Which was way less surprising than her lack of a partner. A man like him neither experienced nor inspired passion and lust and devotion.

At least, he hadn't. Before now.

Poppy's mouth had tightened into a thin, pale line.

"I listen to podcasts about unsolved murders and serial killers." It was a stark announcement, seemingly disconnected from the topic he'd raised. "I read books about psychopathology and Jack the Ripper and forensics. I watch terrible, hilarious reenactments of crimes late at night on cable. I make some tiny dolls bleed and others kill. And I do all that happily. Enthusiastically."

She spoke slowly, giving each word emphasis.

A warning: *Caveat emptor.*

"The last woman I dated and brought home told me I was creepy as fuck. When she saw the workroom in my old house, she was out the door in less than five minutes. And when I'm not being creepy, I'm grading or planning lessons or going to IEP meetings." Her chin had tipped high, and she didn't break eye contact once. "I'm too wrapped up in my work and my hobbies. Which is why my last ex-boyfriend said I was a terrible partner and broke up with me after two months."

He scoffed in mingled disbelief and disdain. "Because you refused to make yourself *less* for him? What a jackass."

Her amused huff flared her nostrils, and her shoulders dropped a fraction. "Can't disagree with you there."

"And you're not creepy." His tone dared her to argue. "You're curious."

"About murder. Which isn't at all creepy," she said dryly. "But enough about me. Why aren't *you* in a long-term relationship, Simon?"

Another question no one had asked him before now.

171

His instinctive response, true but incomplete: *I've never been interested in one.*

But unlike last time, he wasn't going to make her work for the full, honest answer. Not after she'd bared at least a corner of her scarred heart to him, despite her obvious wariness.

"If I were going to invite that kind of upheaval into my life..." The words were slippery, but he was trying to grasp them, trying to explain himself in a way he'd never attempted before. "Sometimes, two people come together and become less than what they were separately. They subtract from one another. One and one making zero."

His mother and father. On their own, decent people. Decent parents. Together: nothing he wanted in his life.

When she nodded in understanding, he continued. "Other times, two people in a relationship make nothing more than the sum of their parts. One plus one equals two." He rested his fists on his hips and made himself say it. "But if I'm going to risk a relationship, I want something more. Something transformative. Not just a sum."

She was listening so carefully, with no attempt to fill in words for him or interrupt, and it was just one more reason he needed to kiss her.

"I want a product. An exponent. I want one plus one to equal eighty, or a thousand, or infinity." He shook his head, exasperated with himself. "It isn't logical. I know that. My entire life, I've doubted that kind of partnership, that kind of love, even existed. I've never seen a hint of it. Not on any date I've ever had."

Until now went unspoken.

With Poppy, he could glimpse the possibility of more.

His gaze dropped to her hand, because his reaction to her burn had been the first warning siren he'd actually acknowledged, the first unmistakable sign he could be transformed by her.

He stepped closer than necessary, closer than was wise. Closer, until her back was pressed against her shelves, her lips soft and parted, her breath hitching with each deliberate step he took.

If he gripped the shelves on either side of her, he could cage her with his body. Lower his open mouth to her jaw. Whisper hotly in her ear, then trace its curve with his tongue.

Instead, their only point of contact was comparatively innocent. His hold on her wrist, raising her hand for his inspection. She gasped at the contact, and he swayed even closer, until the brush of his knee against her thigh sent lightning arcing through his veins.

The burn was a faded pink spot now.

"Does this still hurt?" His voice was raspy and quiet, foreign to his ears.

She shook her head, round cheeks flushed with heat.

"Good."

He turned her hand, exposing the cup of her palm and the pale, velvety skin of her forearm. Blue veins traced just beneath the surface of that skin, curving and branching like the ivy she'd doodled in her notebook.

Beneath his thumb, her pulse was rabbiting.

He slowly stroked that tiny, frantic beat. "Do I scare you?"

She shook her head again, then hesitated.

"Not..." When she licked her lips, he wanted to taste that pink tongue. "Not in that way. Not physically."

He met her half-lidded gaze. "You scare me too."

More truth, offered freely in the hush of a quiet, shadowed home, her bedroom barely more than a heartbeat distant.

He had thinking to do, and it wouldn't happen with temptation inches away, all warm skin and lush curves and sharp eyes.

"Tonight's a school night." He inclined his head in a stiff

little nod, released her hand, and stepped back. "I should head home."

She paused, opening her mouth as if to say something. Her fingers curled into fists. Then her gaze flicked to the floor, and she silently led the way to her front door.

Out on her small porch, the night's autumnal chill transformed their breath to fog. Turning to him, arms wrapped around herself, she spoke before he could take the two steps down to her driveway.

"Simon." Her brow was puckered. "That first conversation in my classroom."

He waited. Listened.

"You hurt me," she finally said, her voice a whisper. "I barely knew you, and you hurt me."

The rest didn't need to be stated aloud.

Please don't hurt me again.

He wanted to tell her he wouldn't, but he might. He wanted to tell her not to worry, but he was terrified too. He wanted to brush a fingertip over that puckered brow and kiss the telltale sign of anxiety away, but he couldn't. Not yet.

Instead, he bowed his head, then left her in the cold.

SIX

THOSE SAME TWO SCIENCE TEACHERS WERE whispering to one another in the faculty lounge as Simon gathered his lunch from the refrigerator the next day.

They were veteran educators, near retirement. Respectable enough in reputation, he supposed, although he generally didn't pay attention to such things. One woman—for reasons he couldn't explain—wore a large brooch in the shape of an arched, hissing cat, its jeweled eyes glinting with malice. The other appeared half-swallowed by her oversized scarf.

And right now, he wanted both of them to eat that fucking scarf and choke on it.

"Can you believe they replaced Mildred with *her?*" Murderous Cat Teacher said. "She's an embarrassment to our school. Have you *seen* what she wears every day?"

Smothering Scarf Teacher shook her head. "Shirts smeared with paint. Jeans. Messy hair. It's a disgrace."

"I can't believe she's gotten away with it." Murderous Cat Teacher sniffed loudly. "I knew Principal Dunn wasn't up to the job. Too soft-hearted, as Mildred and I always said."

"Have you heard about Ms. Wick's little side business?"

Smothering Scarf Teacher's lip curled. "Those dioramas are grotesque and—and *creepy.*"

Creepy.

Poppy had described herself that way too, chin high, hurt darkening her clear eyes.

He didn't slam the door of the refrigerator, but he wanted to. Not just because of his rage at Mildred's cruel cronies, but also because he'd thought—he'd *said*—almost the exact same things such a short time ago, and it shamed him. Gutted him.

You hurt me.

After a fraught, sleepless night, he'd finally solved his problems. He'd found his solutions, unnerving though they might be.

He was done hurting Poppy, and he wasn't about to let others do it instead.

"Excuse me." Rising to his full height, he stepped closer to the table, until he was looming over them. Deliberately. "Or, rather, excuse *you.*"

They blinked up at him, Murderous Cat Teacher's eyes wide and magnified behind her glasses.

"Ms. Wick, your colleague, received administrative permission to dress in a manner appropriate to her daily tasks, which involve ably shepherding bloodthirsty teens through a sea of paint and glue and other horrible substances." His tone was icy enough to freeze them in place. "Furthermore, when I talked to various students this week, I discovered the reason Mrs. Krackel was able to wear formal clothing when she taught."

He planted both his hands on the table and leaned forward, eyes narrowed. "Because, on a daily basis, *Mildred* didn't do a goddamn thing."

The women gasped, and he was almost certain they'd report him for his word choice. He couldn't have given less of a fuck.

"She didn't help students with projects. She didn't help

clean their mess." He spoke slowly, so they had to take in every word. "Ms. Wick's dioramas are stunning examples of meticulous, clever artistry, and they accordingly command a high price. In contrast, from my understanding, Mildred's main talent was collecting a monthly paycheck."

"How—how dare you?" Smothering Scarf Teacher sputtered. "Mildred—"

"—is gone," he finished for her. "I don't know how or why, and for these purposes, it doesn't matter."

He had a theory he intended to run by Poppy later, though. He hoped she'd prove impressed by his reasoning abilities and investigative prowess.

"No matter what happened with Mrs. Krackel, Ms. Wick is an invaluable asset to this school, and she is anything but grotesque. She's kind and warm and talented." Heaving himself upright once more, he stalked to the door, then turned to make one final, chilly statement. "*You*, on the other hand, *are* grotesque."

When he slammed out of the faculty lounge, two of his longtime colleagues staring aghast at him—their cold, controlled colleague, fuming and foul-mouthed—he dimly realized he'd lost his temper. At work. For the first time ever.

But it was for good reason. The best reason.

And quite honestly?

It felt *amazing*.

———

BENDING OVER, SIMON INSPECTED TORI'S DIORAMA-in-progress with a magnifying glass. "It's a coffin. With bloody claw marks and a corpse inside."

Because *of course* it was a coffin with bloody claw marks and a corpse inside. Why had he expected anything else from one of the Goth softball players in Poppy's class?

"It's the first of *two* coffins," Tori corrected with an easy grin. "I'm educating my teachers and classmates about a very special period in our history via my diorama, Mr. Burnham."

He lifted a brow, and she took the gesture as the invitation it was.

"In the nineteenth century, people were very nervous about being buried alive." Turning to her friend, she tucked some of her braids behind her ear. "Do you remember that project we did in Mr. Krause's class, Stacey? About how that one woman in England in the 1600s—"

"Alice Blunden," Stacey provided, face lit with excitement.

"—drank too much poppy tea, which was an opiate, and they thought she was dead, so they buried her, but then kids heard sounds from her grave, so someone exhumed her and saw she'd tried to escape, but they thought she was dead again, so they reburied her, and *then*—"

He pinched the bridge of his nose.

"—the next day, she really was dead, but there were signs she'd revived and struggled a second time before finally, totally, dying. For real."

Jesus, he'd be having nightmares about that.

Tori beamed at him. "So people were scared, and they invented special coffins with ladders and air inlets and bells so if supposedly-dead people woke up in the grave, they could save themselves. My other coffin will be a miniature of that invention. It'll show a woman safely climbing out of her grave, only half-dead, instead of all-the-way dead."

Stacey frowned thoughtfully. "Did you consider including zombies in your diorama?"

"Of course I did." Tori tossed her braids over her shoulder. "But Ms. Wick said zombies were insufficiently educational, and thus did not meet class objectives."

There were many, many things he could say in response to Tori's diorama, but Simon confined himself to one. The truth, however inadequate.

"Impressive work, Ms...." He trailed off, uncertain of her last name.

"Walker," she supplied, then shook the hand he offered. "I'll probably be in your calculus class next year."

"Good," he said, again with perfect honesty. "I look forward to it."

Then he fled back to his accustomed table, before either she or Stacey could inspire further nightmares.

A few moments later, Poppy found him taking notes on his legal pad. "You doing okay, Mr. Burnham? You look...I don't know. Kind of pale and nauseated?"

Her usual buns were slipping from the top of her head, but she was wearing a dress today, for some unknown reason. Rust-red and silky-looking, the material suited her coloring, and the hem flirted around her knees in a distracting way. The garment was also stained with fresh smears of paint and glue, which was exactly why she should have been wearing her jeans instead.

Although he'd been studying her almost nonstop, she'd been cautious around him the entire period. Meeting his eyes for fleeting moments before looking quickly away. Keeping her distance, so they never quite found themselves within arm's length of one another. Addressing him with all the formality due a colleague.

He understood why, and if he had anything to say about it, that professional reserve would disappear within the next hour. But it still made him want to snatch her into his lap and thread his fingers through her hair and yank her mouth to his.

"Tori described her diorama," he told Poppy.

She nodded. "Ah. That would explain your expression." After eyeing him carefully, she strode over to one of her cabinets and returned with a handful of blank paper and a freshly sharpened pencil. "I am absolutely certain you've already written your evaluation, so today's observation is simply a formality."

He dipped his chin in acknowledgment.

In fact, he'd drafted the praise-packed evaluation Wednesday evening, and was prepared to send it to Principal Dunn as soon as the school day ended. The notes he'd been taking on his legal pad weren't about Poppy's teaching talents, manifold though they were. They were his thoughts about Mildred's disappearance, and about the murder in miniature currently sitting on his table, approximately eight inches to his left.

He'd solved the mysteries—he hoped—last night, but wanted to order his thoughts before presenting his findings to Poppy.

She set her stack of paper in front of him, then handed him the pencil. "Since you're done with your evaluation, why don't you distract yourself from the prospect of being buried alive by drawing something?"

"I'm—" He winced. "I'm not much of an artist, I'm afraid."

"It's not about the result, Simon." Her voice was gentle. "It's about the process. There's literally no way for you to be wrong, as long as you try. Just...express yourself."

Her warm fingers trailed along his shoulder as she walked away, and he clenched his eyes shut. Thirty more minutes, and they'd be alone. He could keep control that long. He had to.

By the time the final bell rang, Simon had finished his drawing. Such as it was.

In one of their early conversations, Poppy had said she couldn't predict the contents of her students' hearts or the subjects that consumed their innermost thoughts. That applied to him too, he imagined.

One glance at his paper, which now lay face-down on the table, and she'd know his heart. His innermost thoughts.

He wanted her to know.

As the students filed from the room, he helped her clean up. Then he sat down at the table again and waited for her to venture near.

She fiddled with paperwork on her desk. She typed something into her laptop. She fussed over a splotch of paint on one of the student chairs.

She was nervous.

"Poppy..." At the sight of her right bun, now sagging a millimeter above her ear, he had to smile. "Come here."

Without turning to him, she shook her head. "I just need to..."

She couldn't even finish the breathless sentence, and she still didn't come close. He'd spooked her last night, no doubt. All that heat, all that intimacy, and he'd left her in the cold.

No matter. He knew how to draw her back to him.

"The brother did it. Barron. He set the fire that killed Kaden." He crossed his arms over his chest and leaned back in his chair. "What's my reward?"

At that, she spun around and eyed him suspiciously. "Is that your best guess?"

"It's not a guess. It's a fact." His smile was arrogant, deliberately so. "I solved your murder diorama."

Despite the continued wariness in her expression, she strode to the table and set her fists on her hips. "Explain your reasoning."

This victory didn't feel small. Not in the slightest.

"The brothers came home from work." Simon pictured the sequence of events over and over last night, until the progression finally made sense. "Barron fixed them drinks from their bar cart. He sat on the couch, while Kaden sat on the recliner and smoked. They watched television. Eventually, Kaden fell asleep. Deeply asleep, because Barron put a few of those sleeping pills from the bathroom medicine cabinet in his drink."

Poppy's lips were pressed together as she tried not to smile. "Go on."

"Then Barron sprayed the recliner and the living room with lighter fluid, set everything ablaze, and retreated to his bedroom to climb out the window and feign panic and grief." He lifted his shoulders. "All the other suspects had reasons to dislike Kaden, but they were red herrings. Distractions from the true criminal."

Her eyes sparkled as she edged closer. "What's your proof?"

"The discarded bottle of lighter fluid hidden under a bush outside their bedroom window, so well placed you couldn't see it without a magnifying glass. The papers I found on the bedroom desk, which showed how quickly Kaden was piling up debt and emptying their joint account." He couldn't even imagine how long writing the papers had taken, given the tiny, tiny print. "Those bank and credit card statements required tweezers *and* a magnifying glass to read. Which I employed Wednesday, while you were consulting with Tori about coffins."

She sank into the seat behind her desk, only a foot away. "Good eye, Sherlock."

"But that was all circumstantial evidence. Someone else could have placed the bottle there, and lots of families have money issues without resorting to arson and murder." Unfolding his arms, he tapped his forefinger on the table. "The clinching detail was something entirely different."

"Really?" She was openly smiling at him now, seemingly delighted by his observations. "Tell me."

"Barron's shoes," he said with satisfaction.

Jesus, she could light the entire fucking school with that beam of hers. "I was wondering if anyone would catch that."

"All the shoes were stored in the living room, just inside the front door, and they were all unlaced. Without exception." He leaned forward to rest his weight on his elbows. "So if Barron woke up to a smoke-filled bedroom, saw the living room entirely aflame and realized he couldn't save his brother, then panicked and fled out the window, how exactly did he manage to retrieve a pair of shoes? Much less have the time and patience to double-knot them once putting them on?"

Instead of answering, she waved him on with a grin.

He stabbed his finger into the table again. "The only possible answer: He *wasn't* in a hurry or panicked, because he set the fire himself. He stayed in pajamas to reinforce his story, but didn't want to go barefoot outside. So before dousing his brother's recliner with lighter fluid and setting it alight, he put on shoes and double-knotted them out of habit."

She applauded. "Bravo, Mr. Burnham. You've solved the case."

He gave a little seated bow, his own grin nearly cracking his cheeks. "There was only one thing I couldn't figure out. Why the hair in the sink? At first, I figured it was another red herring, meant to indicate the ex-girlfriend's involvement, but it didn't match her hair color. It was Barron's, not hers."

"Ah. The wet hair in the sink." She plucked at her cardigan, preening a bit herself. "That clue requires a bit of background knowledge or research."

"Which you've done." All those podcasts and books and television reenactments had taught her well.

"Which I've done," she agreed. "Inexperienced arsonists are often surprised by how quickly accelerants flame up once lit, and they frequently burn themselves. Their fingers, their arms—"

"Or their hair." Oh, that was a nice touch. "In the process of killing his brother, Barron set his own hair on fire. So he ran to the bathroom and doused his head in the sink, then cut off the burned parts so the police wouldn't be suspicious. He probably thought the whole house would burn down, concealing the evidence, but it didn't. The bathroom was almost untouched, so the hair remained."

"Precisely." She swiveled back and forth in her chair, eyeing him with open approval. "You're a quick study. What do you want as your reward?"

"I have some ideas." They involved privacy. A quiet bedroom. A soft mattress. Her plump thighs cradling his hips and his name gasped through her parted, swollen lips. "But first, I want to earn another."

"Another reward?" Her brow crinkled. "I don't understand."

"I think I've explained Mildred Krackel's disappearance as well." He held up two fingers. "Two cases, two rewards."

She only looked more confused. "But that's not a mystery."

"It was to me."

"Simon…" Her snort made her breasts jiggle in an entirely distracting way. "You need to gossip more."

Well, that was somewhat dampening. Still, he persevered. "Okay, so here's what I think happened: Mildred didn't simply retire due to old age. There was foul play involved."

"*Foul play?*" Poppy made a sort of choking sound. "In—in a sense, I suppose that's true."

"Let me explain the likely sequence of events." He glanced at his notes, then nodded to himself. "Mildred made enemies. Lots of them."

"Also true." Fingers interlaced, Poppy rested her chin on her hands. "Go on."

"Students resented her lack of care. Other teachers resented her lack of hard work and lesson plans. Candy

184

Albright, as I discovered after speaking with her yesterday, resented Mrs. Krackel's insistence on having students make a Frankenstein collage every Halloween. Complete with green skin and bolts in the neck."

Poppy cringed. "Mildred specified Frankenstein? Not Frankenstein's monster?"

"Even after the English Department's Frankenstein Is *Not* the Monster puppet show. The assignment was a deliberate taunt, according to Ms. Albright."

After the very strong, very loud case Candy had made in defense of that accusation, Simon had to agree. Mrs. Krackel had been mocking her colleague, which was a dangerous game indeed.

"But Ms. Albright wasn't Mrs. Krackel's most devoted enemy." Leaning forward, he lowered his voice. "No, that would be…"

He paused, because apparently he harbored a heretofore unknown love for the dramatic.

Poppy's eyes glinted with amusement. "Yes?"

"Mrs. Denham," he announced.

Her eyebrows beetled, and her smile faded. "Mrs. Denham? Our custodian? Simon, what in the world—"

"Hear me out." For confidence, he consulted his notes one last time. "Please."

Pinching her mouth shut, Poppy waved him on.

"Mrs. Krackel left a horrible mess for Mrs. Denham and the other custodians to clean every day. From what I understand, Mildred refused to either clean it herself or allot sufficient class time so students could do it instead."

Poppy inclined her head. "I've heard the same."

"The rest is sheer speculation, but it would explain everything." He tapped his forefinger on the table. "I think Mrs. Denham finally decided she'd had enough. So she confronted Mrs. Krackel one afternoon and threatened to stop cleaning the classroom unless Mildred or her students did some of the work themselves."

Poppy's brows were now arching toward her hairline, but she didn't interrupt.

"Mildred refused. Laughed her off, or pulled rank. And then—" He spread his hands. "Mrs. Denham made her stand."

Her lips twitched again, possibly at the portentous note in his voice. "Go on."

This final twist in the story, he'd considered for the first time last night. However improbable, it would explain everything. The whispered comments, the horror-filled half-glances toward the table, the unceremonious nature of Mildred's departure. All of it.

"One evening, after Mildred left for the day, Mrs. Denham left a warning. Right here." He dipped his chin to indicate the table where he'd sat every day, the table all the students seemed to avoid so assiduously. "The custodial equivalent of a horse's head."

"Wow," Poppy murmured. "Hadn't expected a *Godfather* reference."

He barreled on, ignoring her. "Maybe a pool of red paint, splattered to resemble blood. Maybe a clay figure stabbed with a carving tool. Something so egregious, so horrifying, Mrs. Krackel had to take action. So she went to Principal Dunn."

"Who said...what?" Poppy's head was tilted as she considered his theory. "Since Mrs. Denham still works here, and Mildred doesn't, I assume Mildred didn't receive the response she anticipated?"

"Exactly." He smiled at her, pleased by her quick understanding. "Tess backed Mrs. Denham, not Mrs. Krackel. At which point, Mildred quit and left the school in a huff, never to return. Mystery solved."

He sat back in smug satisfaction, waiting for praise of his investigative prowess.

It didn't come.

"Um, Simon." Poppy's voice was cautious, its tone familiar. Not quite pitying, but not quite *not* pitying either. "One small problem with your theory. Well, several rather large problems, actually."

Oh, God. He was going to feel like a fool again. He could already tell. "Yes?"

Poppy held up a finger. "First of all, if Mrs. Denham had made that kind of violent threat with Mildred's art supplies, she would no longer be employed at our school. No matter how much our principal might sympathize with the custodial staff or loathe Mrs. Krackel."

Dammit. He'd hoped she wouldn't pinpoint the weakest link in his chain of events so quickly. But the woman made murder dioramas, for heaven's sake. Of *course* she'd immediately spotted the glaring flaw in his theory.

Another finger. "Second, Mildred did make lots of enemies here. But Mrs. Denham wouldn't have done anything to threaten or sabotage—"

"Mr. Burnham is right. At least to a certain extent." The familiar voice came from the open doorway. "I loathed that woman. So did the rest of the custodial staff."

Mrs. Denham stood by her cart, unbowed and unapologetic.

At the sight of their visitor, Poppy turned a shade of red he'd never witnessed in person before. "Mrs. Denham, I'm so sorry. Simon doesn't know the circumstances of Mildred's departure, so he suspects—"

"Oh, there was definitely foul play involved, just like he said." A slow, evil smile emphasized the wrinkles on the older woman's face. "I know that for a fact."

Poppy stared openmouthed at Mrs. Denham. "But—but she was caught screwing the head of security in her classroom after hours! By the superintendent! Who was leading VIPs on a tour of the school! How can that possibly be the result of anything but her own bad judgment?"

Simon's own eyebrows flew to his hairline.

Oh. Oh, my.

That, he hadn't expected. But now that he considered the matter, it still made sense. Mrs. Denham didn't have to threaten Mildred to get rid of her.

No, she could simply—

Mrs. Denham shook her huge ring of keys. "The classroom was locked. I opened it for the group, knowing exactly what they'd find inside." Her mouth pursed. "For her age, Mildred was surprisingly limber. I'm sorry I didn't ask her about joint supplements before she left."

Simon cringed.

"You mean, before she and Harvey were both forced to retire, due to their indiscretions." Poppy's jaw was still slightly agape, and she was shaking her head in disbelief. "When the tour came to this wing...did you—"

"Oh, I definitely encouraged the group to visit this classroom. I told them to expect an eye-popping display inside." Mrs. Denham's cackle echoed in the room. "And they got one."

So much for his theory. Still, he'd chosen the correct suspect, which had to count for *something*.

"Remind me not to piss you off," Poppy whispered, wide-eyed.

"So far, so good." Mrs. Denham winked at her. "No tours scheduled tonight. Just FYI."

Even after the custodian closed the door, the sound of her whistling floated through the classroom, getting fainter as she pushed her cart down the hallway.

Then it was silent once more, and he and Poppy were staring at one another, and he couldn't seem to breathe properly. His palms grew damp where they rested on the—

Wait.

I'll never be able to use that table again, Stacey had said. *Not without picturing what happened...there.*

He looked down at the wooden surface under his hands, and a few other clues fell into place. With a muttered and heartfelt *fuck*, he leapt to his feet and ran to the sink.

Poppy groaned. "What now?"

"Is that—where I've been sitting—" There wasn't enough soap in the world. "Is that Mrs. Krackel's, uh..."

"Sex table?" Poppy's giggle was infectious, much like the germs he'd probably encountered while using that damn table all week. "Why, yes. Yes, it is."

"Dammit, Poppy." He stopped scrubbing and glared in her direction. "You could have said something."

She appeared blithely unbothered by his disfavor, as usual. "It's been disinfected multiple times since Mildred's adventures there. Trust me. I took care of that personally, once I heard the story."

He supposed that was a reasonable response. Besides, his plans for the afternoon didn't involve scowling at Poppy or reenacting Lady Macbeth's endless, frantic hand-washing.

No, he had other priorities. Business first, and then...

And then.

After rinsing and drying his hands, he crossed the room, bent down to open his briefcase, produced a neatly stapled document, and placed it on her desk. "Here's your evaluation. You can read it later. In case you're worried, it's positive. In fact, it's so glowing, it may give you a sunburn."

Her eyes didn't leave his, not even when the paper hit the desk.

"Why, Mr. Burnham." She was grinning at him again, delighted. "What a poetical turn of phrase. Thank you."

"No need to thank me. You earned every word." Now, onto the scary part of this conversation. "We need to, um..."

He rolled his shoulders. Widened his stance slightly. Closed his eyes and swallowed.

"Simon?"

Decades of avoiding vulnerability and risk ended today. Now.

The possibility of Poppy, of entirely illogical transformation, of *more*—it was worth the risk. He had to trust her, and he had to trust his own heart.

When he blinked his eyes open, she was waiting for him, forehead puckered in that endearing, familiar way. Her hazel eyes were cautious, concerned, but so very soft.

She could wreck him. Maybe she already had.

"You may need to find another mentor." He wanted to draw a soothing rectangular prism on his legal pad, but instead he held her gaze. "I'm not familiar with the rules governing the mentor-mentee relationship, at least not the ones that apply to our particular situation."

Quickly, he corrected himself. "I mean, the ones I *want* to apply."

Her brows drew together in confusion. "I'm sorry?"

However embarrassingly inept, his picture would literally tell her more than a thousand words. With a tremor in his hands, he flipped over his drawing and slid it across the table, until she could see it clearly.

He understood his artistic limits, and he hadn't tried to achieve realism.

The stick figures boasted neat labels above their circular heads: POPPY and SIMON. Her figure stood by a table, whose very straight edges he'd achieved with a ruler. There was a little house atop the table. Another tiny stick figure lay beside the house, each of its eyes indicated with an X. A corpse, as best Simon could indicate one.

His stick figure was sitting—awkwardly, with limbs of an odd length—in a chair. The small table next to the chair had a paper on it, marked with an A+.

Poppy's figure leaned toward his. Simon's figure leaned toward hers. Their eyes were hearts. Between them, he'd drawn more hearts.

In his vision, in his dreams, Poppy crafted her dioramas and sang at her workroom desk while he graded nearby, and they—

Well, he'd known his drawing abilities couldn't convey a passionate kiss.

"Simon." The word was a sigh. A caress. "Dearest."

He dared to look up from the drawing, and she was still studying it. Her finger traced one of the hearts that hung in the air between their stick figures, and she was biting her lower lip, eyes glassy with tears.

Dearest was good. He knew that much. But the tears?

"Poppy, is this..." He gulped a breath. Another. "Is this okay? Is this—is this what you want too?"

She touched her forefinger to her puckered lips, then set it gently on his stick figure. A kiss, offered to his penciled counterpart as she blinked back those gut-wrenching tears.

Before he could reach for her, she was speaking, and he listened with every ounce of his being. Every atom.

"If you left my classroom today without kissing me," she said, "I was going to make a diorama of myself, dead of a broken heart, with you as the culprit. It was going to be overly dramatic and much too blunt, but..."

Her eyes lifted to his, and her smile trembled. "I can't be blamed. I make murder dioramas. *Overly dramatic* is kind of my thing."

On the table, her capable hand was shaking too. He covered it with his own, and she immediately parted her fingers so he could slide his in between, and it felt like a buoy to a man lost at sea for years.

"I understand now." He stepped to her side, so close the scent of turpentine and soap filled his lungs. "The importance of process over result. The relief of expression.

If you hadn't already taught me, this drawing would have."

"Good." The corners of her lips indented as her smile turned mischievous. "I only have one complaint about this picture, Mr. Burnham."

"What's that, Ms. Wick?" Fuck, he loved that expression on her.

"Well, unless you count the corpse on the table..." Bending at the waist, she studied his drawing. "There's no crime here."

He bumped into her, hip to hip, and it wasn't an accident.

"On the contrary. A crime has most definitely occurred." Holding out his free arm, he displayed the pencil smudges on his pristine button-down. "Sartorial assault. Attempted murder of my shirt."

Her giggle rang through him, vibrating and joyful as a chime.

"I've changed my mind." She turned to face him. "The crime is that your stick figures aren't kissing, and neither are we."

"That was what I wanted for my reward," he told her. "A kiss from you."

More than his next breath. So much his chest ached.

If they kissed, though, he'd need to keep hold of himself until she was willing to take it further. Until they had privacy and time and a comfortable bed nearby.

"You want a kiss?" She tipped her chin upward, a mute challenge in her bright, sharp eyes. "Take it, then."

So he did.

SEVEN

Poppy's mouth was a revelation beneath his. Soft, warm, eager, sweet with mint.

She must have brushed her teeth between periods, just in case this happened, his rational brain deduced, before his rational brain entirely left the premises.

He took it slow, exploring every corner of those wide, plush lips, her sweet face cupped in his hands as she leaned back against her desk and he stepped into the cradle of her body. The electric charge of the contact dizzied him, buzzing in his ears as she opened her mouth for his tongue.

Her lower lip was trembling between his, its inner surface slick, and suddenly his hand was buried in her hair, twisted below one of those adorable buns, and he inhaled with a gasp before swooping down to kiss her again. Their tongues tangled, and he was sucking on hers, and she was making little sounds in her throat that seared a path straight to his cock.

"Hold on," she panted. "The door—I need to lock it, and maybe wedge a chair—Shit, Simon—"

She tore herself from his arms and half-ran to the door,

locking it, before yanking down the shades over her windows.

"Which chair do you think—" she began, and he couldn't stand it any longer.

He caught up with her partway to the door, removed the student chair from her hands, hauled her close, and backed her into the nearby wall, her mouth open under his even before her shoulders hit the shelves.

Her tongue chased his this time, swirling and exploring until he saw nothing but light behind his eyelids. She shoved up his shirt, yanking it free from his pants, and splayed those capable artist's hands on his hot back, and he lurched against her in reaction.

Both his own hands were tangled in her hair now, angling her head so he could drag his open mouth over her jaw and down the pale length of her neck, then back up. Her short nails bit into his back as he licked the curve of her ear.

"You wore a dress today." He bit her lobe, and she moaned. "For me?"

Her frantic little nod, he rewarded with another fevered kiss.

When he raised his head again, she clutched his hips and whispered, "Wanted to look pretty for our last day together."

"You're always pretty. Always." Disentangling his right hand from her hair, he reached for the hem of that flirty, silky dress. "And this isn't our last day, but—"

Oh, a dress was so much easier than jeans, and her thigh was so soft and dimpled and warm under his palm.

With the hand still buried in her hair, he tipped her head to meet his gaze before exploring further. Higher. "Okay?"

"Yes." Her throat worked as she swallowed, and he sucked at the spot. "Yes, please."

Her cheeks were flushed now, her lips as swollen as he'd imagined, and he wanted to watch her come with an agony of desperation he'd never experienced before.

"Look at me," he rasped. "Look at me as I touch you."

She wet her lips and nodded as much as she could with his fist in her hair, and then he was pulling her cotton panties down those lovely thighs, just far enough so he could explore her without any obstructions.

He palmed her sex, and her head thumped against the shelves as she gasped, but she held his stare. Her hair was coarse between her legs, her flesh slick and hot, and he couldn't wait.

He wouldn't.

Her eyes went hazy with the first stroke of his fingertips, her mouth parted for each rapid inhalation. She was so soft, plump and delicate against his hand, and so responsive to each light, exploring pass over her flesh. Her back arched, the breath seemingly punched from her lungs as he brushed his forefinger over her clit, and he watched her pupils expand with each gentle circle, each rub.

Her shaking thighs spread further, and her cheek was hot against his as he whispered in her ear, "Does that feel good, Poppy?"

"Yes." When his finger sank inside her, her breath hitched. "God, yes."

He drew back enough to watch her swallow and half-close her eyes when he fucked her with one finger, then two. And when he used that slickness to circle her clit again, only his hand in her hair kept that heavy-lidded gaze on his.

She was moving against him, grinding, panting, her face flushed.

"Cover my mouth. Your hand." It was a desperate gasp, her brows drawn as if in pain. "Simon, I'm—"

As soon as he freed his hand from her hair and pressed it over her mouth, she moaned against his palm once, then again, and came hard.

Her legs quaked and her flesh pulsed against his fingertips, and he worked her until the very last spasm of pleasure eased, watching her face turn slack, her expression beatific. Sweaty wisps of hair clung to her temples, and her buns had entirely ceased to exist. She was gripping his bare shoulders —had she unbuttoned his shirt at some point, or had he?— so hard she might leave bruises.

At that moment, nothing else existed but her pleasure and his savage satisfaction at having given it to her. Nothing. Not the danger of what they'd just done, not the fierce throb of his cock.

When she was still, he lowered his hand from her mouth so he could kiss her hard, and she returned the embrace with equal heat.

Then, somehow, his pants were down around his thighs, and so were his boxer-briefs, and she was the one pressing him up against the shelves. Before he could muster a single coherent word, her strong, pale hand wrapped around his dick and stroked.

He made a strangled sound deep in his chest and jerked against her.

When her hand stilled in response, he almost wept.

"I'm sorry, Simon. I should have asked." She touched his cheek. "May I?"

His only response was his hand atop hers, setting it back in motion as she grinned up at him. When she paused to slip her hand between her legs, then resumed gripping his cock with slick fingers, he thunked his head against the shelves hard enough to bruise.

Each squeeze of that capable hand raced up his spine like a line of fire. Lighter fluid set aflame, flaring with such immediate heat, he was surprised his hair wasn't singed.

"Look," she murmured, and he set his forehead to hers as she grasped his neck with her free hand. Together, they watched her pump his dick, his panting breaths and low groans gathering in the space between their mouths.

Helplessly, he was fucking her fingers now, the nape of his

neck sweaty. She was squeezing there too, holding him steady, making him watch, tugging his hair until he was so overwhelmed by sensation he whimpered.

His hands were on her breasts, on that amazing, generous ass, roaming as if she might leave at any moment, as if he needed to touch all of her at once.

He was making too much noise, he knew it, but he couldn't—he couldn't—

With one final squeeze, one more ounce of pressure against the underside of his cockhead, one more lungful of turpentine and musk and sweat, he bucked his hips and buried his face in the damp crook of her neck and sank his teeth into her flesh and came with a muffled shout, jerking hard with every spasm.

She stroked him through it, her grip gentling, her murmur soothing.

When he could see again, when he could stand without her support, he registered what they'd just done. What he'd just done.

If anyone unlocked her classroom door, there was no mistaking the situation.

They were propped against the shelves along one wall. Her panties were still around her knees, and his pants and boxer-briefs rested just below his ass. His shirt was unbuttoned, gaping open, and it wasn't only paint and glue staining her dress now.

If his expression resembled hers at all, they both looked pink and dazed and well-fucked. Her hair bore the marks of his hands. They smelled distinctly of sex. And the pink imprint of his teeth on her pale skin...

That, honestly, was the only thing he regretted.

"Did I hurt you?" He touched the mark carefully, mouth pinched tight. "I'm sorry."

As always, her smile dazzled him. "I'm not."

"Good." He pressed his lips to that mark, then her

197

temple, her cheek, her nose, her round chin. "After we clean up, may I come home with you?"

"Yes." Her fingertips on his own cheek were tender. "Yes, Simon."

When he kissed her again, her mouth sweet and soft beneath his, he found once more what he'd discovered the previous night. The certainty he'd been seeking. The solution to his final mystery. The answer to a problem that wasn't really a problem—not when her heart ached for him the same way his ached for her.

In her presence, one plus one didn't equal two. The two of them weren't a sum, or a product, or even an exponent. Nothing that mundane. Nothing that obvious or simple or safe.

He wouldn't have unraveled so quickly, so thoroughly, for obvious or simple or safe.

No, he and Poppy together made an entirely irrational number, expansive and infinite.

And for the first time, he was delighted there was no known end.

EPILOGUE

Poppy was doodling during a faculty meeting again.

Simon tried to focus on the suit-clad consultant droning at the front of the cafeteria, but how could he? Under the table, Poppy's warm knee pressed against his, and he inhaled paint and sweat and grass with every breath, since she'd taken her students outdoors that day. Her buns hovered mere millimeters above her ears.

They both knew his instinctive response to *that*.

Even after eight months together, those drooping coils made him want to bury his fingers in her soft hair and drag her mouth up to his. He might not be able to explain the reaction, but it was a constant. A fact as reliable as the multiplication tables he'd memorized as a child.

Her doodling was detrimental to his concentration too. He kept glancing over to see what she was drawing, no matter how vigorously he scolded himself for his lapses in attention.

The clean white expanse of her notebook page now featured the bare outlines of...something. An animal. The creature perched with odd stiffness upon a board or slab, its eyes slightly crossed and its head tilted, as if—

Ah. As her distraction of choice, she was sketching the rodent on display in her den, that unmistakable and unfortunate victim of ill-considered taxidermy.

Simon's first morning in her home, she'd introduced him to her lumpy, asymmetrical roommate with a formal little bow and swirl of her hand, as if the three of them were meeting at a royal ball of some sort.

"Simon Burnham, please meet Barry," she'd said. "Barry, please meet Simon. I believe the two of you have a great deal in common. Namely, a tendency toward silence and stiffness."

If she hadn't been stroking a hand over Simon's ass at that very moment, the gesture an unmistakable, loving caress, he might have been offended.

Instead, he'd snorted. "Why Barry?"

After one last squeeze of his backside, she'd retrieved her coffee from a side table and taken a sip. She appeared to be contemplating her answer.

Finally, her shoulder lifted in a desultory shrug. "He looks like a Barry."

He'd had to smile at that, because—yes. The sentiment was precisely Poppy. And that misbegotten animal did sort of look like a Barry, if Simon squinted hard enough.

"What *is* Barry?" It had pained him to ask, but he needed to know. Was Barry a furry, hunched rat? A chipmunk who'd seen better centuries? A rodent creature of myth and legend, descended from a truly cursed gene pool? "For that matter, *why* is Barry?"

Because Simon didn't mean to be rude, but he couldn't imagine plonking a horrific specimen like Barry in his own living room.

Her brow had crinkled, but she was grinning at him, amused by his discomfiture. "Why is Barry? Is that an existential question, or are you confused about his presence in my home?"

"The latter." Although he could definitely make an argument for both interpretations.

"To answer your first question, Barry is a squirrel," she'd told him. "I bought him from a pawn shop around ten years ago, I think."

Good to know. Part of the rodent family, as he'd expected. Maybe an inbred cousin of the squirrels he spotted scurrying across school sidewalks every day?

"As far as why I bought him in the first place..." She'd paused, her smile fading. "I mean, look at him."

Together, they'd turned to contemplate Barry.

"No one else was ever, ever going to buy him. He was just going to sit there, collecting dust in the window, until the day someone tossed him in the trash." Her lips pressed together. "And he seems...sad, doesn't he? Lonely?"

Again. Precisely Poppy.

In response, he'd gently removed the coffee cup from her hand and placed it on a coaster. Then he'd gathered her in his arms and kissed away the blooming ache in his chest.

The first time he'd laid eyes on Barry, he'd known Poppy would have a reason for displaying the creature in her home. A good one.

She did. Of course she did. For all her love of murder and mayhem, her heart was as soft and warm as the enveloping, pillowy duvet on her bed. He also suspected she'd empathized with that lonely squirrel in the pawn shop window more than she might like to admit.

Hell, after that conversation, *he'd* empathized with the rodent too. To the point where he kind of didn't mind Barry's presence in his daily life, and maybe—when Poppy wasn't around—muttered an occasional quick hello to the third member of their household.

Sometimes. No more than once per morning.

Poppy truly was capable of performing miracles.

She'd stolen his heart, when anyone would have told her he didn't have one. She'd inspired him, a man who loved order and rules, a man who'd been alone virtually all his life, to move in with her after only three months together.

It was madness. Color and clutter and violent crime in miniature. Near-constant noise. Off-key singing in the sunshine of her work room as she carefully depicted blood splatter, while he sat with a book in his brand-new club chair, feet propped comfortably on an ottoman.

Then, inevitably, it was her arms around his shoulders, her breath in his ear, his fists in her hair, then his mouth between her legs. She didn't complain about his silence then, and she certainly didn't bemoan his stiffness once they'd tumbled onto her mattress.

It was warmth in the darkness and laughter in the light.

He'd never been happier in his life.

This dream he kept having, the one he'd had again last night—this vision he hadn't been able to shake, not for a single minute all day—was abject foolishness, and he really should be paying attention to the speaker, but—

He nudged Poppy's arm with his legal pad.

She glanced up from detailing the sparkle in Barry's crossed eyes, her brow adorably puckered in concentration. Settling his thigh more firmly against hers, he wrote a note on his paper, beside the neat rectangular pyramid he'd doodled earlier.

Want to play Hangman?

As soon as she read the question, she huffed out a quiet laugh and flipped to a fresh page in her spiral-bound notebook.

Of course, Mr. Burnham, she jotted in her looping script.

He hesitated, then added, *May I choose the phrase?*

Normally, he'd let her go first, but…not this time.

She waved him on with a tiny, subtle gesture, and he carefully drew the gallows and blank spaces beneath, the spaces she'd try to fill by guessing letters, one by one.

Her first choice: an S. There were none of those in his phrase, so he needed to start sketching his stick-figure person. A head within the loop of rope.

According to the normal rules of the game, he supposed that person should be Poppy, perhaps indicated with buns on either side of her circle head. But even within the context of an innocent child's game, he didn't want to imagine her at risk.

He drew his own head instead. A circle with a squiggle of dark hair on top.

When she registered that choice, her eyes went soft, and her knee slid against his thigh so sweetly. With a single fingertip, she skimmed the back of his hand before dropping hers to her lap.

He was sweating now, his breath short, and for once, the reaction wasn't due to lust. It wasn't even due to the somewhat ghoulish sight of his stick-figure head within a noose.

It was nerves. Pure nerves and adoration.

More guesses followed. A. T. N. E. B. R. Slowly, the letters began filling in his chosen phrase, and his drawing sprouted arms and a torso. In a burst of uncharacteristic whimsy, he added buttons down that torso to indicate his usual shirts, even including a striped tie for the hell of it.

ARR _E_

She was sneaking glances at him now, her fingers beginning to tremble, her brow puckered again in seeming confusion.

If he'd gotten this wrong, if her answer wasn't what he hoped, he really was a dead man. Not physically, but in nearly every other way. All the ways that had come to mean everything to him over the past eight months.

Her next guess was a nearly indecipherable scratch, and

her cheeks were blotched with ruddy color as she scrawled the letter. *M?*

She wrote it with a question mark, but there was no need for that. No need for her to worry she'd gotten this, gotten him, wrong. No need for the hectic color on her face, unless—

Oh, fuck, was she going to say no? Was that hot flush prompted by embarrassment for him, rather than fear she'd drawn the wrong conclusion?

His hand was shaking too, but he filled in the appropriate spots.

MARR_ ME_

Her teeth had sunk into her lower lip, indenting its plump surface.

Slowly, so slowly, she made her next guess. *Y.*

If he filled in that letter, all chances of plausible deniability were gone. Not that many five-letter words started with MARR, other than the obvious. So he needed to gather every ounce of his bravery, of his love for the woman beside him, and do it.

MARRY ME_

She was staring at him full-on now, lips parted in a silent gasp, her body twisted away from the speaker and angled toward his. The high color in her cheeks was racing down her neck, spreading over her upper chest, and her eyes were turning glassy.

Tears. Because she was sad to disappoint him?

That consultant might as well have been mouthing his speech. Simon couldn't hear a thing over the echoing pulse in his ears.

Every stroke of the pen was a struggle, but he got the right words down. Or at least, the words he'd intended. Whether they were right or not, he supposed he'd know soon.

The last blank space isn't actually a letter. It's punctuation. Which isn't in the rules, but I thought you would forgive my lapse. What's your next guess?

At that, her tears spilled over, and her lips finally—finally—tipped upward.

A smile. A smile that was so shy and tentative and filled with affection, his heart twisted within him once more. Leaning over her notebook, she slowly wrote something in response, and the air was too thin to breathe as he waited.

Whew. I was confused. She paused, and her smile grew as she kept writing. *I thought you were demanding I marry Meg, from the music department. Or maybe men, plural, because you'd realized how tempting I find bigamy.*

It was funny, that response. What it wasn't: an answer. Despite the beam she was directing his way, despite the way she was now leaning against him, shoulder to shoulder.

He gazed at her, desperate, his free hand fisted on his thigh.

She continued, *You aren't the exclamation mark type, and you're too polite to make a demand. So I'll guess: ?*

He bent over his legal pad. And then—

There it was, immortalized in ink, via the absolute worst handwriting of his life.

MARRY ME?

When he forced himself to meet her tear-glazed hazel eyes, he could have sworn he existed outside time, because every second seemed to encompass an entire millennium. Outside his body too, because he couldn't feel the chair at his back or the tiles under his feet. And, above all, outside the laws of science and reason and even common sense, because —well.

It was preposterous.

There was absolutely no goddamn way he—Simon Clancy Burnham—had just proposed to the woman he loved after less than a year together. In the middle of a fucking faculty meeting. Via *Hangman*, of all things.

He didn't even have a fucking *ring*.

And yet, it seemed…

It seemed he had. There was no other explanation for Poppy's capable hands on his cheeks, cradling his face so tenderly as she cried and nodded and laughed. If he hadn't proposed, he couldn't fathom why his mouth found hers, and her lower lip was soft and slippery between his own, her smile obvious even as they kissed. Under any other circumstances, he would never stroke the warm give of her upper arms and bury his fingers in her hair and haul her close enough to feel her body fit snugly against his own. Not in front of his colleagues, anyway.

"I love you," he rasped against her mouth. "I *love* you, Poppy."

She hiccupped, still beaming. "I love you too, Simon. So much."

So he could only conclude: He had proposed, after all. She'd said yes. They were—in actual reality, not just one of his recent dreams—embracing passionately in the middle of a faculty meeting, Poppy sprawled across his lap and encircled in his arms as they kissed and kissed some more.

In terms of professional appearance and deportment, they were a disgrace.

And in that glorious, blinding moment of joy, Simon simply could not have cared less.

COVER ME

ABOUT "COVER ME"

First comes marriage…

Elizabeth Stone has no health insurance. No savings. No one to turn to when she finds a lump on her breast…except James Magnusson, her friend of over twenty years. When he offers her a marriage of convenience for healthcare coverage, she'd be a fool to say no. But given the emotions she's buried for so long, saying yes might lead to a broken heart.

James won't take no for an answer. Not when marriage could save Elizabeth's life, and not when he's finally realized how much he needs her. Even during his doomed first marriage, James considered Elizabeth a special friend—one he had to keep at a safe distance. Now he's free, and Elizabeth is his wife…but will they finally have the chance to be together, only to have everything torn apart?

For my maternal grandmother, who survived her bout with breast cancer; my paternal grandmother, who didn't; and my mother, who— as of this year—is now a survivor too. This story is dedicated to you.

ONE

THE HOSPITAL GOWN DIDN'T FIT.

Elizabeth tugged at the edges in front, but all that did was pinch her armpits. The worn, thin material couldn't stretch any more. It would tear if she yanked harder. And the young woman who'd led the way to the curtained dressing booths had said to leave the gown open in front, so Elizabeth couldn't reverse the garment.

The jeans covered some of her, but not enough.

She didn't dare look at herself in the mirror. No need to see her breasts and upper belly spilling through the opening, the flesh pale and pebbled by the chill of the Marysburg hospital.

Any other time, the embarrassment and discomfort might have brought stinging color to her cheeks, even though over four decades of life as a fat woman and many visits to this very hospital—and its very inadequate gowns—should have inured her to such indignities. But today, no. She wouldn't pray the hospital would invest in bigger gowns or wonder what those spotting her would think about her weight.

Marysburg General was offering free mammograms today, or at least cooperating with the local breast cancer awareness organization who'd advertised the event. That was good enough for her, even if she had to parade down the antiseptic-scented hallways half-naked.

She didn't know who was really paying for the mammograms, the hospital or the organization. She didn't care. The money wasn't coming from her depleted checking account, and the results from today should relieve weeks of fear.

So she simply held her sweater in front of the gap in her gown, covering all the crucial bits, and drew back the curtain with a metallic rattle. The tech who'd led her to the dressing room was working at a nearby computer, her dark brows knitted.

She looked up after a moment, then winced when she saw Elizabeth's predicament. "I'm sorry." Her ponytail swished as she shook her head. "We've been so busy today, I forgot to get you the right type of gown. If you want to go back into your dressing room, I can bring you one."

No. Elizabeth couldn't wait another moment.

"It's fine." She glanced at the name on the woman's badge, her cheeks aching from a forced smile. "Thank you for the offer, Cailyn. But I figure I'm supposed to be flashing the goods soon anyway, right?"

Cailyn's shoulders relaxed. "True enough. And the room is just down the hall. Follow me."

They proceeded past several doorways and the bustling nurses' station before entering the room with the mammogram machine. It looked newish, shiny and clean, although Elizabeth knew she couldn't expect 3D images from it. Not when someone else was paying.

The machine. The chairs. The table. Everything in this space was familiar. Nothing had changed since last year's mammogram, other than her insurance status.

And one other terrifying, crucial detail.

Despite the coolness of the hospital, slick perspiration had gathered under her arms. Deodorant could throw off mammograms, of course, so she hadn't used any that morning. She suspected she'd have been sweating either way, though.

"Um…" She licked her lips and tasted blood. The dry air of late winter always caused chapping if she wasn't careful, and she hadn't been paying much attention to anything outside her own head in recent days. "You might want to look closely at my right breast."

Cailyn paused in her adjustment of the machine. "All right."

"In the shower last month, I found a—" She faltered, then made herself finish. "I found a lump along the side. Toward the middle. You can't see it, but it's pretty easy to feel. I think it's a cyst, since I tend to get those, but I don't know. It doesn't hurt."

"Hmm." Cailyn crossed the room and flipped through Elizabeth's various registration forms. "Have you discussed this issue with a primary care physician? Especially given your family history and risk factors?"

Her time as a smoker in her twenties. Her grandmothers. The fact she'd never been pregnant. All things she'd noted on those forms. All things she'd been unable to forget since she'd slicked Ivory soap over her breast and felt…something.

Under any other circumstances, she'd have rushed to Dr. Sterling's office weeks ago, and her doctor would have insisted on a diagnostic mammogram, rather than a simple screening.

But much as she'd like to create an alternative reality, one in which she could afford unlimited doctor's visits even without insurance, she couldn't. "No. I haven't seen her."

Since Elizabeth was taking advantage of a program offering free mammograms to uninsured Marysburg residents, Cailyn likely understood the situation without further explanation. At the very least, she didn't ask any more questions.

"All right." Brown eyes kind, Cailyn gave her a reassuring pat on the shoulder. "I'll do my best to get crystal-clear images."

And then the normal routine began. How many times had she had this procedure? Seven? Ten? Definitely every year since she'd turned forty, and Dr. Sterling had ordered at least one baseline mammogram before then. By this point, Elizabeth knew the basics of how to angle her body and her arm, how to lean into the machine when necessary and hold still.

Her left breast compressed between the glass plates, and as always, she noted its resemblance to an unbaked loaf of ciabatta. Dimpled, off-white, and vaguely rectangular.

Two images, like normal. Then the tech helped her switch sides, and her right breast went between the plates. More pressure as they squeezed together once more, spreading her into an even layer as effectively as her favorite rolling pin did pie dough.

Elizabeth tried to concentrate on that vision, letting its familiar sweetness distract her. Rolling out a disc of dough and transferring it into a pie plate. Cutting off the overhang and crimping the edges. Inspecting the little bits of butter within the dough, which would provide flakiness as they melted and steamed in the heat of the oven. Filling the shell with thin-cut apples, tossed with cinnamon-sugar, lemon juice, a few more pats of butter, and a pinch of salt. Weaving a lattice of dough strips for the top and brushing them with cream for extra browning.

From the humid warmth of her mental bakery, she heard and obeyed Cailyn's gentle directives. Position. Freeze. Reposition. Freeze.

Then Cailyn told her to breathe again, and Elizabeth inhaled deeply, her chest loosening for the first time in weeks. The two standard images of her right breast had been taken. Any moment now, the tech would tell her to put the gown back on and return to the dressing room. She'd don her bra and sweater and find out in a few days that the stupid lump was meaningless, nothing of concern.

This horrible month would have a happy ending, and she could go back to worrying about normal things, like that rattle in her car or whether she had enough extra money to maintain her small monthly donation to Planned Parenthood.

All stressful considerations, of course, but not nightmarish. Not anything that would keep her sleepless for weeks on end, waiting for the next free mammogram event nearby.

But Cailyn didn't smile and say they were done. Instead, she bit her lip. Fiddled with the machine, looking at God knew what on the screen.

Another repositioning, and then the tech took one more image. Two more.

Elizabeth coughed as the pressure in her chest returned and ratcheted tighter.

"Are you okay?" The smile crinkling the corners of Cailyn's eyes had disappeared. "Do you need a minute?"

She didn't need a minute. She needed insurance. She needed her mom. She needed a stalwart barrier between her and a world abruptly turned frigid and terrifying.

"I'm fine." Another approximation of a smile, and then she couldn't help but say it. "Does everything look okay?"

Every year, she asked the same question, and she always got the same answer. The tech couldn't make that determination, and the radiologist reading the images would send a report to Dr. Sterling within five business days.

Usually, though, the tech would seem relaxed and smile in a way that told Elizabeth what she needed to know. The images were fine. She was fine.

This time, however, Cailyn remained silent for several heartbeats before speaking, her lips pressed into a tight line. "Your doctor should hear from the radiologist within three to five business days." Another pause. "Or sooner. The radiologist might have time to look at this today. I'll check with her."

The kindness, the probable reason for it, paralyzed Elizabeth in a way a brusque dismissal wouldn't have.

"Even when she sees abnormalities, most of the time it's nothing. Calcifications or a cyst or something harmless. A simple biopsy can tell you one way or another."

Cailyn's voice had become a little higher, the pace of her words a little more rapid, probably because she wasn't supposed to say any of these things to a patient. But she was young and concerned and not experienced enough to disguise either.

"So don't wor—" The other woman cut herself off. "Anyway, you should hear soon. Let's take one more image, and then get you back into your nice, warm sweater."

Elizabeth was pretty sure she'd never be warm again.

Another slight repositioning, another held breath, and it was done. She walked to the dressing area, her sweater held in front of her exposed flesh like a shield. Behind the cloth curtain, she peeled off the too-tight gown, hooked her bra, slicked on the deodorant stashed in her purse, and pulled the sweater over her head, tugging it past her hips.

Then she braced her hands against the wall and dropped her head to her chest.

After a few minutes, Cailyn spoke on the other side of the curtain, her tone gentle. "Are you okay, Ms. Stone?"

The poor kid had asked that question before, and the answer would be the same. The answers, really.

Not at all. Not for months, and definitely not now.

"I'm fine," Elizabeth said.

LATER THAT AFTERNOON, AS CAILYN HAD promised, the call came.

TWO

JAMES GLANCED AT THE DASHBOARD CLOCK, THE numbers bright green and accusatory in the twilit gloom. Ten minutes to six. Dammit, he was going to be late, and he didn't have time to pull over and call Elizabeth.

That last job at the Keplinger house had taken way more time than he'd anticipated, largely because the new kid on his crew had ordered the wrong damn paint for the living room, a semi-gloss blue instead of a matte yellow. An extra early-morning trip to get the right color and finish had set James behind all day.

He'd intended to shower and change before the town hall. Elizabeth wouldn't protest, of course. She'd never been overly concerned with appearances. And Lord knew he didn't give a fuck what some jackass congressman or his supporters thought about him. But meeting his old friend in a paint-splattered sweatshirt and jeans, his hair plastered to his skull by the wool cap he'd worn during trips outside, pained him anyway.

In their better years, his ex had teased him about it some-times, how meticulously he tried to straighten himself before they gave final instructions to the babysitter and met Elizabeth—with or without one of her boyfriends—for dinner.

"We lived with her in a tiny apartment for two years," Viv would say, rolling her eyes as he ran a comb through his hair and ironed his shirt. "She's seen you passed out on a stained sofa with dicks Sharpied on your face. I think she can handle uncombed hair."

"That was in our university days," he'd tell her. "Over a decade ago."

What he carefully neglected to add: *Back when I was drinking too.*

Then, behind the closed door of their bedroom, he'd catch Viv by the waist, press her against the wall, and remind her that the only woman he cared to impress was her. All while hoping he wouldn't taste tequila on her tongue.

In their worse years, when they'd moved cross-country and her drinking had become a constant in their lives, their visits home to Marysburg and occasional dinners with Elizabeth had turned fraught.

"You don't prep like this for our other friends." Viv would watch him in the hotel mirror, her mouth a hyphen.

He'd inhale through his nose, struggling for patience. "There was never anything between Elizabeth and me. You know that. You and I were already together when we lived with her."

Viv would nod, but she wouldn't look convinced. At dinner, she'd go through an entire bottle of wine or half a dozen margaritas and try to drum up arguments with either him or an ever-calm Elizabeth. And once they got out to the car, the slurred accusations and screamed invectives would begin.

Finally, he'd stopped suggesting dinner with their old friend and former roommate during visits to Marysburg. Just another way he'd contorted his life, his relationships, everything he did and was, around his ex-wife's alcoholism. But after the divorce, once he'd returned to his hometown for good, he'd called Elizabeth and apologized. Asked for forgiveness and company at their favorite diner that night.

She'd accepted him back into her life without questions or recriminations. She provided pleasant, undemanding companionship when they both had time. She baked him cookies for every conceivable holiday. She was the antithesis of drama, and around her, he could just *be*.

His history, his choices, his regrets: She knew them all in a way no one else did, not even his parents or his sons. Over the years, he'd hidden so much from his family. From everyone.

He'd wanted to shield his kids from pain. Wanted to protect the privacy and sanctity of his marriage. But because of Elizabeth's unique position in his life, she'd witnessed some of the hardest, most horrible moments of that life.

She hadn't flinched. Hadn't done anything but offer understanding and warmth.

So she deserved him clean and kempt, and she deserved him prompt.

Especially since he'd never, not once in almost thirty years of friendship, heard her make such an impassioned plea for company. For support. As soon as he'd read the Facebook DM, he'd told her she could count on him. He'd be happy to attend a damn town hall or a wake or a wedding or whatever. Anything for her. And it wasn't as if he'd miss another long, solitary evening spent reading or watching HATV before trudging upstairs and tumbling into a big, chilly bed.

There. There was the road leading to the high school.

James arrived in the parking lot two minutes before Congressman Herb Brindle's town hall was due to start, wedged his truck into the first available space, and sprinted for the entrance closest to the auditorium. His back ached with each jarring step, just as it did when he made his sad attempts at jogging four times a week, but he gritted his teeth and kept moving.

The foyer contained two or three clusters of people still chatting and four SWAT officers in polo shirts. They eyed him carefully, but he turned away, still looking for Elizabeth's trademark pale blond hair and solid frame.

She was nowhere to be found, probably because the event was due to start any moment and she'd already taken a seat. Hopefully she'd saved him one too.

To his vague surprise, there was no security check at the door to the auditorium, just a taped-up paper that read "No POSTERS OR SIGNS." Ironic, that. And as soon as he poked his head inside, he saw that glorious hair, glowing beneath the overhead lights like a beacon.

He hustled down the aisle, his boots landing in noisy thuds on the floor. But other than a few more security people around the margins, no one paid him any attention. They were still chatting as they waited for the congressman, who appeared to be filming an interview with a local news reporter at the side of the auditorium.

Elizabeth wasn't chatting with anyone, though. She wasn't even watching the congressman. She was staring at the empty stage, at a spot containing nothing of real interest.

Even when he lowered himself into the seat beside her, she didn't move. Didn't acknowledge him. Was she angry he'd cut the timing so close?

"I'm sorry, Eliz—" he started to say, but then she jerked at the sound of his voice and turned her head in his direction.

Her deep-set blue eyes, usually so clear, were bloodshot, the lids swollen. Her skin had transformed from rosy to blotchy, its paleness mottled by angry patches of pink. Her strong features appeared to have sunken in on themselves somehow, turned creased and saggy when he'd always considered her an ageless wonder.

Only that trademark low blond ponytail was normal, its

brightness incongruous. Almost obscene, given the fear and worry etched across her face.

She'd never looked like this. Ever. Not even at her mother's funeral a couple months ago. Jesus fucking Christ, what was going on?

He wrapped a hand around her upper arm, and the chill of her flesh seeped through her sweater. "Are you okay? What happened?"

Out of the corner of his eye, he could see Brindle moving toward the stage. They only had a minute to talk. Maybe seconds.

Her throat shifted as she swallowed. "I'm fine."

A lie refuted by its telling. He could barely hear her, even though the audience had quieted in anticipation of the congressman's words, and her voice was rough in a way he didn't recognize.

Enough. She didn't belong in a damn high school auditorium, not in her condition.

"Let's go somewhere we can talk. Somewhere warm." He got to his feet and held out his hand to her. "My house is closest."

He'd turn on the gas fireplace and crank up the heat until those tiny shivers wracking her frame stopped. He'd swaddle her in a blanket, get her some of that fancy hot chocolate she liked, and make her tell him everything. Then he'd figure out how to fix it, whatever it was.

She took his hand, but only to tug him back down to his seat. "No."

"But you're—"

Her mouth set, she shook her head. "I need to do this."

"You need to do what?"

But it was too late. A woman in a navy dress had stepped up to the mic stand and started yammering about Brindle's accomplishments, his love for his constituents, and a bunch of other shit James neither believed nor cared about.

He leaned over to whisper in Elizabeth's ear. "Are you sure you want to stay?"

Her soft hair caught on his beard, several strands pulling loose from her ponytail. The scent of baking surrounded her in a nimbus, imbued in that hair and the fabric of her clothing. Vanilla and almond and fresh bread. Sweetness and comfort.

She smelled edible. Always had.

At his words, she shivered again, harder. Then she nodded.

After a round of halfhearted applause from the audience, the woman retreated from the stage, replaced by the suit-clad congressman.

Brindle cleared his throat and gazed out over the auditorium. "It's my honor to speak to you tonight at Marysburg High. As you know, my constituents are the reason I'm here, in every possible sense. And tonight, I'd like to share with you some crucial information about our national debt and the dangers of our ballooning deficit before I open the floor to questions."

Beside James, Elizabeth took a shaky breath, her long, blunt fingers curling into fists on the armrests. Without thinking much about it, he covered the hand closest to him.

Her fingers were stiff under his. Cold. But as Brindle ran through his PowerPoint presentation, complete with endless bar graphs and alarming spikes in various charts, they gradually loosened and warmed, flattening against the plastic armrest.

Abruptly, as the congressman seemed to be reaching the end of his speech, she turned her palm upward, and their fingers intertwined.

Holding hands. They were holding hands for the first time in almost thirty years.

The fit felt natural. Easy, in a way he hadn't anticipated. And her shivers had waned at some point over the last several minutes, which allowed him to take his first full breath in half an hour.

Her distress disturbed him. Immensely. He'd had no clue. Not given her usual self-possession, her seeming imperviousness to damage, the way she'd remained stalwart and cheerful even during the sale of her bakery and her mother's slow, painful decline and death.

Had she been stalwart and cheerful? Or had that been a performance enacted for the comfort of her oblivious audience?

Earlier, she'd told him she was fine when she clearly wasn't. He didn't like to think of her lying to him, and he didn't like to think of how many times she might have done so in the past without him noticing.

Brindle finished discussing his last slide and clicked off the projector. A few audience members, quiet to that point, gave another perfunctory round of applause.

One of the few remaining so-called moderate Republicans, Brindle didn't tend toward fiery speeches or prophecies of doom. His soundbites were reasonable, conciliatory. But he voted with his uber-conservative colleagues every time, no matter how egregious their positions became or how many people—especially women, people of color, and members of the LGBTQ community—their policies hurt.

As far as James was concerned, the man was a fucking coward. Maybe he talked a good game about welcoming immigrants, but he didn't denounce their harassment by ICE or the splitting of families by deportation or the horrific detention camps at the border. Maybe he acknowledged the importance of affordable healthcare for all, but he stood by while the Republicans drafted bill after failed bill that would strip that healthcare from millions.

Brindle was either devoid of principles or lacked the courage to fight for them. Either way: The man was a blight on Virginia and their nation. He needed to be voted out, and soon.

James sincerely hoped someone in the auditorium would ask the congressman where he'd stored his spine, and whether a good ass-kicking would help him find the key.

When Brindle opened the floor to questions, a few audience members raised their hands. Including, to his shock, Elizabeth, the woman who'd bemoaned and feared every oral presentation she'd been assigned in college and never raised her hand in their shared American lit seminars.

This. This was why she'd come, fear of public speaking be damned.

She was shaking again, her fingers squeezing so tight he heard one of his knuckles crack. But she kept her other trembling hand high in the air, gaze pinned to Brindle's nearest roaming flunky with a microphone.

The tie-clad young man—a Young Republican from Marysburg University?—caught her eye, gave a little nod, and headed their way.

Her breath hitched, and her fingers spasmed around his.

When the kid leaned over, his outstretched hand holding the microphone, Elizabeth slowly, clumsily rose to her feet. James expected her to disentangle their hands at that point, but she didn't. And he wasn't letting go until he knew she was okay, whether that happened in a minute or an hour.

So he scooted forward in his chair so she didn't have to lean to the side and held her hand as she spoke into the microphone, her voice quavering.

"My name is Elizabeth Stone, and I'm a lifelong resident of Marysburg. My question concerns your stance on healthcare." She licked her chapped lips. "I'm very concerned about—"

"Let me stop you for a moment, Ms. Stone." The congressman held up a hand. "I want to be clear that I understand the importance of healthcare to Virginians and all

Americans. Every time I hear the story of an innocent child's illness driving a family into bankruptcy, I grieve more than I can say." Lips pursed, he shook his head. "Health insurance needs to be affordable and readily available. But as my presentation just demonstrated, we also have to find a solution that won't bankrupt our government in the long term. That's a tough challenge, but it's one my Republican colleagues and I are more than willing to take on. We'll keep working on it until we find the right answer. For you, and for everyone."

He paused, clearly waiting for applause. When it didn't come, he turned back to Elizabeth. "What's your question, ma'am?"

She was breathing fast, but she didn't avert her gaze from the congressman. After one more squeeze of James's hand, she began talking again.

"Let me tell you a little about my family medical history, Congressman. My Grandma Stone died of breast cancer before I was even born. My father didn't talk about it much, but from what I hear, she had a lump under her arm the size of a grapefruit before she went to a doctor, and by then it was too late. She was dead before my dad even graduated from college." Her fingers had turned cold against his once more. He covered them with his free hand, surrounding her as best he could as she spoke. "Grandma Barker had a mastectomy in her late forties. She survived for a couple more decades before she got lung cancer."

Elizabeth cleared her throat. "Both of them were smokers, unlike my mom. And my mother never got breast cancer, although she had a few questionable mammograms over the years. My sisters haven't had any issues either. But you can understand why I've always been concerned about breast cancer. Terrified of it, actually."

He'd had no idea. None.

"Last month, I—" She paused. "I found a lump in my

right breast while I was showering. But I don't have health insurance, and I wasn't comfortable going into debt to pay for a mammogram."

James must have made some sort of sound, because she stopped speaking for a moment and glanced down at him. With a nod, he encouraged her to keep going, but he barely heard her next few words.

When the fuck had Elizabeth lost her insurance? And why hadn't she said something to him? He could have paid her premium. He could have paid for a fucking mammogram. Shit, he'd have *begged* her to take his money and go to the damn doctor.

They'd been friends for decades. Unlike most of their circle, she hadn't blinked when he'd decided to shift from teaching English to painting houses. She'd tolerated Viv's abuse and tried to stay close to them both, even in the midst of all the alcohol-soaked drama. She brought him homemade soup when he came down with a cold or fever. She baked him cookies for every conceivable holiday—including Arbor Day, for Christ's sake—and fed him basically every time she saw him. He figured he could blame ninety percent of his belly on her, and the other ten percent on the Rita's frozen custard place near his house.

She'd been a steady, supportive, undemanding presence in his life almost as long as he could remember.

And she'd been without insurance and terrified, and she hadn't fucking told him?

No. This was unacceptable. And as soon as this damn town hall ended, he was going to tell her so. Right after he held her until she stopped shaking.

"—and the radiologist said I needed a biopsy as soon as possible, but if I couldn't afford a mammogram, how can I afford a biopsy?" Elizabeth's voice was so shredded now, he could barely make out her words. "And if it's cancer, how can I afford treatment without spending the rest of my life in debt? What if my lack of coverage means I don't get the care I need?"

Even as her tears spilled over, she jabbed a finger in the congressman's direction. "But let's say the lump is nothing, I survive this year, and I try to get coverage next year. If the latest Republican healthcare bill passes, I won't be able to pay for health insurance anyway, because of all my preexisting conditions." She jerked the hand twined with James's against the softness of her stomach. "I'm fat. I smoked for a while in my twenties and have occasional asthma. And since the abnormal mammogram is in my records now, that'll probably disqualify me for an affordable plan too."

For the first time since James had known her, she'd raised her voice. She was yelling now, those blotches on her face standing out in relief against the bone-white paleness of her skin.

"So, yes, I hear you saying that innocent babies born with health conditions shouldn't die, and their families shouldn't go bankrupt. How generous of you." Her trembling lip curled. "But what about people like me? I'm not innocent. I'm a flawed human being, and I've made some bad decisions. Does that mean I no longer have value to you or to our society? Does being fat and a former smoker mean I deserve to d—"

Her chest hitched, and he brought their twined hands to his cheek, desperate to provide some sort of silent comfort.

After a moment, she continued. "Does that mean I deserve to die? Does that mean I deserve to spend weeks or months awake in bed, wondering whether I have a tumor growing from something treatable to something that will cause me a slow, agonizing d-death?" She was sobbing between every word now. "You need to think hard, Congressman Brindle. About people like me. About what you believe. About whether your conscience will allow you to bankrupt and kill an untold number of Americans in the name of the free market and deficit reduction, even as you increase military spending and cut taxes for the wealthy."

The congressman, his brow furrowed, had extended a hand to her. "Ms. Stone, I'm so sorry that your—"

"No." She cut him off without hesitation. "You've gone on record as supporting every one of your party's failed health-care bills. So I don't want your sympathy. I want your vote. A no on every cruel healthcare plan your Republican colleagues propose. A yes on universal healthcare. If you can't give me both, save your prayers and platitudes for someone who can afford them. And that's all I have to say."

The crowd erupted into whistles and applause, drowning out Brindle's attempted reply.

Elizabeth wasn't even paying attention to the congressman anymore. Instead, she lowered her chin to look at James. "Can we go now?"

Her nose was red and running, her eyes swollen. But her shoulders were straight, no hint of apology evident on her face. The local news stations' cameras were trained on her, but she wasn't flinching away from them or hiding herself.

She wasn't just kind and pleasant and smart. She was fucking phenomenal. A powerhouse of a woman, even in the midst of such pain and fear.

Why hadn't he seen it before?

He stood. "I'll drive us home. We can get your car later."

Without another word, she slung her purse over her shoulder and headed for the exit, James in tow. At her sudden movement, the SWAT guys headed in her direction, but they stood down when they saw she was leaving.

And as James and Elizabeth walked hand-in-hand to his truck, he started formulating a plan.

THREE

Halfway to the truck, Elizabeth came to a sudden halt. "Wait. I forgot your blueberry cheesecake in my car."

To James's relief, she sounded more like herself again, cheerful and steady. But was that reality or just an attempt to smooth over any awkwardness and shield her vulnerability?

And for God's sake, why had she brought him yet more food when she couldn't even afford necessary medical care?

"It's colder than a witch's t—" He cleared his throat. "Colder than a witch's nose out here. Why don't you get in the truck and I'll grab the cheesecake for you?"

"I would, but we're approximately two feet from my parking spot." Faint amusement curved her wide mouth. "Didn't you notice?"

He hadn't, actually. He hadn't been thinking about anything but her. Her glorious takedown of Brindle and her predicament, of course, but also the icy chill of her fingers and how much he wanted to bundle her into his truck, turn on the heated seats, and adjust the thermostat until they could roast a good-sized turkey in the cab.

He smiled back at her. "Guess not."

233

Within moments, she'd produced her favorite springform pan from her old Honda's trunk and locked the car tight, and they continued on their way.

While digging for her keys, though, she'd let go of his hand, and it felt odd without hers in it. Empty. An inexplicable reaction, since before tonight, he hadn't held a woman's hand in at least four years. Maybe longer, since he and Viv had abandoned hand-holding long before they divorced.

After James helped Elizabeth into the truck, he paused. "Do you want me to take you home? Or would you like to order Carmelo's at my house?"

She had a decided soft spot for their chicken parmesan pizza, and he was prepared to employ every trick, every advantage he had to keep her with him. Because if he gave her any time to recover herself, he suspected those defenses of hers—the ones he'd just noticed—would snap into place, and she'd be back to pretending that everything was fine. That she was fine.

In thirty years, she'd never asked for help, even though she'd surely needed assistance at some point. He wanted to know why she hadn't reached out. Why she hadn't trusted him to care for her. But no matter her reasoning, suffering alone was no longer an acceptable alternative for her. Not now. Not given the terror he'd seen in her eyes tonight.

"Pizza sounds good." She strapped herself in. "We can have the cheesecake for dessert."

"Perfect."

By the time he buckled up and backed out of the tight space, she was slumped in the seat, her eyes half-closed, and his heart ached at the exhaustion painted in blue shadows beneath her eyes. But he couldn't let her sleep. Not until he understood the situation and whether it required immediate action.

"Elizabeth..." He turned left out of the lot and headed

234

home. "You were incredible in there. But based on what you said, I have a few questions."

He kept his eyes on the road, but he could hear her let out a slow breath. "I bet you do."

Might as well cut right to the heart of the matter. "When did you lose your insurance coverage?" He snuck a quick glance her way, but it was long enough to see her drop her chin to her chest. "And how?"

Dammit, he didn't want to hurt or embarrass her. But he needed to know the story, so they could work out a happy ending together one way or another.

She deflated against the seat, and her words emerged one by one, slowly, as if she were forcing them from her mouth. "You know I work two jobs now."

Yup. Since she'd sold her bakery a couple years ago, which he still didn't understand. Every time he'd visited, customers had been lined up at the counter and poised to order boxes and boxes of doughnuts and pastries and cookies from her fleet of clerks, and she and her assistant had been working in the back, laughing and swaying to terrible, synth-heavy music from the eighties.

But since she'd said she was happy about the sale, he hadn't inquired further.

Tonight, he was going to find out what had happened. Because it was rapidly becoming clear she'd been a much better friend to him than he'd ever been to her, and that was going to stop right this fucking second, even if it made them both uncomfortable.

He told her the sum total of what he knew. "Last I heard, you worked part-time at the art supply store on Tidewater Avenue and a few hours a week for that custom art company."

"Yeah." Her voice was quiet. "Artify Yourself! I'm a customer service rep for them, and they let me work from home."

"Let me guess. Neither job offers health insurance for part-time workers." When she nodded, he decided to wade into deeper, choppier water. "And you couldn't afford to pay for your own insurance?"

At that, she sat up straight, her chin tilted high. "Actually, I could. I did, thanks to the ACA."

"Then what happened?"

"Mom..." Abruptly, she turned to look out the window. "I tried to keep her home as long as possible, but those last few months, she was in and out of the hospital so many times. And since I was the only kid left in Marysburg, I was the one to be there with her. I went anytime I wasn't working. Sometimes I slept in a chair by her bed for days on end."

Her mom had struggled with dementia for years by that point, and Elizabeth had seemed to handle the situation with her customary ease. She'd moved her mother into her home, set up the sunny basement suite as a virtual nursing facility, and hired nurses to care for her mom during work hours and when she needed to run errands or take a break.

Thinking about it now, that must have been fucking expensive. But somehow, his friend had still managed to smile whenever she saw him, to chat about his work and his pitiful attempts to jog and the movies they'd streamed recently.

Late last autumn, though, she'd essentially disappeared from his life for a few months, only to reemerge after her mother's funeral in January. She hadn't told him the reason for her absence, and he hadn't thought to ask. Fuck, why hadn't he thought to ask?

"Oh, God." In a rush, Elizabeth turned to him, her face frantic with apology and wet with tears. "I'm not complaining, James. I swear I'm not. She deserved all the time and love I could give her."

Jesus, she broke his heart. "I know you're not complaining."

He reached out his right hand and clasped hers again. It felt right, and she didn't move away. Instead, she gripped him tight. Tighter, as she continued her explanation.

"Late last year, I chose a new, cheaper plan through the ACA and set up autopay. Or at least I thought I did." Defeat and grief freighted her voice, turning it heavy and slow. "When Mom got pneumonia, things became disorganized at home, and I never confirmed anything. I just assumed the payments for this year were going through, but they weren't. And I wasn't opening my mail or checking my e-mail very often, so I didn't notice until it was too late."

Even during college, she'd been the responsible roommate. The one who'd ensured their landlord got his check on time. The one who'd researched the least cruel ways to evict the mice in their little pantry. The one who'd forced him and Viv to drink water when they partied and drank too much.

And she'd failed to notice her health insurance hadn't gone into effect?

Even before the mammogram, she'd obviously reached the limits of her endurance.

And he'd been nowhere to be found. Other than when they'd met for dinner and he'd accepted her offerings of food.

He was dirt.

So was her insurance company. "They kicked you off your plan?"

"Yes. And I'm not allowed to get a new one until the end of the year, during open enrollment." She gave a shaky laugh. "I was just hoping to ride out the year without any major health issues. But here we are."

"So you found the"—he swallowed hard—"lump and got a free mammogram. You must have been terrified."

Another too-loud laugh. "An understatement."

"And you went alone?"

She paused. "Yeah."

He'd known that. Somehow, he'd known that before even

237

asking the question. "Why didn't you ask me to come with you? Or one of your other friends? Why did you go by yourself?"

The thought of her scared and isolated gutted him, and he didn't understand the necessity for it. He knew she had a trusted, faithful circle of friends. Why hadn't she called them into service?

Most of all, why hadn't she called him?

And why did that omission sting so fucking badly?

She shifted in her seat. "Most of them have kids at home, or they work during the day. I didn't want to bother anyone."

He had to ask. He couldn't stop himself, much as he didn't want to make this—any of this—about him.

"What about me? You know I can set my own schedule most days, or at least take an hour off if I need one. And my kids are already out on their own, so I've got nothing but time."

"Most guys are uncomfortable with female stuff."

He slanted her a look.

She immediately caved. "Okay, okay. I know you're not like that. Viv always bragged about how you'd buy her tampons without an ounce of self-consciousness." Another look, and she squirmed again. "But...I guess I thought you'd..."

When she trailed off, he narrowed his eyes on the road. "I'd what?"

He'd be too busy? Or impatient? What?

Her tone was reluctant, but she said it. "You'd been through enough drama already. You'd spent enough time trying to help everyone around you. I didn't want to be one more burden."

Viv. This was about Viv.

And maybe Elizabeth wasn't entirely wrong about his current stance on drama. He avoided it whenever and however he could, which meant no contact with his ex. No

238

dating. No plans for another marriage. Nothing but work and occasional visits to the D.C. area so he could help his boys settle into their adult lives.

But there was drama, and there was need, and Elizabeth should know he could differentiate one from the other. "Helping a friend isn't an imposition. I would have come with you to the mammogram. Gladly. You're my friend, for God's sake."

"I asked you to come with me to the town hall." She offered the reminder like a gift, something to pacify his obvious discontent. "I didn't bother DMing anyone else."

He could feel his chest puff out a tad. God, he was pitiful.

"Because you knew I'd say yes?"

"That." With a faint rustle of clothing, she turned to him, and he could feel her gaze against the side of his face like the sun. "And you'd support me no matter what I said or did. You're a rock in times of trouble."

She knew about the failed rehab attempts near the end of his marriage. The way he'd tried to patch together his splintering relationship despite late-night phone calls from unfamiliar bars and police reports and texts from Viv's boss wondering where she was.

He wouldn't go back to any of that. But a few years of therapy had left him able and willing to handle everyday trouble. The grief and problems of normal life, not addicted life.

Pulling into his driveway, he hit the remote for the garage door. After positioning the truck inside the oversized berth, he turned off the engine.

Her fingers, now warm, were still laced through his.

"Then let me be your rock," he told her.

"What..." Her broad forehead creased. "What does that mean?"

She needed a financial buffer. His wasn't huge, not after divorce expenses and alimony and lingering rehab bills, but he had one, and he was more than happy to share it with his friend in distress.

She needed support through the biopsy process and—God forbid—any necessary follow-up treatment. He could provide that. He *wanted* to provide that.

And most urgently, she needed health insurance. He had that, and he could give it to her. Under one circumstance.

It was an extreme solution, out of character for them both. But how would he feel if he did nothing, and she suffered unnecessarily? If she—fuck, he didn't want to consider it, but he had to—

What if she died when he could have helped?

How would that feel?

Could he stand by and watch her waste away because he refused to act?

No. Shit, no.

The steady, warm light of her goodness wasn't getting extinguished on his watch. No fucking way.

"James?"

She was smiling uncertainly at him, despite her exhaustion and fear. Even under the harsh light of the garage door opener, her hair glowed like a halo. Her bloodshot blue eyes were deep and kind and so beautiful he almost wept.

And he finally understood.

That was why he hadn't insisted on getting answers from her before. Why he hadn't dug deeper and tried to get closer and discovered the heart of her.

First, he'd been with Viv. Then he'd needed to recover from the disastrous aftermath of his marriage. Either way, he'd chosen not to play with fire.

For him, Elizabeth was a flame.

If he'd insisted on answers, if he'd learned her inside and out, he'd known what would happen. On some level, he'd always known.

If he got too close, he'd care too much. She'd incinerate his marriage. She'd incinerate him.

But for the first time in almost three decades, he was ready to get burned.

He took a deep breath and met the gentle, confused eyes of his longtime friend.

"Elizabeth," he said, "will you marry me?"

FOUR

ELIZABETH ARGUED FOR HOURS. OH, HOW SHE argued.

Blinking away the prickle of tears—because how could she not cry at so much kindness?—she told him her circumstances didn't require such a gallant gesture. She told him she'd find another way to pay for her medical expenses. She told him he'd meet another woman he wanted to marry and regret either the illegality of bigamy or the hassle of divorce.

They stayed in that garage long enough for the overhead light to switch off. But even in the dark, she could see the very real distress in his eyes when he mentioned her biopsy, hear the certainty with which he told her he wouldn't be able to live with himself if he didn't help her this way.

So despite all her arguments, he didn't budge. Instead, he led them into the warmth of the kitchen, fiddled with something in his microwave, and upped the ante.

"The only logical path forward is for you to marry me." After handing her a steaming mug of way-too-expensive hot chocolate—her favorite brand, damn him—he leaned back against the counter. "And we might as well save some living expenses in the meantime. Why don't you move in?"

She promptly burned her tongue on the cocoa. *"What?"*

"We've been roommates before." He crossed his arms over his broad chest, completely calm. "I know we can live together comfortably."

She put down the mug and gaped at him. "We were *twenty*, James. I'm forty-seven now. Set in my ways."

"Maybe so, but I'm flexible," he said with a shrug.

That was a damned lie.

Still, he kept looking at her, a virtual wall of a man. Maybe he wasn't overly tall, but he was strong and built solid, with enough extra heft around the middle to make her feel sheltered in his presence. In her mind, he'd always taken up more space and oxygen than was justified by his size, just through sheer, quiet force of personality.

His appearance, its subtle handsomeness and flagrant maleness, didn't help either. Those navy-blue eyes were magnetic. Always had been, always would be. That thick, silver-touched russet hair, ruffled from the winter wind, made her want to smooth it with gentle fingers. And that new, post-divorce beard, the way it outlined his jaw and contoured his cheeks, only made looking away from him more difficult.

She knew that squinty, challenging expression, the way his thick brows drew together. She knew that low, measured tone. He wouldn't give up, on her or on his cockamamie plan.

He'd even pushed up the sleeves of his sweatshirt, a tell-tale sign he meant business.

And in the end, they both understood she didn't have a choice. Not really. Even though the prospect of a loveless marriage with James made her ache in ways she didn't care to consider further.

"Please, Elizabeth." His voice had turned coaxing, liquid and sweet as her cocoa. "Please marry me."

She took a long sip of that cocoa for fortitude before she surrendered.

"Okay." Another sip, and then she met that intent blue gaze, now flaring with victory. "Okay, James. I'll marry you."

He sagged against the counter and let out a slow breath, his arms finally uncrossing. Then he smiled at her, his cheeks creasing beneath that way-too-attractive beard, and despite her worry, she couldn't help smiling back.

The relief of the decision, however hard-fought, dizzied her.

She wasn't alone in her battles. Not anymore. Not as long as they were married.

Praise God, soon she'd have good health insurance. The moment her coverage became effective, she could get her lump biopsied and afford any necessary treatment. She could schedule her yearly skin exam at the dermatologist. Hell, she could see any doctor she needed to for any of a thousand reasons.

And James would be her husband. Hers. After almost thirty years.

But only for a brief stretch of time.

She didn't realize she was crying again until he brushed away her tears with gentle, careful sweeps of his thumbs. When he tugged her up from her seat and into his arms, she didn't resist.

Why did this one man always smell like home to her?

Why did his arms around her always feel like a fortress?

She pulled away after a few seconds to blow her nose and recover herself, but it was too late. The sudden, unexpected release of weeks of tension had weakened her, and so had that devastating smile of his and the safe clasp of his embrace.

She had no more resistance left. She was accepting the inevitable, much as it might hurt in the end.

So after only a few more minutes of discussion and

persuasion, she lowered her chin to the kitchen table and closed her eyes. "Fine. I'll move in with you."

"Good," he said, patting away the last wetness on her face with a soft cotton dishcloth.

Within seconds, he'd planned how they'd pack up any necessities from her house and transfer them to his before the wedding ceremony. Talked about using his truck and the help of his construction buddies. Worked out all the details with obvious satisfaction in that deep voice.

But before he could get too smug, she insisted on a few addenda.

"First, we need a prenup." She sat up straight. "Not to protect me. To protect you and reassure your kids. I'm not the rightful beneficiary of any of your possessions or money, and I want that clear to everyone involved."

That prenup might also provide her with a reminder, if she needed one, of the precise terms of their marriage. The document's strict bounds would confine her. Corral any wayward emotions.

He shook his head. "You won't take advantage of me, Elizabeth. Everyone knows that. And if they don't, they should."

"We're doing it," she told him. "Or else the deal is off."

Despite his narrow-eyed death stare, she didn't falter or flinch.

He sighed. "Fine. We'll get a prenup."

"Second, we need to make a list of all our expected household expenses and divvy them up fairly." Fishing in her purse, she located her phone. "Let's do that over pizza. I'm paying."

He took the cell from her hand and gave his own credit card number for the order, despite her protestations. A fitting start to the expense-allotment discussion, which—to her complete lack of surprise—didn't go smoothly either. Even Carmelo's truly excellent chicken parmesan pizza couldn't make the stubborn man across the table see reason.

"If you cook for us, we can consider that ample repayment for your portion of the utilities and all the other bills." James set aside his cleared plate and patted the gentle mound of his stomach. "We both know how much I love your food."

She glared at him as she removed the blueberry cheese-cake from his refrigerator. "No. Absolutely not. I'll pay an equal share."

But after a few more rounds of argument and a couple wedges of the cheesecake, she found herself agreeing to a compromise. She'd get a discount on the bills in exchange for cooking, largely because he told her, his mouth set in a mulish line, that he wouldn't eat her food otherwise. And that was unacceptable to her.

They tackled her third and final addendum over decaf coffee. By then, he'd stripped off his sweatshirt and was—rather distractingly—only wearing a worn, thin t-shirt and jeans that molded faithfully to his strong thighs.

It was unfair, to say the least.

"We need to discuss what we should do if we find ourselves interested in other people." She looked down at the sturdy blue mug in her hand, trying not to picture the situation. "While we're still married, I mean."

A long silence stretched between them, and he didn't say a word. Finally, she raised her gaze to him again.

For some reason, he looked...odd. Agitated, almost. Above his reddish-brown beard, his cheeks had flushed, and those crossed arms had tightened until she could see his biceps pulling at his tee.

She didn't understand. Was he embarrassed at the awkwardness of the question? Or was the thought of another romantic relationship *that* repugnant to him after the slow-motion train wreck of his marriage?

His blue eyes rested on her, sharp and intent. "Do you think it's likely you'll want to date another man?"

"Of course not." She waved a hand. "I don't have the energy for dating. And if I haven't found someone I loved enough to marry in forty-seven years, what's the likelihood I'm going to locate him this year?"

"You're marrying me," he pointed out, his shoulders dropping a fraction.

"That's different, and we both know it."

He made a kind of humming sound in response.

"But we should come up with a plan in case *you* meet someone." And God, why did that thought send a lightning bolt of pain through her chest?

He dismissed her statement with a shrug. "Nah. I'm good."

She didn't have the strength to argue more. Or maybe she didn't *want* to argue more, not about that. "Fine. Forget about it."

Then, to her shock, he added one final addendum of his own.

"We can divorce once you're eligible for individual insurance again." He reached out to clasp her hand, a gesture he seemed to make all the time now. As always, it felt warm and comforting in a way that discomfited her. "But we don't have to. I want that clear. As far as I'm concerned, we can stay married forever."

Why? Why would he make that offer?

She laughed through the ache and the longing. "I'm unfit for human company before I've had at least two cups of tea in the morning. When I cook or bake, I manage to dirty every dish, measuring cup, and utensil available. And I like to take nightly hour-long baths that use up all the hot water in the house. You don't want me as your permanent wife. Trust me."

He didn't laugh in response. "I do trust you. That's my point."

Oh, God. The sweetness of that stung.

"I don't see myself marrying anyone else, Elizabeth. Not soon, not ever. I also think we'd make a good team. And as far as your baths, my hot water heater has way more capacity than yours." He raised an eyebrow. "As you'll soon find out, there are benefits to marrying someone in the building trades. You don't have to give up those benefits if you don't want to. Again: not soon, not ever."

When she pursed her lips and looked down, he directed her eyes back to his with a gentle finger under her chin. "Just promise me you'll think about it. That's all I'm asking."

So in the end, she agreed to that too.

If tonight's discussion was a preview of their married life, she was pretty sure she'd never win an argument with James. Not a single one. Which should be a terrifying thought for someone who'd always prized her freedom, her ability to make whatever decisions she thought best.

And even through her haze of relief, she *was* unnerved.

Not because he might trample on her independence—but because marriage to him already felt like so much more than a convenience.

THE WEDDING SHOULD HAVE ENDED WITH A perfunctory embrace.

The courthouse judge, his face expectant and wreathed with a smile, had pronounced them husband and wife and invited James to kiss Elizabeth. It was the standard end to a standard civil ceremony. The judge didn't understand the situation, of course.

This wasn't a marriage born out of love, but necessity.

They'd planned it in less than a week and invited only a

few local friends and James's kids as witnesses. Other than the bouquet of lace-wrapped pink roses James had unexpectedly produced for her that morning, there were no flowers. No bridesmaids or groomsmen. She was wearing a knee-length cream dress purchased for her niece's christening twelve years before, while James's suit pulled a bit at his shoulders and middle. God only knew how long he'd owned it. The rings they'd just donned were thick and gold but completely generic, despite his repeated offers to find other options.

So at the end of the ceremony, she expected a peck on the cheek. Maybe even a brief buss on her lips, for the sake of anyone who might question the wisdom or validity of the marriage.

Instead, James cradled her face in his warm, rough hands with deliberate care. His thumb stroked her cheek in a gentle arc. And he lowered his mouth to hers as her brain fogged with the scent of sunshine and clean cotton. James's scent.

Then he was kissing her.

Not a peck. Not a buss. A kiss. A tender, exploratory greeting of a kiss.

His beard brushed against her cheeks as he courted every corner, every curve of her mouth. He took his time, and she responded without thinking to the dizzying pleasure of it.

When her mouth opened, the kiss transformed. Still slow, still careful. But no longer innocent or friendly, not with her knowledge of how he tasted and the hoarse rumble in his chest when his tongue met hers for the first time.

Her hands, which had come to rest against that broad barrel of a chest, curled in on themselves. So did her toes.

But somewhere inside, a brittle, hidden part of her unfurled like a fern under his touch. A part she'd deprived of oxygen and nourishment for almost three decades, shoving it deep when it threatened her friendships and her self-respect. Coiling it tight whenever she caught herself imagining things that didn't exist, possibilities that would never come to fruition.

You cause me bitterness and grief, and I reject both, she'd told it.

Over the last hellish couple of years, she'd forgotten it existed entirely.

Deep-rooted, though, it had apparently remained. Waiting. Dormant. Hopeful.

James's thick arm encircled her waist and hitched her against his body, and he was surrounding her with heat and strength. If she teetered, he'd keep her upright. If she wanted to hide, she could burrow her face into that delicious-smelling neck and trust he'd shield her. Her secrets. Her vulnerabilities.

Oh, the relief of it. Her eyes prickled, even as her limbs grew warm and languid.

Then he raised his head, arm still tight around her waist, and she dimly registered the hush of a half-dozen stunned wedding guests. All people who knew the situation. Who knew this wasn't a real marriage, blindingly sweet kiss notwithstanding.

No doubt they were wondering what exactly they'd just witnessed.

Funny. So was she.

FIVE

AFTER THE SMALL, POST-WEDDING GATHERING OF family and friends at James's house ended, Elizabeth headed directly for the master bathroom. Like the rest of the house, it wasn't huge, but it was impeccably maintained and impressively outfitted.

"Is it okay if I take a bath?" she called out, already halfway up the stairs.

He appeared at the lowest step a moment later, shaking his head. "Of course it's okay. This is your house too, Elizabeth. Take a million baths."

She didn't need a million. She just needed one, right this second.

She needed water so hot it would melt away her foolishness. She needed bubbles, reminders of how fleeting beauty could be. She needed a wet, warm washcloth over her eyes, simply because this was her damn wedding day. She deserved some pampering.

But most of all, she needed a few minutes alone to remember the circumstances of her wedding.

She hadn't married for love.

He hadn't either.

They'd agreed to wed for one reason and one reason only: so she could share his excellent healthcare benefits, get a biopsy the first of next month, and afford any necessary treatments thereafter. It didn't matter how sweetly and thoroughly he'd kissed her in front of the judge, or how firmly he'd held her hand as they chatted with his amiable sons, or how often he'd told her she looked lovely in her cream dress.

None of that changed anything.

An hour spent naked, wet, and on her back should get her head straight.

Although, now that she'd thought about it in those terms, maybe not.

Still, she filled the gorgeous soaking tub with steaming water and poured her foaming bath salts. Then she stripped, wiggled her toes against the warm tiles underfoot—James had seriously undersold the benefits of a husband in construction—and grabbed two fresh towels and a washcloth from the quartz-topped vanity.

Was that...was that a heated towel rack off to the side? Really?

Shit, she was never leaving this bathroom again. And since James had offered her the master suite, explaining that he found it too big for a man alone and had been living in the guest room since he'd moved in, she supposed she didn't really *have* to leave.

Marriage rocked.

A quick ponytail later, she slid beneath the bubbles with a sigh and positioned a rolled-up towel under her neck. After wetting the washcloth, she draped it over her eyes and waited for clarity.

And waited. And waited.

Instead, she remembered how she'd taken James aside at their gathering and told him she'd pull her weight. She'd make sure he didn't regret his decision. She'd never take advantage of him or burden him more than she already had.

He listened patiently, although he didn't appear overly concerned.

But when she told him he could divorce her whenever he wanted, for whatever reason he wanted, he rolled his eyes, then leaned down and kissed the tip of her nose.

"Stop worrying," he told her.

Then somehow, old-school Madonna began playing on his stereo system, which he'd mysteriously wired throughout the house. Another construction-husband perk, no doubt.

He swung her into his arms and pressed his cheek against hers while pre-English-accent Madge—Elizabeth's favorite version, which James clearly knew—sang about how crazy she was for her lover. How her heart raced at his nearness. How their bodies merged in the dark.

Elizabeth clung to James, unable to do anything else. And when the music faded, when the small crowd applauded and he loosened his hold, she'd cried again, and he'd tenderly wiped away those tears too.

She'd stared up at him through blurry eyes, speechless.

It was their wedding song. He'd given her a wedding song.

So how exactly was she supposed to keep her feet planted on solid earth? How was she supposed to stop herself from floating away like one of those bubbles, only to pop in a cold splatter at the first touch of reality?

This. This was why she'd never asked him for anything. Why she'd never let herself rely on him. Sure, she hadn't wanted to burden a man who already struggled under the weight of an addiction-ravaged marriage, two wonderful but needy kids, and the expenses attendant with all three. Sure, she was accustomed to dealing with her problems on her own.

But more than that, she'd known. If she ever let him closer, she'd fall.

And he'd been married for over twenty years.

With a hysterical half-giggle, half-sob, she remembered: He was now married again. This time to her. And given the circumstances, it was simultaneously the best and worst thing that had ever happened to her.

At a quiet knock on the bathroom door, she froze.

"Are you okay?" His voice was concerned. "It sounded like you were crying."

Oh, God, how embarrassing. He'd caught her laughing at herself like a loon.

"I'm fine!" she called back.

"Good." A pause. "I was also wondering what you wanted me to do with your friend Jenny's wedding gift. The painting. I can"—he must have turned away from the door, because his words became indecipherable for a moment—"while you're in the bath, if you'd like."

She sat up straight. "I'm sorry. What did you say?"

"I said I can take the painting and"—more indistinct mumbles—"if that's what you want."

This was ridiculous. She wasn't exactly a shy virgin, and they were both adults. Hell, they were *married* to each other. They didn't need to shout at one another through a door.

Her layer of bubbles was still thick and opaque, and she had a handy towel nearby for emergency coverage. Good enough.

"Let's make this easier on both of us, James." She slid back down and rested her head against the towel. "Why don't you come in, and we'll talk?"

Another, longer pause. "Are you sure?"

"If I weren't, I wouldn't have offered."

The door cracked open an inch. "If you're certain, there are a few toiletries I should move to the other bathroom too."

"Be my guest." She snorted. "Or be the homeowner, I suppose. I mean, this is your house."

"*Our* house."

The door opened all the way, and he entered the bathroom, his eyes averted from the tub. And if she wasn't mistaken—

"Are you holding a plate of petits fours? In a bathroom?"

He chewed a bit, and then swallowed audibly. "I make no apologies. I didn't know you'd invite me inside. And you made them, so they're delicious, just like all the other snacks and sweets you cooked for the party. I wanted to eat them while they were fresh."

No wonder she hadn't been able to understand him through the door. He'd probably been chewing then too.

He set his plate down on the smooth, speckled vanity countertop and selected another petit four. Holding it carefully between his thumb and forefinger, he studied the poured fondant glaze and the sugared rose petal on top. The swirls piped along the sides with such care.

All shiny white and sparkling pink. All more wedding-cake-like than she'd intended.

He nodded his head a little, seemingly to himself.

When he spoke again, his voice was low and soft. "Do you want one?"

His eyes met hers in the half-fogged mirror, and suddenly, even though she didn't slip an inch, she was drowning. She nodded too, and he slowly walked toward her. Slowly knelt on the thick mat by the bath and offered the petit four to her.

When she took it from him, their fingers brushed. She shivered, and his eyes narrowed.

"Are you cold? Do you want me to run more hot water?"

She was plenty hot. For the first time in years, maybe.

"I'm..." She swallowed. "I'm good. Thank you for the snack."

She popped the petit four into her mouth, not knowing what else to do. The moist loft of the vanilla sponge, the welcome tartness of lemon curd against sweet raspberry jam, made her smile in pride. Made her close her eyes in pleasure.

After two years away from her bakery, she still knew her shit.

When she opened her eyes again, the heat from the bath had coaxed a flush along James's cheekbones.

He cleared his throat. "Another?"

"No, thank you. I'm still full from everything I ate earlier." A huge bubble was clinging to the side of the tub, just on the water line, and she lifted a toe to pop it. "Didn't you say something about the painting Jenny gave me?"

He blinked, hard. "Uh, yeah. I was wondering if you wanted me to hang it in your bedroom. I can do that while you're bathing, if you'd like."

"Oh, what a lovely idea." She smiled at him, delighted by the thought. "She shouldn't have given it to me, not considering the prices she gets for her originals these days, but I've always adored that painting. I'm so glad to have it." She scrunched her nose. "Does that make me vain?"

He rested his elbows on the edge of the tub. "Because you love a gorgeous, colorful portrait created by a good friend? One where you're painting your toenails and looking happy? Why would that make you vain?"

"Well, it's sort of like admiring myself, right?" Flicking a bubble with her finger, she considered the matter. "But I think what I love most about it is remembering how much fun we had while she painted me. I can't even tell you how many layers of polish I went through. It took me buckets of acetone to get it all off between sessions."

"You're not wearing polish on your toes now."

Startled, she glanced down at the end of the tub and saw that her feet were visible through the thinning layer of bubbles. But her important bits were still covered by a thick foam, so she relaxed back into the water.

"I used to get pedicures before Mom got really sick." At a local spa, where they soaked your feet in water strewn with flower petals. "When I couldn't afford that anymore, I'd take a couple hours and set up a sort of home spa and paint my own toenails." Her smile faded. "Then I ran out of time and energy."

When she immersed her hand in the water, her arm brushed against the side of her breast, and she remembered everything. Her parents, both gone now. Her bakery, sold. Her house, in which she had almost zero equity because of the burst housing bubble years ago. Her mammogram, concerning enough that the radiologist had contacted her within hours. Her marriage, proposed in the name of convenience and kindness instead of love.

The bath water had cooled while she'd been talking to James.

She was cold again.

With an effort, she tried to smile at him. "Why don't you grab your toiletries, and I'll see you in a few minutes? We can fill out the last bits of paperwork and call the insurance company. I want to make certain I'll be covered the first of next month, in time for my biopsy."

His brows had drawn together. "Are you okay?"

"Fine. Just getting pruney," she said, and shooed him out of the bathroom.

Later, they hung her painting. They finished the paperwork. They called the insurance company. They argued about whether he should just pay for the damn biopsy—his words—and get it done tomorrow, instead of next month. It was one of the rare arguments he lost.

After an awkward farewell and brief hug, they retreated to separate bedrooms for their first night as a married couple.

All the while, she attempted to make sure any lingering bubbles of foolishness were well and truly popped. But try as she might, they seemed to keep appearing faster than she could vanquish them.

By THE NIGHT BEFORE HER BIOPSY, SHE AND JAMES had fallen into a comfortable—if occasionally worrisome —routine.

At dawn, he headed out on jobs while she worked at home for Artify Yourself! After lunch, she reported to Bradshaw's Art Supply for her afternoon shift. Since he left work earlier than she did, he picked up any groceries she'd listed on the notepad by the refrigerator. They usually arrived home around the same time, and then he poured her a glass of wine, grabbed a can of soda for himself, and kept her company while she cooked.

He did the dishes while she took care of bills or watched the Food Network.

Then he joined her on the couch, and her favorite part of the evening began. The scariest part. The part where he sat next to her, put an arm around her shoulders, and cuddled her close.

At first, she'd resisted leaning on him. But gradually, she'd started giving him more of her weight. She'd started resting her head against his chest, where she could hear the steady thump-thump of his huge, generous heart. She'd started slinging one leg over his, and in turn, he'd started resting his cheek against the top of her head and encircling her with both arms.

Oh, it was glorious.

She'd never enjoyed cuddling with other men, not as much as they had. But with James, she wanted to crawl inside him and never emerge.

Especially tonight.

Especially given what would happen in the morning. What she'd find out soon thereafter.

But she needed to stay strong, so she didn't lean on him. She sat on the armchair instead of the couch after dinner and held her hands very tightly in her lap. So tightly they were vibrating. She was vibrating.

Maybe Bobby Flay was beating someone in a competition involving a secret ingredient or a signature dish. Maybe not. She had no idea, even though her eyes never left the television screen. Between her fears and the proximity of James, her brain didn't have room for anything else.

When he finished with the dishes, he strode toward the couch, then came to an abrupt halt. She turned her head to look at him, and he studied her for a moment, his face gentle.

"I picked up something special on the way home today." He nodded toward a canvas bag he'd deposited near the front door. "Want to see?"

She didn't, but she nodded anyway. "Sure."

He brought the bag to her, laid it in her lap, and perched on the arm of her chair.

With trembling fingers, she opened the ridiculously heavy sack and found a rainbow.

Dozens of bottles of nail polish, from electric blue and black to pearly white. Reds and oranges and too many shades of pink to count. And beneath them—

"The lady at the counter said you needed those weird wooden sticks and emery boards. And some polish remover and things to spread apart your toes, although they look like they'd be incredibly uncomfortable to use." He leaned over to eye them suspiciously. "I assume you already have toenail clippers, but if you want new ones, I got those too."

This was beyond sweet. Beyond caring. But she just didn't have the energy tonight, and oh, God, he was going to be so disappointed.

"You..." She looked up at him. "You want me to paint my toenails? Because I'm not sure I—"

"No." Plucking the bag from her lap, he poured its contents over the coffee table with a clatter. "I don't want you to paint your toenails. *I'll* paint your toenails. Badly." He paused. "Sorry about that. I'll try not to injure you in any permanent way, although I make no promises when it comes to those pointy sticks."

She started laughing helplessly, and then at some point the laughter turned into sobs, and she was in his arms again. Finally.

SIX

After she finished crying and James finished painting her toenails—a kind term for the toddler's finger-painting project he inflicted on her cute, chubby feet—they cuddled on the couch again and talked. For hours.

"Are your kids okay with us marrying?"

She sounded worried, and he could understand why. He should have reassured her days ago, but they'd been settling into their new routine, and he'd wanted to make her life in this home, as his wife, as easy and relaxing as possible. So he hadn't mentioned biopsies or families or money or anything stressful.

But maybe she needed to talk about all those things. Maybe they both did.

If so, he was more than willing.

"My boys are fine with it." The simple truth. "They've always liked you, and they want me to be happy, whatever form that might take."

For all Viv's struggles, she'd managed to shield their sons from the worst of her alcoholism. She'd sometimes gone years sober, especially when the kids were young. And even during relapses, her heaviest drinking had been reserved for late nights or so-called business trips, at least until the boys had both left for college. So they were as well-adjusted as could be expected, especially after years of family and individual therapy.

They were good kids, and they loved him. They'd supported the marriage.

Elizabeth raised her head from his chest. "But they know the truth, right? They know why you asked me to marry you?"

He smoothed her silky, pale hair back from her forehead. "They know exactly why I married you."

Another simple truth, although maybe not as simple as Elizabeth believed.

She collapsed back down onto his chest, her soft warmth a welcome weight. "Good."

"They're happy for us. But let me be clear about something." He ducked his head until their noses almost touched. "I neither asked for nor needed their permission. My marriage to you is the business of only two people, and we're both here on this couch."

"Okay." She blinked up at him, and he wanted to kiss her. The need ached in his joints and throbbed with every beat of his heart.

But he held off, because he also wanted to prolong this moment. All of it—the embrace, the conversation—was intimate. As intimate as lovemaking, maybe, for a woman as intensely private and self-contained as Elizabeth.

Her seeming openness was a façade. He knew that now.

"I was wondering..." He sent up a silent prayer that the question wouldn't offend her. "Why didn't you ever marry? Before me, I mean?"

The instant rush of pride every time he thought about their marriage was probably foolish, given why she'd agreed to his proposal. But he couldn't help it. She was beautiful, smart, talented, kind, and married to *him*. James Magnusson.

A man of average height and average income, with an unused degree in American literature and an ever-growing belly.

A man who was pretty sure he loved the woman he'd married.

No, that didn't quite capture it. He'd loved her for almost thirty years, without question. As a roommate, a friend, and a person he admired. But now he was falling *in* love with her.

So he needed to make sure they stayed married. But he was working on that, day by day. Taking down her walls and learning her, piece by piece.

Her voice was quiet when she answered his question. "My parents got divorced when I was ten, and it was..." She sighed. "It was hard on all of us, especially when Dad moved away. I kind of had to take care of my sisters and brother for a while. And at some point, I promised myself I wouldn't get married unless I was sure, totally sure, I'd never get divorced, because I didn't want to experience that sort of rupture ever again."

"And you were never sure?"

Because she'd had serious boyfriends over the years, some of them clearly in love with her. Guys with sharp clothes and office jobs and vacation homes. Ones who'd sat pressed up against her in restaurant booths and played with her fingers over dessert. And though he'd been married for most of those boyfriends, he couldn't say he'd enjoyed watching them with her.

"No. I was never sure. So I stayed single." She gave a laugh that didn't sound amused. "And now I'm in a marriage with an expiration date. Kind of ironic, huh?"

No. He wasn't letting that stand. "It doesn't have an expiration date. Not if you don't want it to."

She bit her lip for a moment. "Before we got married, you never asked me about my finances. About why I didn't have any money. Weren't you concerned I was a spendthrift or a compulsive shopper or an online gambler?"

"Once I took the time to think about it, I was pretty sure I understood the situation." He pressed a kiss on her furrowed forehead, because he was only human. "In-home nursing for an elderly woman with advanced dementia couldn't have been cheap."

"Mom..." She took a shuddering breath. "Her grandmother spent years in a nursing home. The conditions there were apparently terrible. Horrifying, actually. And as Mom got older and more confused, she would get hysterical at the thought of going to one. She'd sob and scream and promise to—" When Elizabeth's breath hitched again, he ran a soothing hand down her back. "She'd promise to kill herself if we tried to take her to a group home."

Another stroke of her back, and her breathing evened.

"But once the dementia got worse, it wasn't safe for her to be in her house anymore. Too many steps. Too much risk of falling or fire. And all my siblings are across the country."

"So you took her in and paid for nursing care during working hours."

She nodded, her hair bunching against his chest. "I made a good living at the bakery. But not good enough for that. Not after a year or so. So..." A long, painful pause. "I sold the bakery and used the money to keep Mom home."

The agony of the decision carved deep lines beside her mouth, and everything about this fucking situation, especially how he'd left her swinging alone in the cold breeze for so long, gutted him.

"What about your siblings? Couldn't they contribute too?"

"They didn't have the resources I did, but they gave what they could."

He tried to remember the date of the funeral. "She passed away...two months ago?"

At that, her back began heaving with her renewed sobs, and he wanted to sew his own mouth shut. Why had he

264

pushed her this way the night before her fucking
Christ's sake?

"I'm sorry." He hugged her tighter, waiting for the
of grief to pass. "I shouldn't have asked. It was such a si
time ago, and it must still hurt so—"

She lifted her head, her lips puffy with tears. "No, James.
That's the worst part. It *didn't* hurt. Not really." She
hiccupped. Then, fisting her hands in his sweatshirt, she met
his eyes. "When she died, I was...relieved. So relieved. I
know that sounds monstrous, but I had no more money. I
was out of options. And I loved her no matter what, but she
deserved some peace, and I felt like I'd already lost my mom
years ago."

"No, honey, it doesn't sound monstrous." He rubbed her
back. "It sounds human."

More sobs, and no wonder. Between her guilt and worry
and grief, he could hardly believe she'd still been functioning
at all.

He held her for a long time after that. But just when he
thought she'd fallen asleep, exhausted from her tears, her
quiet voice drifted from his chest.

"Let's talk about you." She sounded hoarse but calm. "Do
you like your work? Is it something you want to keep doing
until retirement?"

"Yeah." Reaching behind himself, he grabbed the fleece
blanket draped over the back of the couch. Carefully, he
covered them both, making sure to tuck the edges around her
feet on the ottoman. "At some point in the next few years,
though, I'll probably want to go out on my own. Get my own
crew and work for myself."

She stiffened against him. "I'm delaying you. If you didn't
need to keep your current insurance—"

"I'm in no hurry. Like I just said, I enjoy my job. And I'd
be a fool to open my own business without doing plenty of
research and planning first."

Maybe he'd thought about pulling the trigger next spring, but that could wait. Elizabeth was his priority, now and—if he had his way—forever.

Her frame hadn't relaxed. "If you want to do it this year, I'll figure out something."

For a woman who'd sacrificed her savings, her business, and years of her life for her mom, she certainly had trouble accepting minor sacrifices made on *her* behalf.

And they were through with this topic. He wanted her lax and warm against him once more.

"I'm not changing anything until I'm sure you're taken care of." When she started to say something, he shushed her. "That's not negotiable, so don't waste your breath arguing."

"Stubborn son of a gun," she muttered, her words muffled by his sweatshirt.

"Which I guess would make you a stubborn daughter of a gun." He snorted. "Weird how that particular idiom never took hold."

Her smile warmed her voice. "It never took hold because, compared to men, most women are fonts of sweet reason. Also, it doesn't rhyme."

"Good points." He considered the matter. "Glad we're putting our lit degrees to good use at long last."

She made a sort of sleepy hum.

He should let her rest. But he had one more question, and he wanted to ask it while her defenses were still down.

Lowering his head, he whispered softly into her ear. "Speaking of stubborn, why were you feeding me all this time when you barely had enough time or money to feed yourself?"

Her words were barely audible. "Because someone needed to care for you."

He swallowed. Hard.

In mere days, she'd burrowed so deep in his heart, she'd destroy it if she left him. Either voluntarily or...not.

266

For the millionth time since that town hall, he sent up a prayer that her biopsy would be fine. She'd be fine. They'd navigate their new marriage without the specter of cancer haunting their every breath.

"I appreciate that, honey." Gently, he removed the elastic from her hair. There, that should be more comfortable for her. "But who cares for you?"

She didn't answer. So he closed his own eyes, disregarded what a night on the couch would do to his poor back, and followed her into sleep.

The Marysburg General Hospital Breast Health Center let James accompany Elizabeth into the inner waiting room. Which was convenient, since he wasn't sure he could have let go of her hand if a hospital employee had tried to separate them.

Together, they trudged through all the usual hoops. Registration for Elizabeth's core needle biopsy. Reading and signing the informed consent document, which was—like all its brethren, in his experience—pretty horrifying.

That document confirmed the basics of what the radiologist would do to his wife. Guided by an ultrasound, the doctor would use a hollow needle to remove several tissue samples from the lump, and a pathologist would analyze those samples. Elizabeth should get the results within two to five business days.

Such dry language for such a fraught, terrifying process.

With each form, each explanation, Elizabeth's fingers turned more icy. He chafed them, wishing to God he could do all this for her. Take the worry, take the needle, take the agonizing wait for answers, and leave her calm and content.

But he couldn't. She had to go through this process, but she didn't have to do it alone.

As far as he was concerned, she didn't have to do anything alone. Not anymore. Not if she didn't want to.

And he made sure she knew it. "Do you want me in the room with you during the biopsy? The form said it's okay if I come. But if you'd prefer that I wait out here instead, that's fine too."

He'd honor her wishes. Even if the thought of her going through the procedure alone made him want to howl.

"I want you with me." No hesitation, and those deep-set blue eyes were beseeching. "Please, James."

God, she wrung his heart to pieces sometimes.

He pressed a kiss against her furrowed brow. "You don't need to say please, honey. If you want me, of course I'll be there."

The next few minutes were a blur of exchanging her sweater and bra for a gown, getting her vitals taken, and walking to the ultrasound room. And then she was lying on her back on the bed, naked from the waist up, and for the first time in his life, he wasn't even tempted to look at a beautiful woman's bare breasts.

Instead, he maintained eye contact with a pale, trembling Elizabeth. Smiled at her as the ultrasound tech located the lump, marked it with a pen, and cleansed the area. Held her cold hand when the tech covered the surrounding bare skin with sterile drapes and then retreated to the ultrasound machine.

"I want you to look," Elizabeth suddenly told him.

His heart seized. "I don't know whether—"

"I'll want to know what happened, but I can't watch. I need you to do it for me." Her voice wavered. "Please, James."

"Okay." He squeezed her hand and steeled himself. "Okay."

The radiologist glanced up from where she was spreading some sort of clear gel over the uncovered part of Elizabeth's breast. "I'll also describe what I'm doing, which might help. Unless you'd prefer I didn't."

"Please do." Elizabeth nodded. "I want to know."

So they listened and he watched as the radiologist located the lump with the ultrasound, numbed the area with shots of local anesthesia—a process that looked remarkably violent for something meant to help ease pain—and waited for the medication to take effect.

When the doctor made a small incision and inserted the biopsy needle, he wanted to look away, but he didn't. His wife needed him, and he wouldn't fail her.

The radiologist seemed perfectly calm. "Clicking sound in three, two, one..."

Elizabeth still flinched, and so did he. On the ultrasound screen, beside the tech's head, he could see that damn needle grab the sample, and then the radiologist transferred the scrap of flesh to a bottle of clear liquid.

He had to clear his throat a couple times. "How...how bad was that?"

"Not bad at all," Elizabeth said, and it sounded like the truth. "The anesthesia felt like a bee sting, but this is just tugging and pressure, not pain."

Three more samples. Four. Five.

Then the radiologist looked up again. "I'm about to insert that titanium clip you heard about. It'll help mark the spot for future mammograms or if you need surgery."

After the clip's insertion and a few minutes of pressure on the area, they were almost done.

"One more mammogram to document the location of the clip, and then we'll bandage you. No stitches necessary." The doctor smiled at Elizabeth. "You did great."

He helped Elizabeth sit up, and after the mammogram and bandaging, a young nurse produced a list of post-procedure instructions and handed it to him.

She held up a blue square, making eye contact with Elizabeth. "First of all, you'll want to put this cold pack inside your bra right away. It'll help with the tenderness and bruising." Passing him the pack, she continued running down the list of instructions, her voice gentle. "Please keep the bandage in place for forty-eight hours. No strenuous activity for the first twenty-four. We suggest wearing a soft, supportive bra and continuing to use cold packs as needed. Acetaminophen for pain relief. No aspirin or ibuprofen for a couple of days."

She turned to him. "The paper I gave you lists a number to call if you have questions or concerns. If anything seems odd or worrisome, just use it. We're here to help. And we'll contact you later today and tomorrow no matter what, just to be sure the recovery is going well. Within two to five business days, you should have the results from the pathologist." She paused. "Questions?"

"I think we're good." Elizabeth stood. "Thank you."

When the nurse was gone, Elizabeth headed for the dressing booths. He halted next to the curtain, expecting her to drop his hand at that point, but she didn't. Instead, she pulled him inside. So he helped her put on her bra and tuck the cold pack inside. Tugged the sweater carefully over her head, attempting not to jar her.

Then they were in the parking lot and headed home. The procedure itself had taken thirty minutes, tops, but the various steps before and after had eaten up over two hours.

"I don't know why I'm so tired." She sagged against the back of her seat, her eyelids heavy. "I did nothing but lie there."

He knew why. "Just sleep, honey. We'll be home soon."

At the stop sign marking the exit from the hospital onto the county road, he brought the car to a gentle halt. Then he took another quick glance over at his wife.

Already asleep. Good. He smoothed her pale hair back

from her peaceful face before checking both directions for traffic.

"You," she said quietly.

Not asleep, then. Did she need pain medication?

He pulled out slowly. "Me what?"

Her eyes were still closed. "Last night, you asked who cared for me."

He couldn't respond, not with his throat so thick.

"You." She reached for him with a seeking hand, and he laced their fingers together. "You care for me."

SEVEN

THREE DAYS LATER, ELIZABETH TURNED OFF THEIR cells and woke James with a kiss.

Not their first, which had happened at their wedding. Not even their second or third.

Since the biopsy, they'd taken to sleeping cuddled together on the master bedroom's king-sized bed. And before they drifted off each night, he would cradle her face in his hands and kiss her. Claim her mouth like a man who knew exactly what he could do with his. Settle her comfortably against him and tunnel his strong fingers through her hair and tangle their tongues until she was breathless and aching somewhere other than her breast.

He kissed her with gentle but unmistakable expertise. With lust.

Then he tucked the covers around them, nuzzled his bristly cheek against hers, and rumbled a quick good night, as if she were supposed to sleep after that. As if *anyone* could sleep after that.

To be fair, she did sleep after that. Quite well.

But it was still annoying. She wanted more, and she planned to show him so right now.

The morning sun streamed through tiny gaps in the blinds and struck fire in his russet beard. In sleep, the lines beside his eyes were barely visible, and he almost looked twenty again.

But he wasn't. She wasn't. And she was glad for it.

She leaned down and pressed a kiss on his lips, and even in sleep, his mouth clung to hers. But when he blinked those gorgeous blue eyes open and saw her, he bolted upright, almost head-butting her. She sprang back in a hurry, and he steadied her with a hand wrapped around her upper arm.

"Shit." He rubbed his eyes with his free hand. "Sorry about that."

So much for seduction. "It's okay. I didn't mean to scare you."

"You didn't scare me, honey. It's just that I was all, um..." A faint flush crept over his cheeks. "I was all happy about the kiss when I woke up, and then I remembered morning breath. Give me a minute."

He was *still* happy about the kiss, from what the tented sheet was telling her.

"Fine." She'd already made her morning bathroom stop, and she supposed it was unfair to deny him his. "But hurry."

His eyes suddenly didn't look so sleepy anymore. Instead, they were wide and alert. "Really?"

She patted the bed beside her. "Yeah."

He hurried. But when he emerged from the bathroom a minute later, he didn't leap back into bed. Instead, he halted in the doorway, his mouth pressed tight. Not the expression of a man about to get some with a wife he adored.

Did he have doubts? Did he not want her after all?

Had she misunderstood everything?

"Honey, you can wipe that look off your face." With a sigh, he cast his eyes downward. "One glance at my pajama bottoms will tell you what you need to know."

Oh. Good point.

"But your breast…" He shook his head. "It's still bruised and tender. I don't want it to, um…"

When he paused, clearly searching for the right words, she had to laugh. "Rhythmically jiggle up and down?"

"That's it." He paused. "Although maybe I misinterpreted your little pat on the bed, and you don't actually want to make love. Am I assuming too much here?"

"No. You're not." Still, that didn't solve their problem. Because he was right: Bouncing boobs didn't sound particularly comfortable at the moment. "I think we can make it work. Maybe I can wear my bra?"

He closed his eyes and let out a slow breath. "The first time I'm inside you, I want us both naked and sweaty and completely unconcerned about anything but how hard and often I can make you come."

Ooooh. That gave her a nice little tingle.

The situation sucked, though.

"So no making love today?" She frowned at him. "I won't lie to you. That's a grave disappointment, James. You've been teasing me with your stealth sex-bomb kisses for days now."

He blinked at her for a moment, and then his lips curved into the widest, most wicked grin she'd ever seen on his handsome face. "You like my mouth, huh?"

She rolled her eyes. "Of course I like your mouth. You clearly took some sort of seminar while I was writing my senior thesis about Melville's weird whale-penis chapter in *Moby Dick*."

"No seminar. Just enthusiasm." His blue eyes glinted in the morning sun. "And speaking of my mouth and my enthusiasm, why don't you lie back nice and slowly?"

She should insist on taking care of him first, given how attentive he'd been since the procedure. How sweetly he tried to distract her when she started worrying. How gently he held her when the cell rang and she could barely speak, could barely hold it in her shaking hand until she glanced at the display and saw it was a friend or her sister. Not the pathologist or Dr. Sterling. Not the news that would free her or signal more struggles ahead.

She was still waiting for that call. But she wasn't waiting any longer for the man she loved. The man she'd married. The man who was walking toward their bed with a definite swagger.

So yes, maybe she should take care of him first. But he seemed content to hold out a little longer, and she was too weak to deny herself that mouth.

He was atop the bed now, his eyes hot and expectant on her.

Before she lay back, she stripped off her simple cotton nightgown and tossed it to the floor. No panties. No bandages. Just her, warm and naked for her husband's eyes.

Propping himself on one elbow, he smoothed a gentle hand down her left side, from shoulder to knee. "I want to create a dictionary of you." He paused, then shook his head. "No, an encyclopedia. One with entries delineating your history." A careful kiss beside her bruised breast. "Your dreams." Another brush of his lips against her temple. "Your preferences."

He cupped her left breast and circled her nipple with a light stroke of his rough thumb.

"Important names." His mouth covered hers, and they kissed until she was squirming beneath him, arching into his hand. "Crucial dates."

He moved to kneel between her thighs, and then opened her with a slow, deliberate stroke of his thumbs.

The cool air of the morning dueled with his warmth against her secret flesh, and she shivered at the feel of both. She stared up at him, but for once he didn't meet her eyes.

He was gazing at her body, rapt, a haze of heat painted across his cheekbones.

"Your topography." He removed his hands from her

center, sliding them down her inner thighs, and they trembled under his touch. "Every dip."

He gently lifted and spread her knees, his fingers hot on the sensitive hollows behind them. Then he lowered himself until his mouth was an inch from where she ached.

"Every furrow." He licked her then, along labia separated by his careful fingers, and then his tongue flicked lower. "Every river."

He must have taken a thousand seminars. A million.

"Every rise." A slow, languid circle of her clitoris. "Every bit of you, mapped and known."

He sucked her lightly, and she almost came out of her skin.

When she jerked at the bolt of pleasure, though, he lifted his head. "Honey, you have to stay still, or we can't do this. I won't hurt you."

God help them both, he wasn't joking. He was willing to end this, and she wanted to cry.

"I'm not sure I can." She raised herself on her elbows. "Please, James—"

"You don't have to say please, and you don't have to worry. I'll help." He glided a hand up her belly, where it rested heavy and warm. A reminder to stay still. "Hold onto the headboard, Elizabeth."

So she laid back down and held on, frantic but still as he licked and circled with that talented tongue and drew her between those soft lips. His beard abraded her skin, an inciting friction she'd never known to want before now.

The slow penetration of his fingers pressing deep inside. Another tender suck and flick of her clitoris. The weight of his hand, steady and warm. Holding her down, holding her together.

She burst with a sob, her body clenching around his fingers as she arched a bare inch toward his mouth, and he allowed it. Allowed her to grind against him as she came like a cataclysm. Soothed her with light strokes of his tongue all the while, a deep hum in his chest comforting her as she shattered and reformed stronger. Less brittle.

The words broke free, and she didn't bite them back. "I love you. I love you, James."

One last tender nuzzle, and he lifted his head.

"You're my world, Elizabeth Stone." His navy-blue eyes blazed with heat and light. "I love you too."

Someone had called her cell while they were otherwise occupied.

A quick check of the display, and she knew her moment of reckoning had arrived.

"Dr. Sterling left a message." She held up the phone when James emerged from the bathroom, and her hand was steady. "I haven't listened to it yet."

He was at her side in a heartbeat, wrapped around her, his arms thick and strong and so warm she couldn't imagine ever being cold again.

"We can listen together." He edged back enough to catch her eye. "But first, I want to say something, and it has to be now."

She blinked up at him. "Okay."

"Marry me."

She couldn't help it. Even in the midst of real, gut-clenching fear, even with James essentially vibrating with protectiveness and intensity beside her, she had to laugh.

A semi-hysterical laugh, but a real one. "Pretty sure we already did that, baby. Don't you remember? It was like ten days ago? I had a bouquet and you ate three plates of petits fours?"

"I remember." His intensity hadn't diminished. "But that's not what I mean."

She licked lips turned suddenly dry. "What *do* you mean?"

"We had a wedding, but I didn't ask you to commit to a real marriage, because that wasn't the point. Not then. Not for you." He stroked her cheekbone with a sweep of his thumb. "But I don't want to be your husband for a year or two, Elizabeth."

That fragile thing inside her, buried and dormant for so long, unfurled further. Reached for light and oxygen and nourishment, with complete faith all three were there, waiting for her.

The first tear spilled down her cheek. "You don't?"

"No matter what that phone message says, I want to stay by your side. Not only as your friend and lover. As your husband. Not until you can get your own health insurance, but forever." He took a shuddering breath. "That's what I want, and I hope that's what you want too. So please, Elizabeth. Marry me."

She wanted to agree. To fall into his arms and weep with joy, and then tackle whatever future awaited them together. But she had to know one thing first.

"Baby..." She cradled his bristly cheek in her palm. "You're a natural-born fixer and caretaker. Are you sure you don't just want a new project?"

He leaned his forehead against hers. "I don't want to fix you. You're perfect as you are."

Why couldn't she stop crying?

"I just want to love you." He smiled at her, sure and patient. "That's all."

She pressed her lips against his. Once. Twice.

"Marry me." He spoke the words against her mouth. "Be with me forever."

She sniffled and smiled and said yes. Again.

And then they listened to the message together, hand in hand.

EPILOGUE

James arrived home to find his wife in the master bathroom, buried under a mound of bubbles, a washcloth draped over her beloved face. A sight he'd seen almost daily for years now, but which never failed to both amuse and arouse him.

He set his offering down on the vanity and perched on the edge of the tub. "Honey, how long have you been in here?"

She peeled back a corner of the cloth to peer at him. "I don't know. Possibly hours."

"Tough day at work?" He trailed his fingers in the hot water. "Do you need a little pick-me-up?"

Around the holidays, she toiled for endless hours in the back room of her bakery, cranking out an astounding number of pies, decorated cookies, and other delicious seasonal treats on a daily basis. She started her days early and ended them tired, and he always worried about her at this time of year. But winter was his own business's slow season, so he helped out however he could.

Like now, for instance.

The bubbles near her hip were thinning, he noted with approval. He helped them along with a few swirls of the water, and suddenly he could see Paris, he could see France, he could see his wife's total lack of underp—

"A *pick-me-up*, huh?" She removed the washcloth from her face, tossed it onto the bath mat, and eyed his busy fingers in the water. "If I'm interpreting that phrase correctly, consider me completely on board with your plan."

Then she glanced at the counter, and her eyes widened. "But first, is that...uh..."

"A cake?" He turned his head to contemplate the monstrosity. "In theory. I baked it yesterday and hid it in my workshop until today."

"You made me a cake?" Now she was squinting at him, her head tilted. "You realize I own an actual bakery, right?"

He shrugged. "You're busy. And I wanted to do something special for you today."

A wicked grin curved her wide mouth. "Move your hand about six inches to the right."

"Something *else* special." He got up and brought the cake closer to her. "Something involving exploding eggs and melted icing and a call from the fire department."

"Baby, you're all the sweetness I need." She wasn't even looking at the misshapen mound on the plate anymore. Instead, she was gazing at him, her blue eyes soft. "But thank you for making the cake."

"You're welcome." Keeping the plate carefully level, he leaned forward to drop a kiss on her mouth. "I love you."

She smiled up at him. "I love you too. That said, I'm not sure what's so special about tod—"

She sat up with a jerk. The water splashed over the edge of the tub, then settled to just below her breast. He was only human, so he took a moment to admire the view.

Her smile transformed into a pleased laugh. "Eight years! Today makes eight years!"

She'd finally deciphered what he'd drawn on the cake with two shaky loops of the premade icing. In her defense, it did look more like the outline of a mangy owl than a number, so a certain amount of confusion was understandable.

"Yup. It's your anniversary." It was also a long, promising time to remain cancer-free, although he hoped the number of years would eventually stretch into infinity. "Congratulations, honey."

He put the cake on the counter. Bending down, he kissed the scar from her mastectomy, the smooth curve of her shoulder, and her temple, where her hair swept back into its ever-present ponytail.

That distinctive hair glowed pale in the light of the setting sun, framing her pretty face like a nimbus. Not blond anymore, not since it grew back after chemo. Silver.

Just as beautiful as blond. More so, in fact.

He loved her hair. Loved her scar.

That halo of silver was not only gorgeous, but undeniable, physical proof of what a gloriously stubborn fighter he'd married. And because of that scar, the surgery it represented, she was still his wife. Still his partner and friend and—

His heart. She was still his heart and his world.

"Eight years. Which means next week is *our* anniversary." She walked her wet fingers up his leg. "I have big plans for you."

Given where her hand strayed, he could guess at some of those plans, and he approved.

But his were more urgent.

He'd promised her a pick-me-up, and he was a man of his word.

Stripping down to nothing took less than a minute, and then he stood naked in front of his wife with his fists on his hips and his interest more than evident.

She shook her head. "Show-off."

Maybe just a little. But soon enough, his hands would make her forget all about it.

281

"Move over, woman." More water splashed over the edge of the tub as he climbed inside. "I have work to do."

Work he loved, for the woman he loved.

He figured he could do work like this for a lifetime.

Elizabeth was giggling as he nibbled at her neck, her hands sliding over his chest and moving downward, beneath the warm water.

And more, he amended. *A lifetime and more.*

THE END

THANK YOU FOR READING *Sweetest in the Gale: A Marysburg Story Collection*. ♥ If you'd like to stay in touch and hear about future new releases, please visit me on the web at oliviadade.com and/or sign up for my newsletter, the Hussy Herald, at https://go.oliviadade.com/Newsletter.

PREVIEW OF SPOILER
ALERT

ONE

Between takes, Marcus did his best not to acknowledge the obvious: This was a stupid-ass way to die.

Still, at the director's call of action, he let out a guttural howl and rode amidst the chaos of warfare once more, adrenaline metallic on his tongue as he galloped through choking smoke-machine clouds. Bellowing stunt performers on horseback whizzed past while his own horse jolted rhythmically between his thighs. Mud—or some foul combination of mud and horseshit, from the smell of it—splattered against his cheek. The special rig raced ahead of him, the camera on the SUV's rushing arm capturing all his determination and desperation.

He didn't love this season's script, true. But he loved *this*. The physicality of it all. The way their show's big budget bought those enormous smoke machines, wired the spider camera tracking overhead, hired those stunt actors, and paid for his training on horseback. That money reserved acres and acres of Spanish coastline for the sole purpose of the series' final, climactic battle, and it allowed them to rehearse and film for weeks and weeks and endless, miserable *weeks* to get just the right shots.

And it was miserable. Often. But because their behind-the-scenes crew of almost a thousand consummate professionals had set the scene so thoroughly, so convincingly, he didn't have to pretend quite so hard, didn't have to fight to lose himself in the moment. The hazy, chaotic landscape around him helped him drop into character, even as the literal and metaphorical choreography of a successful show and this particular scene came to his hand like a well-trained hound.

There was no cut when Dido—Carah, his talented colleague of over seven years now—appeared through the fog at exactly the place they'd rehearsed, sword aimed directly at him. The showrunners had specified long, continuous takes whenever possible for this battle sequence.

"I have come for my revenge, Aeneas the Betrayer!" Dido shouted, her voice raw and cracked with rage. Real-life exhaustion too, he imagined.

At a safe distance, he brought the horse to a standstill and swung down. Strode up to her, knocked aside her sword in one swift motion, and gripped her shoulders.

"I have come for *you*, my beloved." He cupped her face with one dirty hand. "As soon as I heard you lived once more. Not even the return of the dead from Tartarus could stop me. I care nothing for anyone or anything else. Let the world burn. I want you, you alone, and I would defy the gods to have you."

If those lines in the script contradicted seasons' worth of character development, not to mention the books that had inspired the series, he wouldn't dwell on that. Not now.

For a moment, Carah softened against his touch. Leaned into his palm.

By this point in the long filming day, she stank. So did he. So did everyone else. So did the entire horseshit-strewn field. Mud had burrowed into places he didn't care to consider.

Portraying misery and perseverance against all odds wasn't much of a stretch.

Dido shoved him away.

"You *are* a demigod," she reminded him with a sneer. "Married to another, and an adulterer besides. You lay with my sister, and she fell on her sword in disgrace at such a betrayal upon word of my return from Hades. I can only hope she too rises today and takes her own revenge."

Shame, so easy for him to muster, bowed his head. "I thought you lost forever. Lavinia may be my wife in name, but she has no hold on my heart. And Anna—" His brow furrowed, a plea for understanding despite his seeming betrayals. "She was a tarnished mirror of you. Nothing more."

The thought appeared, unbidden. *Unapologetic Lavinia Stan is going to fucking* detonate *when she sees this scene.*

"You've betrayed mortals, and now you betray the gods as well. *Pius Aeneas* indeed." With her crouching swipe, Dido's sword returned to her fist. "I'll have my own revenge first. All others will have to settle for your torment in the afterlife."

Her grip was sure and steady on the weapon, and she brandished it easily. Despite a heavy bronze handle, the sword's blade itself was blunt, lightweight aluminum for the safety of everyone involved, exactly like his. Still, the impact of metal against metal rang out as they began the dance they'd been learning for weeks now.

His movements flowed without much thought, the product of endless thought and repetition. The fight coordinator and choreographer had carefully planned each motion to emphasize the one-sidedness of the battle: Dido was trying to hurt him, but he was attempting to disarm her and avoiding wounding her in the process.

After driving him back with a sudden, violent surge, she rasped, "No man will defeat me!"

More horses galloping past. Partially obscured by the smoke, escapees from the underworld bit and kicked and swung and aimed discarded weapons at their mortal and immortal foes, who were attempting to drive them back to Tartarus. Groans and death and shouts surrounded his own fight.

Precise footwork, back toward Dido. Precise. Precise. Block her wild swing.

"That may be true." He offered a smile, sharp and predatory. "But as you just reminded us both: I'm more than a man."

A clumsy callback to the famous lines in both the second *Gods of the Gates* book and the second season of the series, when Dido had murmured in his arms that no man could seduce her. *I'm more than a man*, he'd returned, and then they'd paused filming to incorporate Carah's body double for the rest of the scene.

More swings of the sword. Some connecting, most not. And then the fatal moment came: He fended off her last, impassioned attack, inadvertently shoving her onto the green-tipped, rubber sword of one of his own men.

The VFX department would fix the sword and blood later. The audience would see a fatal wound where only muddy silk existed now.

Tears. Final, whispered words.

As he knelt in the field, she died in his arms.

When she was gone, he took one last, wet-eyed look at the battle all around him. Saw that the forces of Tartarus were losing, and his men no longer had need of him. Then he gently laid her on the ground beside his own sword, a cherished gift from Dido from their time in Carthage, strode into the chaos, and allowed himself to be fatally stabbed by one of the dead.

"In the Elysian Fields, I'll see you once more, my beloved," he murmured on his final breath.

For that extended stretch of time, Marcus was gone. Only Aeneas, disoriented and desolate and dying and hopeful, existed.

"Cut!" the director called, the order echoed by other crew members. "I think we got everything we needed this time. That's a wrap for this scene!"

As the director and production manager turned away to discuss something, Marcus surfaced, blinking back to himself. His head floated above his shoulders, buoyant and uncluttered, as it sometimes did after he'd truly slipped his own skin and lost himself in a character.

Bliss, in its own way. For so long, the sensation he'd lived and labored for day by day.

It wasn't enough. Not anymore.

Carah recovered more quickly than him. Levering herself up out of the mud and to her feet, she heaved a heartfelt sigh.

"Thank fucking Christ." She held out her hand to him. "If I wanted mud in my ass crack, I'd pay for one of those full-body detox treatments, and that motherfucker would smell like tea tree or lavender, not horseshit."

He laughed and allowed her to steady him as he stood. His leather armor seemed to weigh as much as Rumpelstilt-skin, the Friesian the horse master was now leading away. "If it's any consolation, you have a healthy, just-been-stabbed glow."

"A goddamn shame they did all the closeups in earlier takes, then." After sniffing her armpit, she wrinkled her nose and gave a resigned shrug. "Shit, I need a shower *pronto*. At least we're done for the day."

Carah generally didn't require much response. He simply nodded.

"Just one more scene for me," she continued. "Back at the studio, later this week. My sword-training montage. How about you?"

He sounded out the words in his head, checking for falsity.

Somehow, they were true. "No. This is it. They filmed my immortality scene before the Battle for the Living."

This scene would be his own last memory of filming *Gods of the Gates*, but for the television audience, Aeneas's ascension to full-god status would be their final glimpse of the character. Ambrosia and nectar and a healthy swallow from the river Lethe, rather than blood and filth and despair.

After said swallow, Aeneas would forget Dido and Lavinia both. Poor Anna too.

And after the final season aired, fans were going to slaughter R.J. and Ron—the series' head writers, executive producers, and showrunners—online and at cons. For a multiplicity of reasons, since the abrupt reversal of Aeneas's character arc was only one of many storytelling failures in the last episodes. Marcus couldn't even estimate the number of pointed, aggrieved fix-it fics that would appear after the finale.

Hundreds, definitely. Maybe thousands.

He'd be writing at least one or two of them as Book!AeneasWouldNever, with Unapologetic Lavinia Stan's help.

Squinting through the residual smoke, he eyed the swords on the ground. Bits of torn costume. A plastic water bottle hopefully hidden from the camera's sight, behind a dummy dressed as a dead member of Aeneas's fleet.

Should he take something from the set as a memento? Did he even want to? And what on this filthy field could both encompass over seven years working on the show and smell acceptable enough for display in his home?

Nothing. Nothing.

So after a final, heartfelt hug for Carah, he headed empty-handed toward his trailer. Only to be stopped by a palm clapped to his shoulder before he'd gone a dozen steps.

"Hold on, Marcus," an all-too-familiar voice ordered.

When Marcus turned around, Ron beckoned several cameras closer—they were rolling again, somehow—and called back Carah and all the nearby crew.

Shit. In his exhaustion, Marcus had forgotten this little ceremony. In theory, a tribute to each main series actor at the end of their last day on set. In reality, a behind-the-scenes extra to tempt their audience to buy physical copies of the show or at least pay more to stream the special content.

Ron's hand was still on his shoulder. Marcus didn't shrug it off, but he tipped his face toward the ground for a moment. Gathered his thoughts and braced himself.

Before he could finally leave, he had yet another role to play. One he'd been perfecting for most of a decade, and one he'd wanted to leave behind with greater fervency as each of those years ticked past.

Marcus Caster-Rupp.

Friendly. Vain. Dim as that smoky battlefield surrounding them.

He was a well-groomed golden retriever, proud of the few tricks he'd miraculously learned.

"When we began looking for our Aeneas, we knew we had to find an athletic actor. Someone who could portray a leader of men and a lover of women. And above all else..." Ron lifted a hand and pinched Marcus's cheek, lingeringly enough that he might have felt the flush of sudden rage. "A pretty face. We couldn't have found prettier, not if we'd searched for another decade."

The crew laughed.

Marcus's stomach churned.

Another pinch, and he forced himself to grin smugly. To toss his hair and shed his armor so he could show the unseen audience the flex of his biceps, even as he moved out of Ron's reach. Then the showrunner and the crew were urging Marcus to say something, to make a speech in honor of all his years on the series.

291

Impromptu speaking. Would this fucking day never fucking *end?*

The role, though, surrounded him like an embrace. Familiar. Comforting, if increasingly claustrophobic. In its confines, he knew what to do. What to say. Who to be.

"Five years ago…" He turned to Ron. "Wait. How many years have we been filming now?"

Their boss chuckled indulgently. "Seven."

"Seven years ago, then." Marcus gave an unembarrassed shrug, beaming toward the camera. "Seven years ago, we started filming, and I had no idea what was in store for all of us. I'm very grateful for this role, and for our audience. Since you needed"—he made himself say it—"a pretty face, I'm glad mine was the prettiest you saw. Not surprised, but glad."

He arched an eyebrow, settling his fists on his hips in a heroic pose, and waited for more laughter. This time, directed and deliberately elicited by him.

That bit of control settled his stomach, if only a little.

"I'm also glad you found so many other pretty faces to act alongside." He winked at Carah. "Not as pretty as mine, of course, but pretty enough."

More smiles from the crew and an eye-roll from Carah.

He could leave now. He knew it. This was all anyone outside his closest colleagues and crew members expected of him.

Still, he had to say one last thing, because this *was* his last day. This *was* the end of seven damn years of his life, years of endless hard work and challenges and accomplishments and the joy that came from doing that work, meeting those challenges, and finally, finally allowing himself to count those accomplishments as worthwhile and *his*.

He could now ride a horse like he'd been doing it his whole life.

The sword master said he was the best in the cast with a

weapon in hand and had the fastest feet of any actor she'd ever met.

At long last, he'd learned to pronounce Latin with an ease his parents had both acknowledged and deemed a bitter irony.

Over his time on *Gods of the Gates*, he'd been nominated for five major acting awards. He'd never won, of course, but he had to believe—he did believe—that the nominations didn't simply reward a pretty face, but skill. Emotional depth. The public might believe him an acting savant, able to ape intelligence despite having none of his own, but he knew the work he'd put into his craft and his career.

None of that would have been possible without the crew.

He angled away from the cameras to look at some of those people, and to obscure the change in his expression. "Finally, I want to thank everyone behind the scenes of our show. There are nearly a thousand of you, and I—I can't—" The sincere words tangled his tongue, and he paused for a moment. "I can't imagine how any series could have found a more dedicated, knowledgeable group. So to all the producers, stunt performers, location managers, dialect coaches, production designers, costumer designers, hair and makeup artists, VFX and SFX people, and so many others: Thank you. I, um, owe you more than I can express."

There. It was done. He'd managed to say it without stumbling too much.

Later, he'd grieve and consider his next steps. Now, he simply needed to wash and rest.

After a final round of embarrassing applause and a few claps on the back and hugs and handshakes, he made his escape. To his trailer for a quick wash at the sink, and then to his generic Spanish hotel room, where a very, very long and well-deserved shower awaited him.

At least he thought he'd made his escape, until Vika

Andrich caught up with him just outside the hotel lobby entrance.

"Marcus! Do you have a minute?" Her voice somehow remained steady, even though she was jogging over from the parking lot in sensible heels. "I had a few questions about the big sequence you're filming now."

He wasn't entirely surprised to spot her. Once or twice a year, she'd show up wherever they were shooting and get whatever on-site impressions and interviews she could, and those articles were always especially popular on her blog. Of course she'd want to cover the end of the series' filming in person.

Unlike some other reporters, if he asked for space, she'd respect his privacy. He even liked her. That wasn't the problem.

The other qualities that made her his favorite entertainment blogger-slash-paparazzo also made her his least favorite: She was friendly. Funny. Easy to relax around. Too easy.

She was also smart. Smart enough to have spied something... off... about him.

Offering her a wide smile, he stopped inches short of freedom. "Vika, you know I can't tell you anything about what's happening this season. But if you think your readers want to see me covered in mud"—he winked—"and we both know they do, then feel free to take a picture or two."

He posed, presenting her with what he'd been told was his best side, and she got a couple of shots.

"I know you can't tell me anything specific," she said, checking the images, "but maybe you could describe the sixth season in three words?"

Tapping his chin, he furrowed his brow. Playacted deep thought for long moments.

"I know!" He brightened and turned a pleased grin on her. "Last. One. Ever. I hope that helps."

Her eyes narrowed, and she studied him for a beat too long.

Then, confronted with the blinding gleam of her own innocent smile, he had to blink.

"I guess…" She trailed off, still smiling. "I guess I need to find one of the other actors to ask about how the show's ending deviates from both E. Wade's books and, of course, Homer's *Aeneid*. Aeneas ended up married to Dido in both those stories, but the show might have taken a different approach."

Homer? What the fuck?

And Dido was long, looooong dead by the end of the *Aeneid*. By the final page of the third *Gods of the Gates* book, she was alive but decidedly no longer interested in Aeneas, although he supposed that could change if Wade ever released the last two books in the series.

Somewhere, Virgil was probably uttering Latin curses as he shifted in his grave, and by all rights, E. Wade should be side-eyeing Vika from her lavish compound in Hawaii.

He pinched his forehead with a thumb and forefinger, absently noting the dirt beneath his nails. Dammit, *someone* needed to correct such grievous misapprehensions.

"The *Aeneid* wasn't—" Vika's brows rose with his first words, and her phone was recording, and he saw the trick. Oh, yes, he saw it. "The *Aeneid* isn't something I've read, sadly. I'm sure Homer is very talented, but I'm not much of a reader in general."

The last bit, at least, had once been true. Before he'd discovered fanfic and audiobooks, he hadn't read much beside his scripts, and he'd labored over those only until he'd learned them well enough to record them, loop the recording, and play the words back to himself over and over.

She tapped her screen, and her own recording ended. "Thank you, Marcus. It was kind of you to talk to me."

"My pleasure, Vika. Good luck with your other interviews." With a final flash of a vapid smile, he was finally inside the hotel and trudging toward the elevator.

After pressing the button for his floor, he leaned heavily against the wall and closed his eyes.

Soon, he was going to have to grapple with his persona. Where it chafed, how it had served him in the past, and how it served him still. Whether shedding it would be worth the consequences to his personal life and career.

But not today. Fuck, he was tired.

Back in his hotel room, the shower felt just as good as he'd hoped. Better.

Afterward, he powered on his laptop and ignored the scripts sent by his agent. Choosing his next project—one that hopefully take his career in a new direction—could wait too, as could checking his Twitter and Instagram accounts.

The only thing that definitely needed to happen before he slept for a million years: sending a direct message to Unapologetic Lavinia Stan. Or Ulsie, as he'd begun calling her, to her complete disgust. *Ulsie is a good name for a cow, and only for a cow*, she'd written. But she hadn't told him to stop, and he hadn't. The nickname, one he alone used, pleased him more than it should.

He logged onto the Lavineas server he'd helped create several years ago for the use of the lively, talented, ever-supportive Aeneas/Lavinia fanfic community. On AO3, he still occasionally dabbled in Aeneas/Dido fanfic, but less and less often these days. Especially once Ulsie had become the primary beta and proofreader for all Book!AeneasWouldNever's stories.

She lived in California, and she'd still be at work. She wouldn't be able to respond immediately to his messages. If he didn't DM her tonight, though, he wouldn't have her response first thing in the morning, and he needed that. More and more as each week passed.

Soon, so very soon, he and Ulsie would be back in the same time zone. The same state.

Not that proximity mattered, since they'd never meet in person.

Only it did matter. Somehow, it did.

TWO

DIRT. MORE DIRT.

This particular dirt would tell a story, though, if April listened hard enough.

She squinted at the site's final soil core through her prescription safety glasses, comparing the different shades of brown to her color chart, then noted the sample's water content, soil plasticity and consistency, grain size and shape, and all the other relevant data on her field form.

No discoloration. No particular odor either, which didn't surprise her. Solvents would emit a sweet smell, and fuels would smell like—well, fuel. Hydrocarbons. But lead would simply smell like dirt. So would arsenic.

After wiping her gloved hand on the thigh of her jeans, she jotted down her findings.

Normally, she'd be talking to her assistant sampler, Bashir, about their most egregious coworkers or maybe their most recent reality-show binge-watches. But by this point in the afternoon, they were both too tired to make idle conversation, so she finished logging the sample silently while he filled out the label for the glass sample jar and completed the chain-of-custody form.

After she filled the jar with soil and wiped her hand on her jeans again, she labeled the container, slipped it into a zip-top bag, and placed it in the ice-filled cooler. One last signature to confirm she was handing off the sample to the waiting lab courier, and they were done for the day. Thank God.

"That's it?" Bashir asked.

"That's it." As they watched the courier leave with the cooler, she blew out a breath. "I can take care of cleanup, if you want to relax for a few minutes."

He shook his head. "I'll help."

Other than their thirty-minute lunch break, they'd been on task and focused since seven that morning, almost nine hours ago. Her feet hurt in her dusty safety boots, her exposed skin stung from too much sun exposure, dehydration had her head throbbing inside her hard hat, and she was ready for a good, long shower back at the hotel.

Her cheek also itched, probably from a stray smear of dirt. Which was unfortunate, because soil-to-skin contact was, in technical terminology, an exposure pathway. Or, as April would put it, a fucking bad idea.

Uncapping her water bottle, she wet a stray paper towel and swiped until her cheek felt clean again.

"You still have some…" Bashir's finger scratched at his spot near his temple. "There."

"Thanks." Despite her headache, her smile at him was sincere. She could count the number of genuine friends she had at her current firm on one hand, but Bashir was among them. "Good work today."

After one last swipe and Bashir's affirmative nod—she'd gotten rid of all the mud this time, apparently—the paper towel ended in the same garbage bag as her used gloves, and good riddance.

The soil was dirty in more ways than one. Until midcentury, a pesticide factory had operated on the site, polluting the facility's surroundings with lead and arsenic. Because of that history, April had spent the last several weeks gathering samples of the soil to analyze for both chemicals. She wanted neither directly on her skin. Or on her jeans, for that matter, but paper towels were just a pain in the ass at the end of the day.

"Did I tell you?" As she gathered their paperwork, he slid her a sly grin. "Last week, Chuck told that new kid never to drink water in the exclusion zone. Because it's bad practice, and goes against health and safety guidelines."

Together, they turned to stare at their red cooler filled with water bottles, which she'd placed on the tailgate of their field truck that morning.

"Chuck's a self-congratulatory twenty-two-year-old prick who's spent almost no time on actual job sites." At her flat statement, Bashir's eyes widened. "He doesn't know what the fuck he's talking about, but is happy to tell everyone how to do their jobs anyway."

At that, Bashir snorted. "Not just our jobs."

"Oh, Jesus." April rolled her eyes skyward. "Did he lecture you about hummus *again?*"

"Yes. Even though I don't even eat much hummus, or give half a shit about chickpeas. I guess he just assumes I do, because..." Bashir waved a hand at himself. "You know."

Together, they began carrying the paperwork to the company truck.

"I know." She sighed. "Please tell me he wasn't telling you to try—"

"The chocolate hummus," Bashir confirmed. "Again. If you'd like to hear about its fiber and protein content, or perhaps how it's a vast improvement over more traditional versions of hummus—*the hummus of your people*, as he put it— I've been well informed and would be delighted to share my newfound knowledge with you."

He opened the passenger door for her, and she tucked the paperwork inside the latching case of her clipboard.

"Ugh. I'm so sorry." She grimaced. "If it's any consolation, he also has very definite opinions about how his few female colleagues should dress to score more jobs."

In a small, private firm, consultants like her had to hustle for clients, woo them over lunches and at professional meetings, draw them aside at conventions and conferences about remedial technologies. Convince them she should be taken seriously and they wanted to pay her company for her geological expertise.

To remain optimally billable, she had to look a certain way. Sound a certain way. Present herself in the most professional possible light at all times.

Billable had become an epithet to her in recent years.

Reputation in her industry could be a fragile thing. Could be damaged. By, say, the revelation that a seemingly serious and practical colleague liked to play dress-up as her favorite pretend TV character and spent most of her free time discussing fictional half-gods.

Bashir rolled his eyes. "Of course he has opinions about women's clothing. You told management, right?"

"Literally five minutes later."

"Good." Bashir walked by her side back toward the sampling table. "Hopefully they'll fire his ass before much longer."

"He knows nothing. Less than nothing, if that's possible." A pluck of her fingers at her shirt demonstrated how it clung damply to her. "I mean, look at how much we sweated today."

"Copiously." He glanced down at his own sweat-soaked orange shirt. "Disgustingly."

Stopping by the table, she shook her head. "Exactly. Someone needs to set that new kid straight. Unless she wants to end up in the hospital for dehydration, she needs to bring water."

Bashir inclined his head. "You would know."

"I would know."

And she did. Up until now, almost a third of her work hours as a geologist had been spent staying upwind of drill rigs like the one on this site, poring over soil samples to be logged and shoved into jars and sent off for lab testing. For a long time, she'd loved the processes and the challenges and even the physicality of doing field work. Some part of her still did love it.

Not all of her, though. Not enough of her.

As they flipped the table on its side and folded its legs, Bashir paused. "You're really leaving, huh?"

"Yup." This was her last day visiting a contaminated site in her current role, her last week as a consultant at a private firm, and her last time washing dirt from her jeans. "I'll miss you, but it's time. Past time."

In less than a week, she was moving from Sacramento to Berkeley. And in less than two weeks, Future April would begin her new job at a state regulatory agency in Oakland, overseeing the work of consultants like Current April, which would mean more meetings and document analysis, and less time in the field.

She was ready. For so many reasons, personal and professional both.

Once she and Bashir had all their supplies back in the truck, she changed into her regular glasses, and removed her other personal protective equipment. With a sigh of relief, she untied her dusty boots and deposited them in a plastic bag, then put back on her battered but clean sneakers. Beside her, he did the same.

Then she was done. Finally, blessedly done, and desperate for a shower, a cheeseburger, and approximately a gallon of ice water. Not to mention some more Lavineas fanfiction, group chats on the server, and DMs with Book!Aeneas-WouldNever. Hopefully BAWN had written while she was working.

First, though, she and Bashir needed to say their goodbyes.

"I don't know if you already have plans for the weekend, but Mimi and I would love to treat you to dinner. To celebrate your new job and say farewell." Even after several years of working together, he was still shy enough to fidget while issuing the invitation. "She knows you're my favorite colleague."

As he was one of hers, and she considered his wife Mimi a genuine friend too.

But even they didn't know everything about her. Specifically, that she spent most evenings and weekends immersed in the *Gods of the Gates* fandom: tweeting about her OTP, writing and beta-ing and reading fanfic, chatting on the Lavineas server, and employing her vast enthusiasm and infinitesimal costume-construction skill to cosplay Lavinia.

One stray pic at a con, one slip of the tongue, and her professional reputation might suffer. She could devolve from an experienced professional into a silly fangirl in less time than it took for her to log a soil sample.

So she hadn't attended *Gods of the Gates* cons. She hadn't told work friends about her fandom. Not even friends she liked as much as Bashir.

The state regulators at her new job, though...

Well, the difference in culture couldn't have been clearer. The personal and the professional were inextricable there. Intertwined in the most joyful and hilarious ways.

When she arrived in less than two weeks, she'd become the fifth person on their team of geologists. The third woman. When she'd gone in to complete her I-9 last week, the other women, Heidi and Mel, had offered April a slice of the cake the team had brought to work in celebration of the women's tenth anniversary as partners.

Mel and the two guys on the team—Pablo and Kei—were in a freakin' band together. *A band.* One that evidently performed for retirement parties and other gatherings in which their unique folk music talents couldn't successfully be avoided.

They're terrible, Heidi had whispered, her mouth half-hidden behind her water bottle, *but they all enjoy it so much, we can't say anything.*

At that moment, in that dreary state-government-bureaucrat's office suite, something taut to the point of snapping inside April had eased. Any remaining doubts had disappeared.

She'd made the right decision to change jobs, even with the pay cut. Even with the price of housing in the Bay Area. Even with the hassle of moving.

At her new workplace, she wouldn't need to shield different parts of herself for fear of others' disapproval. As of next week, billability no longer concerned her.

In fact…

It didn't concern her now, either. Not anymore.

"Thank you so much for the invitation, Bashir." When she hugged him, he patted her back tentatively. "I'm busy this weekend, unfortunately. I have to be at my new apartment, getting it ready for the move. But I'll be back in town late next week. Can we do dinner then instead?"

When she pulled away, he smiled down at her, looking pleased. "Of course. I'll check Mimi's schedule and text you later tonight, after we get back from dinner at her family's house. They live nearby, so she's picking me up at the hotel, and we'll drive home afterward."

Fuck billability, she thought.

"I plan to spend the evening eating a room service burger

and writing *Gods of the Gates* fanfiction," she told him. "Your night sounds much more exciting."

He blinked at her for a few seconds before flashing an impish grin. "You only say that because you haven't met my in-laws."

She laughed. "Fair enough."

"When we have dinner, I want to hear more about your writing." His head tilted, he was studying her curiously. "Mimi loves that show. Especially the pretty dude."

"Marcus Caster-Rupp?" Honestly, it could be any one of a handful of actors, but Caster-Rupp was undeniably the prettiest dude of all. Also the most boring. So boring, she sometimes wondered how one man could be so shiny, yet so incredibly *dull*.

"That's the one." He directed a pained grimace at the heavens. "He's on her freebie list. Every time we stream an episode, she's always very insistent about that."

April patted his arm. "Think about it this way: She won't ever actually meet him. None of us will, unless we move to LA and start selling vital organs to pay for our haircuts."

"Huh." His expression brightened. "That's true."

Before leaving the site, they thanked the drill crew. Then, after she exchanged one last round of goodbyes with Bashir, he climbed into his car while she boosted herself into the driver's seat of the truck. With a farewell beep, she headed toward her hotel, while he drove to his in-laws' home.

For each mile she traveled, invisible tethers surrounding her seemed to snap free, leaving her oddly, giddily buoyant. Yeah, she still had a personal drilling rig operating in her skull, but a few glasses of water would take care of the headache, no problem. And so what if she had dirt all over her jeans? Even contaminated soil couldn't sully the essential, joyful truth.

She caught a glimpse of herself in the rearview mirror.

Her smile was so wide, she might as well have been starring in a toothpaste commercial.

And no wonder. No wonder.

This was her last day in the dirt.

She was starting now.

When she got back to the hotel, she dumped her jeans into a waiting plastic bag and got naked. In the shower, she scrubbed her body pink under the hot spray.

Her clean flannel pajamas felt like a cloud against her skin as she drained a glass of water and read over BAWN's latest messages. At long last, he'd decided what to write for his next fic. Monday's prompt for their upcoming Aeneas and Lavinia Week requested *a showdown between Aeneas's two lady loves*, and BAWN had been contemplating the best way to handle it for days.

Since the two women haven't met in the books or on the show, you could always come up with a fluffy alternative-universe story, which is what I'm doing, she'd written before work that morning, already knowing how he'd respond to *that* suggestion. *Or—and I really think this idea might work for you —maybe Aeneas could dream about the showdown, so you can keep things canon-compliant and in his POV? What do you think?*

The latter option offered plenty of opportunity for angst, so of course he'd chosen that one. BAWN was such an insightful writer, but April had to admit it: Some of his fics were depressing as hell.

Less so now than when he'd started, though. Back then, even his Aeneas/Lavinia stories had been bursting with their hero's guilt and shame when it came to Dido, all dirges and funeral pyres and lamentations. April's first real conversation with BAWN on the Lavineas server, in fact, had involved her half-joking suggestion that he use the tag *misery ahoy!* on some of his fics.

For his mental health alone, it was better for him to focus on the Lavinia-Aeneas OTP. Clearly. Writing occasional fluffy fics wouldn't do him any harm, either.

Tonight, though, she didn't have time the Good Gospel of Fluff. By the time she finished describing her own fluffy AU fic idea—Lavinia and Dido would meet as teenage combatants in a trivia contest, their feelings for Aeneas making each round of questions and answers increasingly fraught and hilarious—she was on the verge of losing her courage. Again.

Months ago, when she'd applied for her new job, she'd decided she was done shielding different parts of herself for fear of others' disapproval. That applied to her fandom too.

On Twitter, to dodge possible professional disaster, she'd always cropped her cosplay pictures to exclude her face. But she'd failed to share her Twitter handle with fellow Lavineas stans for an entirely different reason.

Her body.

She hadn't wanted her friends on the server to see her body in those Lavinia costumes. Particularly one of those friends, whose opinion mattered more than it should.

For a ship whose essential heartbeat was all about love for goodness, for sterling character and intelligence, over appearance, Lavineas fics included a surprising, disappointing amount of fat-shaming. Not BAWN's, to his credit. But some of his favorite fics, the ones he'd bookmarked and recommended to her, did.

After a lifetime of struggle, April now loved her body. All of it. Red hair to freckled, chubby toes.

She hadn't expected the same from others. Still didn't. But she was tired of fucking hiding, and she was done with more than just contaminated mud on her jeans and colleagues she only allowed so close.

This year, she was attending her fandom's biggest convention, Con of the Gates, which always took place—appropriately enough—within a sunny day's view of the Golden Gate Bridge. Countless bloggers and reporters showed up to that con, and they took pictures, some of which always ended up going viral or printed in newspaper articles or splashed across the television screen.

She wouldn't care. Not anymore. If her colleagues could openly discuss their terrible folk-music trio, she could certainly discuss her love for the most popular show on television.

And when she came to the con, she was finally going to meet her fandom friends there in person. She might even meet BAWN in person, despite his shyness. She would give all of them an opportunity to prove they'd truly understood the message of their OTP.

If they didn't, it would hurt. She couldn't lie to herself about that.

Especially if BAWN took one look at her and—

Well, no point in imagining rejection that didn't yet exist.

Worst-case scenario, though, she'd find other friends. Other fandoms more accepting of who and what she was. Another beta reader for her fics, whose DMs were beams of sunshine to start her morning and the warmth of a down comforter at night.

Another man she wanted in her face-to-face life and maybe even her bed.

So she had to do this tonight, before she lost her nerve. It wasn't the final step, or even the hardest. But it was the first.

Without letting herself think too hard about it, she checked a thread on Twitter from that morning, still going strong. The *Gods of the Gates*'s official account had asked fans to post their best cosplay photos, and the responses now numbered in the hundreds. A few dozen featured people her size, and she very carefully didn't click to see replies to those tweets.

On her phone, she had a selfie from her most recent Lavinia costume. The image was uncropped, her face and body both clearly visible. Her colleagues, present and future, would recognize her. Her friends and family too. Most nerve-racking of all: If she told him her Twitter handle, Book!AeneasWouldNever would finally see her for the first time.

Deep breath.

She tweeted it. Then immediately shut her laptop and ordered some damn room service, because she deserved it. After dinner, she began her one-shot, fluffy, modern AU fic so BAWN could give her some feedback over the weekend.

Right before bedtime, she couldn't stand it anymore.

Block finger ready, she checked her Twitter notifications.

Holy fuck. Holy *fuck*.

She'd gone viral. At least by her modest standards. Hundreds of people had commented on her photo, with more chiming in by the second. She couldn't read her notifications fast enough, and some of them she didn't want to read at all.

She'd known how certain swaths of the Gods of the Gates fandom acted. She wasn't surprised to find, scattered amongst admiring and supportive responses, a few ugly threads.

Looks like she ate Lavinia seemed to be the most popular among those tweets.

It stung, of course. But no stranger on the internet could truly hurt her. Not the same way family and friends and coworkers could.

Still, she didn't intend to inflict that sort of harm on herself longer than necessary. It might take time, but she needed to wrestle her mentions into submission.

But... Jesus. Where had all these people *come* from?

Blocking all the haters in one particular thread took a while, as did muting—at least for the moment—certain key, livestock- and zoo animal-related words. Hog. Cow. Hippo. Elephant.

By the time she finished, she had dozens more notifications. These seemed friendlier, for the most part, but she didn't plan to tackle them until the morning.

Until she noticed one at the very top, received seconds before.

The account boasted a bright blue bubble with a check inside. An official, verified account, then.

Marcus Caster-Rupp's account.

The guy playing Aeneas—fucking *Aeneas*—had tweeted to her. Followed her.

And...he appeared to have—

No, that couldn't be right. She was hallucinating.

She squinted. Blinked. Read it again. A third time.

For reasons yet unknown, he appeared to have—

Well, he appeared to have asked her out. On a date.

"I read a fic like this once," she whispered.

Then she clicked on the thread to find out what the fuck had just happened.

Spoiler Alert will be available October 6, 2020! To preorder, go to https://oliviadade.com/books/spoiler-alert/. And for more news and release-day alerts, sign up for my newsletter, the Hussy Herald, at https://go.oliviadade.com/Newsletter.

ALSO BY OLIVIA DADE

SPOILER ALERT

THERE'S SOMETHING ABOUT MARYSBURG

Teach Me

40-Love

Sweetest in the Gale: A Marysburg Story Collection

LOVE UNSCRIPTED

Desire and the Deep Blue Sea

Tiny House, Big Love

LOVESTRUCK LIBRARIANS

My Reckless Valentine

Mayday

Ready to Fall

Driven to Distraction

Hidden Hearts

ABOUT OLIVIA

Olivia Dade grew up an undeniable nerd, prone to ignoring the world around her as she read any book she could find. Her favorites, though, were always, always romances. As an adult, she earned an M.A. in American history and worked in a variety of jobs that required the donning of actual pants: Colonial Williamsburg interpreter, high school teacher, academic tutor, and (of course) librarian. Now, however, she has finally achieved her lifelong goal of wearing pajamas all day as a hermit-like writer and enthusiastic hag. She currently lives outside Stockholm with her patient Swedish husband, their whip-smart daughter, and the family's ever-burgeoning collection of books.

If you want to find me online, here's where to go!
Website: https://oliviadade.com
Twitter: https://twitter.com/OliviaWrites
Newsletter: https://go.oliviadade.com/Newsletter

ACKNOWLEDGMENTS

I'd intended "Sweetest in the Gale" to be a light, fun, extremely short story, one in which a new teacher in the English Department would woo Candy via linguistics-based bickering. Instead...well. It's a novella, not a short story, and it's not especially light. It's about linguistics, yes, but also about grief and poetry and guilt. Thank you to Emma Barry, Kate Clayborn, and Maria Vale for making sure I got the story and its tone right, even if it wasn't the story I'd intended to tell or the tone I'd intended to take. Thank you too to everyone I met through my volunteer work at the Hospice of Washington County in Maryland: the dedicated staff, the loving families, and—most of all—the patients. I haven't forgotten you. I won't forget you.

I am so proud to have worked with my incredibly talented friends while writing "Unraveled." I owe a huge debt of gratitude to Emma Barry, Adriana Herrera, Ruby Lang, and Cat Sebastian for agreeing to the *He's Come Undone* anthology and ensuring there was nothing but joy in the process of making it reality. Thank you too for reading over this story and providing notes, encouragement, and emoji-laden DMs! You're all the literal best. :-)

With "Cover Me," I veered so far outside my prior romantic-comedy lane that I required a great deal of handholding (even more than usual!). So I owe an enormous thank-you to everyone who read this story and gave me the help and reassurance I needed: Alexandra Haughton, Gwendolen Crane, Emma Barry, Sonoma Lass, Cecilia Grant, Molly O'Keefe, and Ruby Lang. I can't tell you how much I appreciate your kindness and the care with which you considered my words.

Finally, a huge thank-you to Sionna Fox for all her help, and to Leni Kauffman for my gorgeous cover and illustrations.

And of course, all my love to my family. Without you, I'd be lost (if somewhat better-rested).

Made in the USA
Middletown, DE
01 July 2022